The Cop Reporter

P.J. JONES

LONESOME CREEK CHRONICLER

Paperback ISBN; 979-8-9877919-5-0

E-Book ISBN: 979-8-9877919-4-3

Library of Congress Number 113454328231

Cover by Dana Nicole Joiner

Dedication

For Margie Morelock Hughes, my best friend of life, whose likeness inspired that of Katherine.
Margie is beautiful, bright, strong-willed, and fearless.

In Gratitude

I'd like to express my appreciation to two men who remember what it was like to work in news and criminal investigations before the advent of software and DNA technology.

Glenn Dromgoole, longtime editor of *The Abilene Reporter-News*, member of the Texas Literary Hall of Fame, and author of thirty-plus books, took time to ensure my memories of our newsroom in the early 1980s were correct. I forgot the sports guys got the windows. Of course, they did.

I write nothing about law enforcement that isn't run through my partner in writing true crime, retired DeSoto Parish Sheriff's Deputy Det. Lt. Robert (Robbo) Davidson, who still serves on the Louisiana Commission for Law Enforcement. His memoir, The Evil I Have Seen, received the Readers' Favorite Gold Medal for True Crime in 2022. Thank you, gentlemen.

Contents

Prologue

News reporters never earned much money, but I refused to believe our pay reflected our significance to society. Quite the opposite. Like law enforcement officers, firefighters, EMTs, and nurses, newspeople worked nights, weekends, and holidays to do what we loved.

We, members of the press, fancied ourselves as guardians of the people's right to know, leading us to clash with representatives of government, particularly cops, who regarded themselves as guardians of the people. Period. Police held tight to each shred of information in their possession lest it become common knowledge and thus, at least in their minds, threaten the integrity of their investigations. We tugged for every tidbit to enlighten our readers.

Despite our opposing goals, a kinship existed between the police and the press. We were dancing partners stepping all over each other's toes until, after enough times around the dance floor, we finally got the rhythm right.

Chapter 1

ABILENE, TEXAS 1980

I worked the night shift from two to ten. We put out the morning newspaper. The old guys, the ones who had been there forever, got the day shift, working for the afternoon edition. Their big stories got refreshed for the following morning edition. A new headline didn't necessarily mean anything was new—just a different audience for a different day.

As the newest hire, my first stop every day was the cop shop. Nobody wanted to be the cop reporter chasing wrecks and fires, interviewing people who just lost loved ones, and dealing with cops who regarded you as chewing gum stuck to the soles of their shoes.

But that's who I was. The cop reporter.

Go to work, clock in, and drive to the county jail. Check the log. Who got arrested for what? Is there anything interesting or unusual? Chat with the jailer. Sometimes, he would give you a wink or a nod to nudge you in the right direction.

Head to the arresting agency. Since most crimes were committed inside the city limits, more often than not, it was Abilene cops I butted heads with.

Check the clipboards. Ask for a copy of newsworthy incidents.

Endure the condescending sneer of the desk sergeant, who grumbled under his breath as he riffled loudly through papers, trudged to a back office to make the copies, and returned to sling them on the counter. Sometimes, they sailed off.

Finally, ask to speak to the officer who signed said reports.

Then—and this was the worst part—you had to deal with their gum-smacking, guard-dog secretary. She glanced up from her typing to acknowledge me standing at her desk. She snarled. "What do you need today?"

"I need to talk to ... let me see ... Detective Callahan about the arrest of ... James Billingsly."

"Callahan ain't in." She resumed her typing. I wasn't sure how she did it so well with such long fingernails.

"Well, can I speak to whoever is in charge? I need to know more about this arrest for robbery and aggravated assault."

"What's your name again?" She knew my name. I'd endured her every day for the past month.

"Kat Coe. I'm with the *Reporter-News.*"

She ceased her typing to leer at me and snicker. She was a big-chested blonde with poofy hair and round blue eyes. The kind of woman men ogle. "Like catch cold?" She tilted her head back and chuckled at her joke. "Ka-choo?"

"No, ma'am." I flashed her my best fake smile. "Kat is short for Katherine. It's what my family and friends have called me all my life. Kat. Coe. C-O-E. That's my name."

She eyed me up and down, smacking that gum. She didn't need all that make-up. She had pretty eyes. "If I was you, I'd go by my real name." She leaned toward me with a full-frontal sneer. "Because we ain't your family or friends."

"Can I talk to whoever is in charge or not?" Yes, I was loud. The smile was gone.

She narrowed her eyes. "Callahan's married you know."

My arms swung high and wide. "Who gives a flying fig? I'm not here to screw the man. I'm here to get a damned news story if you'll let me do my job." As it spewed forth, I regretted it. Sometimes, words like that flew out of my mouth, and I'd yet to be able to grab one and shove it back in.

If she complained, I'd be in trouble. Already.

But maybe she needed that. She looked at me wide-eyed, picked up her telephone receiver, and punched a button. A moment later, "Reporter's here to see Callahan ... Yeah." She eyed me up and down. "A Ms. Kat Coe. I'm not sure if she's a miss or a missus ... from the newspaper ... okay." She punched a big red button on top of her desk, releasing the lock on the heavy wooden door to her left, and tilted her head toward it. "You can go back."

Wow. My first time entering the hallowed halls of the Abilene Police Department Detective Division. I should snap at her more often. Usually, an officer met me in the lobby to answer my questions. This time, I would get a glimpse of their inner sanctum.

Stepping into a long corridor with polished tile floors and long fluorescent lights on the ceiling, as the door clicked shut behind me, I wondered, "Where do I go?" No one was in the small offices I peered into, walking down the hall.

The corridor dead-ended with a righthand turn.

The first open door on the left looked like a meeting room, filled with men standing around, smoking, and talking. A red-headed detective near the door spotted me. Our gazes latched. As I stepped forward, extending my hand to introduce myself, he reached over and slammed that door shut right in my face before I got a word out. *Bam!* It reverberated through the empty hallway.

Jackass.

Glancing right and left, I walked back to peer down the long corridor toward the lobby. I'd be damned if I'd walk past Dolly Parton with my tail tucked between my legs. I couldn't go back to the newsroom empty-handed. I had to have a story, and so far, this robbery and assault was it.

So I leaned against the wall in front of that door and waited, studying the incident report.

Offense: Aggravated Assault & Robbery Time: Blank. Address: Blank. Name of Victim: Blank.

Narrative: Victim found suffering extensive injuries. Taken by ambulance to Hendrick Medical Center.

I turned it over. Blank.

That's it?

Who's the victim? Where did the crime occur? What time did it happen? Unbelievable. This was as slim an incident report as I'd ever seen. I could surmise the victim was probably beaten. If the injuries were from a weapon, the officer would have charged the assailant with attempted murder and tagged on aggravated assault.

Aggravated indicated severity. Hit someone with your fist? That's assault. Send them to the hospital from blows by your fist, or use a baseball bat, knife, or gun? That's aggravated.

Or the victim was underage. Anything you did to a minor was aggravated.

It didn't say sexual assault, so for the time being, I ruled that out.

Law enforcement always left blank or whited out the name, age, and gender of sexual assault victims and juveniles. Even if the cops didn't protect them, which they did, the newspaper would never print the name of a sexual assault victim or a juvenile. With all the blanks, this was probably an underage victim. But robbery? It didn't fit.

Arrest Report: Suspect: James Edward Billingsly. Charge: Aggravated assault and robbery. Time of arrest: 8:17 a.m. Place of arrest: 3517 South First.

Abilene was divided north and south on either side of the railroad tracks that ran east and west. Numbered streets ran parallel with the tracks. North and South First Streets were almost all businesses.

Tree streets crossed the tracks—Cypress, Sycamore, Elm, Walnut, Hickory.

Narrative: Suspect taken into custody without incident.

Okay, he didn't fight or run. I flipped through my reporter's notepad. Back to the jail log. Name: James Billingsly. Booking Time: 8:50 a.m. White male. Thirty-eight years old.

You don't wake up at thirty-eight and start assaulting and robbing people. Chances were, Billingsly had a sheet. Somewhere.

I peered up from my notes. Let me get this straight. We don't know who got robbed and assaulted, when, or where, but they arrested James Billingsly for the crime a little after eight o'clock this morning on South First Street.

This probably happened in the middle of the night. With so many blanks, this was either a sexual assault or an underage victim. Or both. Robbery didn't fit with a juvenile victim.

I heard the door open. All those men were still in there. It wasn't an organized meeting, just an afternoon gabfest they didn't want me privy to. The redhead who slammed the door in my face opened it. "You're still here?" His hair was short and wavy.

"It would appear."

Red's brows drew together. "I thought you'd take the hint." His short-sleeved shirt exposed fair skin and freckles, matching his green eyes.

"I can't go back empty-handed. I need the story on James Billingsly."

Red called over his shoulder. "Callahan! Reporter here to see you." As he walked out of sight, I heard Red say to someone, "At least this one's got some stones."

It was a minute before a tall drink of water rounded the corner wearing cowboy boots and Wranglers. Black hat. White shirt. Rodeo buckle on his brown leather belt. Had to be Detective Callahan. He stepped into the hall, closing the door behind him. "What can I do for you?"

"My name is Kat Coe with the *Reporter-News*. Are you in charge of this robbery and assault case? The arrest of James Billingsly?"

"Yes, ma'am." He walked past me down the long hall toward the reception area, me trailing behind with my notepad. A big guy. I hadn't gotten a look at his face shaded by the hat.

"What can you tell me about the case?"

"Not much beyond that report."

"Oh ... Come on. You can give me more than that." I guess the snark in my voice stopped him.

He turned around, towering over me. I'd say Callahan was six feet one inch or two or even three, but something—maybe the hat and boots—made him seem, I don't know, bigger. He tucked his chin, peering down at me. "You know we don't talk to reporters."

"I just need the basics." I cleared my throat. "Like, who is the victim? What happened to the victim? Where did the robbery and assault occur? What time? You want me to go on?"

He stared at me for a moment. I wasn't sure of his expression. Was he dumbfounded? Disgusted? Or was he just about to laugh? He turned his back to me again. "Come in and sit down."

He entered an office big enough for his desk and a file cabinet, with two small, round-back wooden chairs in front of his desk.

For sure, I need to bark at the secretary more often.

He took off his hat and hung it on a hat rack in the corner behind his desk, ran his fingers through his hair, squeezed behind his desk, and started to sit down. He stopped and straightened, extending one hand toward the chairs. "Go ahead. Have a seat."

His hair, which had been hidden by the hat, was dark. I'd say almost black. Parted on the side and cut over his ears, the same as every respectable cowboy in Texas. He stood as I sat in one of the chairs and put my purse in the other, my reporter's notepad and pen in hand.

Then he sat.

The detective shuffled through papers on his desk, avoiding my eyes. Finally, he said, "James Billingsly was taken into custody for questioning in connection with a robbery and assault because he was a known sex offender in the vicinity. But he was released after his alibi was verified."

Anytime any cop talked about a case, they sounded mechanical.

Our gazes met and held. "So this is a sexual assault?"

"I didn't say that. I said he was a known offender in the vicinity." His eyes were a golden brown.

"Do you have a physical description of the offender? We could help get it out there."

Callahan rested his forearms on his desk, his hands folded in front of him, his gaze direct. "Broadcasting the description of an offender usually just gets us a bunch of bogus calls. We end up chasing our tails."

I might as well try to prime a plugged well as get information out of this guy. "Do you have a description? Yes or no?"

He leaned back in his chair and scratched his left brow with his little finger. He had a strong brow ridge. He tweaked his mouth to one side, his gaze bored into me. I was patient. At last, he said, "There were no witnesses." He paused, maybe waiting for me to ask another question. I didn't. He added, "And the victim can't talk."

"Can't or won't?" There was another gritty pause as he maintained that blank stare. I stared back, waiting for an answer.

He leaned his forearms back on the desk, his hands clasped together. He clenched his mouth and said, "The victim is dead."

My eyes felt like they popped out of their sockets. "So this is a murder?" My story just went to front page.

"As of thirty minutes ago, yes ma'am. It's a murder. The victim expired at Hendrick Medical Center."

Why did cops always say expired? The victim died. Just say it. "Can I get the name of the victim?"

"Your victim is a sixty-three-year-old white female." He cleared his throat, peering at his folded hands, which he tapped on the desk several times before he lifted his eyes to rejoin mine. "She was robbed and beaten … to death."

"And sexually assaulted," I added.

His dark brows bunched together. "I didn't say that."

"Yes or no? Was the victim sexually assaulted?"

"At this point, as far as we know, she was not." He had a low, slow West Texas drawl.

"Name of the victim and address where the crime took place?"

He turned his head aside and coughed into his fist. Rubbed his thumbnail across his lower lip. Cleared his throat again. "For the time being, we aren't releasing the name of the victim and to help keep her identity protected, I will not release the address of the assault."

I blinked. "You're kidding me, right? If she's not a sexual assault victim, that's public record."

He shook his head softly, the lips drawn tight.

"Seriously?" I leaned forward. "The legislature passed the Open Records Act while I was still in college. Has it not made its way to Abilene?"

A flash in his eyes slapped back. Ice was in his voice. "The law says we've gotta give you the documents you request without asking why." He aimed an index finger at me with his hands folded in front of him. "Looks to me like you've got it in your hand."

I held it up. "This is a bogus report."

"It is what it is."

My jaw sagged along with my shoulders. "I never—"

Detective Callahan ran his hand over his face and leaned in. "Listen. It's as bad as I've seen. Let's spare the woman's family more misery."

I was mute for a few seconds. Dumfounded, I leaned back in the chair. "This is unbelievable. You're really not going to give me the name of the victim or the address where the crime occurred?"

The corners of his mouth turned downward, his chin jutted, and he shook his head just enough to convey his message.

"How about when?" My pen was in hand, resting on my notepad. So far, it hadn't moved. "What time did this robbery and murder occur?"

"Hasn't been determined."

"What was taken? Money? Jewelry?"

"No comment."

I lifted my hands, flabbergasted. In my five years of reporting, I had never been this stonewalled. "Will you at least say, did this happen in a—"

"Residence." Those brown eyes would not let up. They called that color honey brown. Put those eyes in a tanned face accentuated by hair and eyebrows the color of rich chocolate fudge—and they grabbed you. And held you.

I cleared my throat and glanced at my notepad. "Did this occur near where Billingsly was taken into custody?"

He squinted at me. "What's your name again?"

"You said Billingsly was in the vicinity—"

"I said, 'What's your name again?'"

"Kat. Kat Coe. C-O-E." I dug into my purse and handed him my business card.

He leaned back in his desk chair, studying it. "Is that Kat, as in Kathy or Katherine or Kathleen or Katri—?"

"Katherine. Why do you people have a problem with Kat?"

He slipped the card into his shirt pocket. "I don't know what people you're talking about, but Katherine suits you better." He rested his forearms back on his desk. This guy had a unique ability to make you feel like he was looking right inside you, his gaze a tad narrow. A little unnerving, actually.

"Now, Katherine or Kat, I've told you about all I'm going to tell you—"

"You haven't told me anything."

His dark brows shifted high, perturbed at my interruption. "I've got work to do. You can say Abilene police questioned a person of interest in the robbery and murder of an elderly white female. The suspect was released after his alibi was checked out. If I were you, I wouldn't print his name because some people will automatically think he's guilty and try to lynch him. You can say Detective T.J. Callahan said…" He paused and glanced away, maybe gathering words from high in the room. "It's one of the most sickening, violent crimes I've investigated." His gaze came back, meeting mine. "And we will find the killer." He leaned back with a head nod, effectively dismissing me. "There's your statement, Miss Coe. More than that, you'll have to get somewhere else."

I finished jotting his quote. A flurry of questions crowded my mind, but there was no point in trying to get answers from him. Callahan was a giant boulder blocking me from the facts. "May I get your card to make sure I spell your name and title correctly?"

He dug in his top desk drawer and handed me one. Didn't keep business cards on him. Interesting.

I tucked the card in the notepad, the notepad in my purse, stood and offered him my hand. "Thank you. I appreciate this." *Not.*

He stared at my hand—didn't take it—and lifted his eyes to meet mine. "You screw me on this, Katherine, and you'll never get another chance."

I drove as fast as the law allowed and ran into the newsroom. Jack McPherson was my city editor. Jack answered to a managing editor, who answered to the editor, who answered to the publisher. I seldom saw any manager other than Jack. They had private offices and seemed to live in the clouds like news gods. They were about the big picture and budgets.

I was just a reporter.

As city editor, Jack ran the room. His reputation for mentoring and developing reporters was one of the main reasons I took the job.

The *Reporter-News* was the daily newspaper of record for a vast swath of middle Texas, circulated from Ranger to the west of Sweetwater, Ballinger to Stephenville, Breckenridge to Goldthwaite. *ARN* was a respected newspaper, and I was delighted when Jack offered me the position.

The *San Angelo Standard-Times*, where I'd worked since college, and the *Abilene Reporter-News* were sister newspapers owned by Hart-Hanks, so it was an inner-company transfer that offered me a chance to grow and get away from San Angelo.

"Jack!" I ran across the room, waving my notepad. "I've got a murder! Front page!" A month in Abilene, and I hadn't had a front-page story.

He peered at me over black-rimmed reading glasses with an amused grin. "Okay. Tell me." Leaning back in his swivel desk chair, Jack twirled his red ink pen as I filled him in on what little I had. Elderly female, robbed and beaten. Died at the hospital later.

"That's not much more than a blurb on page three." He waved me away and went back to scanning wire copy. "Go knock some doors if you want to make front page."

"I've got a hunch there's more to this. They're too vague."

His gaze lifted. "How vague?"

He hadn't been paying attention. Dammit!

"I told you, Jack. He won't give me the address where it happened or the name of the victim and it's not a sexual assault. All I have is the name of the man who was booked into the jail and released, and the address where he was picked up. It was an aggravated assault and robbery, but the victim died at Hendrick this afternoon, which makes it murder." It hit me. "Actually, she died in the commission of another felony, so this is capital murder."

Jack pushed his glasses on top of his head, leaned his forearms on his desk, and squinted. "Who wouldn't release the victim's name or address of the crime?"

I heard Callahan in my head. "Screw me on this, and you'll never get another chance."

I didn't need Jack chewing out the chief of police because Callahan wouldn't release information. I'd just gotten my toe in the door. "They won't release the address of the assault to protect the identity of the victim, someone said."

Jack's face hardened before my eyes. His chin jutted, and he rubbed it with his fist. A pointed chin on a narrow face. Slowly, his gaze broke away from mine, and he bellowed the name of the chief photographer. "King!" Jack waved. "Get over here!"

Jimmy King all but ran across the newsroom. Jimmy was wiry and nimble. The best news photographers were as flexible as a bull rider. I'd seen those guys contort their bodies to get the proper lighting and angle for the shot they wanted.

Jimmy had shaggy, dishwater blonde hair and light blue eyes, and his work had garnered tons of awards from the Texas Press Association. Somehow, he was always the one who managed to get *the* shot. Suffice it to say, everyone held Jimmy King in awe.

We stood side by side in front of Jack's desk. Two kids in front of the principal.

"What have you heard on the scanners today?" Jack asked him. Photographers carried portable scanners attached to their belts.

Jimmy glanced at me, then answered Jack. "I haven't heard squat. The morning shift said there was some activity in Rolling Meadows early, but Mikey said he cruised the neighborhood. Didn't see anything."

Jack took off his glasses and stood. He was a tall, thin man with dark brown hair. He wagged those glasses. "When they hide stuff, it means there's something to hide." His eyes were on Jimmy but landed back on me. "Kat, you've got the murder of a VIP and the cops are trying to keep a lid on it. Now blow that friggin' lid off." He aimed those glasses at us like a magic wand. "It'd be damned nice if you could beat the bastards at their own game." He shooed us. "Go to the address where they arrested the suspect. Start there."

It was still in my head. "They got him at 3517 South First a little after eight this morning."

"That's a business," Jimmy said.

I checked my watch. "It'll close before long."

"Probably where he works," Jimmy said. "I'll drive."

Chapter 2

I was moving up in the newsroom. My first time on assignment with a photographer, and I drew Jimmy King. "That should be a car lot," he said. "Maybe a mechanic or car salesman."

"They let him go. His alibi checked out."

Swerving around a car he considered to be moving too slowly, Jimmy cut his eyes at me riding in the passenger seat. "Put on your seat belt. What time did the offense occur?"

I buckled up. "He said it hasn't been determined."

"Who said?"

"Detective Callahan."

"Oh, man." Jimmy groaned. "I hear he's a giant asshole."

"He's a giant something."

"You don't have the name, time, or place? Sneaky bastard." Jimmy stomped on the accelerator.

I white-knuckled the door handle. "So we get the story anyway."

Jimmy grinned, passing another slow Joe. "That'll piss them off. I like the way you think."

News photographers had city maps imprinted on their brains, and they could cross town as fast as any emergency vehicle. Jimmy thought 3517 South First was a car lot. It was an oil change place next door to a car lot. We walked in together. "Is James Billingsly here?"

"Who wants to know?" asked a brawny guy wiping big, greasy hands with a red rag already smudged with black oil. He wore a dark blue uniform.

"I'm Kat Coe, with the *Reporter-News*. This is Chief Photographer Jimmy King."

The guy had bulging chest muscles. His biceps and forearms were those of a bodybuilder. You couldn't miss the muscles flexing as he aimed his oily red rag at Jimmy, who had a camera hanging around his neck. "Don't take pictures, asshole."

Jimmy didn't respond. The two stared at each other as I coaxed. "I just need to talk to Mr. Billingsly. I understand—"

"I'm James Billingsly." His gaze left Jimmy to meet mine. "Yeah, they picked me up. They always do. They let me go. They always do. Because I didn't do a damned thing. I never do. I was at home with my wife and kids when Mrs. Bennett was beaten."

Jimmy and I exchanged glances. "Mrs. Bennett?"

Billingsly eagle-eyed us with new caution. "Yeah. That's why you're here, right?" Those eyes were sea green, and his close-cropped hair was the color of the sand on South Padre Island.

I pried. "Can you tell me what the cops said? They treat us like they treat you."

Billingsly shook his head, just barely. "Listen, if it makes any difference, yes, I'm a known sex offender. But they don't tell you that was twenty years ago, and the so-called sexual offense was consensual. I did time for having sex with a sixteen-year-old girl when I was eighteen."

I wasn't going there, but Billingsly wouldn't stop. "She was in big trouble with her rich family when we got caught, so they made it sound like an assault when it wasn't. But I still did time. Fuckers branded me for life."

"About this incident today," I said.

He waved his arm toward the street. "They come screeching in here after I opened up shop. Took me into custody. Wanted to know where I was between the hours of ten p.m. and six a.m. I told them at home with my wife and kids. My wife told them the same. So did my neighbor, who saw me leave for work at seven-thirty."

"They said you were in the vicinity. The offense report doesn't give the address."

Billingsly snorted and scratched his cheek, depositing grease on it. "You're a reporter and you don't know where the Bennett mansion is?"

"I do," Jimmy said. "Let's go."

"Can I get a statement from you, Mr. Billingsly? About this? Being arrested and released."

"Hell no, lady!" He waved us away with those still-greasy hands. "Get the hell out of here before you ruin my business."

Abilene only had a couple of genuinely affluent neighbor-hoods. One was by the country club. The other was Rolling Meadows, a subdivision of sprawling houses surrounded by acreage with white post-and-rail fences, some with wrought iron fences.

All were gated, with lush green lawns. Sprinkler systems were a sure sign of prosperity in a perennially parched part of Texas. Abilene might get twenty inches of rain on a good year. In a dry year, water was more valuable than oil.

"So, you know I'm new to Abilene. Who are the Bennetts?"

Jimmy cut his eyes at me as he weaved through traffic. "Henry Bennett. Bennett Construction. They build hospitals, schools, big shopping centers, and office complexes all over this part of Texas. I don't know, maybe all over Texas and Oklahoma. They're big."

This part of Texas was known as the Big Country.

You climbed Ranger Hill on Interstate 20, about eighty miles west of Fort Worth, and from that point on, almost all you saw was sky all the way to New Mexico and Kansas. The West Texas sky was usually empty, anywhere from dusty blue to cobalt, depending on how much of the Panhandle was blowing in it.

The windswept prairie was broken here and there by high plateaus—mesas, we called them. Abilene was about halfway between Fort Worth and Odessa, smack dab in the great big, wide-open middle of Texas. Those endless skies afforded kaleidoscope-colored sunrises and sunsets, their glory unobstructed by mountains, big trees, or buildings.

Prickly pear, mesquite, sage, and cedar dotted the land where deer and buffalo once roamed. Yes, this was cow and cowboy country where the air always moved. Some people hated the West Texas wind, but I reveled in it. Something about the wind made me feel free.

Jimmy stopped on the paved road in front of a particularly grand house. It was a two-story mansion built of Austin stone with a round turret on one corner.

Who lives in a house like that? A glistening white castle, out of place on the Texas prairie. The arched, wrought-iron gate, which hung between tall, white stone columns, was open.

Jimmy studied me for a moment. "You want to go up and knock on the door?"

I hated that part of the job. I had to gird myself every time I had to intrude on the privacy of a grieving family. We were more likely to be run off than well received. "I don't know how else I'll get a story."

Jimmy winked and twisted his neck. "Like I said, I like your style."

The house stood half a football field from the road, with a roundabout in front of it. There were no cars in sight.

Jimmy parked in front of the porch.

"I hope someone's here," I said as I exited the little white news car. "Otherwise, I'm striking out."

As we walked the cobblestone path to the steps leading up to the house, an oversized, arched, wooden front door swung open, and a small black woman stepped outside onto an uncovered porch, also paved with cobblestone. Tall black vases with red-berry holly stood on either side of the door, dwarfing her. Petite but plump with short gray hair. Her face was round like she was. "Deliveries are in the back." She wiped her hands on her apron.

"We're not delivering." I stepped toward her. "I'm sorry to intrude at this time, but I'm Katherine Coe with the *Reporter-News*, and this is Jimmy King. We wanted to talk to you about—"

She retreated into the house and closed the door, not with a slam but with a well-mannered, definitive *Click.*

Jimmy and I exchanged glances.

A man's voice mocked me from behind. "No, you're not sorry to intrude at this time." We turned. He was forty-ish, standing on the sidewalk. "It's your job. I'm Bass Bennett. I guess I know why you're here." He was tall and striking. That was black hair, not brown, and it fell into his dark brows. Long black lashes framed crisp, topaz blue eyes. They stood out.

"I am sorry, Mr. Bennett. I understand loss. But it is my job. Let us tell your story, in your words, rather than rely on the police." I glanced around the property. "What happened here?"

"What did you say your name was?"

"Kat Coe." I fished out my business card from my purse and handed it to him. "This is Jimmy King, our chief photographer." Jimmy handed over his card, too.

Bass peered at each, studied me momentarily, and then pointed at the house. "The housekeeper found my mother early this morning." He shoved his hands and the business cards into his tan pants pockets and lowered his head, talking to the ground. "She was in the dining room ... tied to a chair." He hesitated, then lifted his head, his gaze meeting mine. "She was beaten. Her face...." He spun around and took a few steps away. His head hung again, and his shoulders heaved for a moment.

Jimmy and I exchanged glances. Jimmy wasn't taking photographs, just watching Bass Bennett. He knew this wasn't the time. I was just glad he hadn't thrown us off the property. Yet.

Bass collected himself and then wiped his eyes as he faced me. "She was ... unrecognizable."

Unrecognizable?

My hand covered my mouth. "Oh, Mr. Bennett, I'm so sorry." I gave it a moment, remembering Callahan saying, 'It's as bad as I've seen.'

"May I get your mother's full name? We know almost nothing from the police."

"Marilyn. Marilyn Bass Bennett." He wiped the corner of one eye with a knuckle.

"And how old was she?" I was scribbling.

"Sixty-three."

"Your father?"

"My father's Henry Bennett. Hank. Dad's been gone a little more than a year. Mom lives here alone." He cleared his throat. "Lived here alone. The housekeeper and gardener come each day around seven. Like I said, Miranda found her when she came to work."

If I scribbled too fast, I'd have trouble deciphering my shorthand, so I did my best to keep up and write legibly. I peered over my shoulder at the front door. "Was that Miranda who just came out?"

"No. I sent Miranda home. She was too upset to work."

"And that lady?"

"She works for me. I asked Sadie to stay here today. I'm not sure why. But after Mother passed, I just ... needed to come back here ... and I didn't really want to be alone." He lifted his shoulders. "I grew up here. Anyway, back to this morning. Miranda called me in a panic. When I realized what she was saying, I told her to hang up and call an ambulance. I called the police and headed this way. I got here before they did." He pointed. "I just live about a mile that way."

"Your mother was alive when you got here?" I asked.

"Yes."

"Please, Bass. Let us tell your mother's story. Who was she, and what happened here?"

"My mother was...." He lifted his shoulders again, his blue eyes searching the empty sky. His gaze came back to mine. "My mother was a wonderful human being. Ask anyone. She was a leader. Head of the Junior League. Compassionate. Mom volunteered at the hospital. Active in church, First Baptist. She played golf and tennis. Loved her grandchildren." He lifted his palms. "I mean, everybody loved my mother. Why would anyone do this? To her?"

Still scribbling, I asked, "Was the house ransacked? Robbed?"

"Yes. Dad had a safe. They got what they wanted. Why do that to her?"

"Show me," Jimmy said. "Can I take a picture of the safe?"

Ballsy, Jimmy.

Bass paused a moment, stared at Jimmy, and lifted his shoulders. "I don't see why not."

Oh. Wow.

We followed Bass into the house, exchanging glances, both of us a little in shock. Jimmy was forging a new frontier, getting interior crime scene photos. I'd never heard of it happening. Anywhere. You could take and publish all the photographs you want from the public road or sidewalk, but inside? That wasn't done.

The mansion's foyer was what you'd expect: ostentatious, lofty ceilings, polished marble floor, large, framed oil paintings on the walls, not prints. Floor-to-ceiling windows across the back showcased a landscaped swimming pool and cabana.

Bass turned left off the foyer, leading us through a large sitting room into a smaller office, a round room inside the turret. I took that to be mahogany paneling. A portrait of a stately-looking, silver-haired man hung on the wall directly behind a massive mahogany desk. He was, I presumed, Bass's father. A banker's lamp with a green shade illuminated the desk.

A few feet to the right of the portrait was the safe, set into the wall. Its door hung open on one hinge. "Dad's safe was hidden behind a painting. They took it."

Jimmy started snapping shots as I kept Bass talking. He swung his arm wide. "This room was ransacked. I checked the whole house. "The only other room trashed was the master bedroom. All of Mother's jewelry is gone."

Police had dusted for prints, evidenced by little poofs of white powder all around on the walls and furniture. "The safe was empty. I have no idea what was in it. Dad was a sportsman. He owned a lot of rifles and handguns. They're all gone." A large, empty gun case stood to the right of the safe, and on either side of it hung the mounts of trophy deer and elk.

"Do you know if the police got any fingerprints?"

He shook his head gently. "They said it looked like they wore gloves."

If they wore gloves, this was no crime of opportunity. It was planned, and Callahan knew it.

"Can you tell me about the painting that was stolen? I asked.

"It was a Bierstadt."

My expression reflected my ignorance of art. Bass clarified, his voice and expression condescending. "Albert Bierstadt...." He got nothing back from me. "Western landscape."

"Was it valuable?"

"Yes."

"Do you want to say how—?"

"No."

Jimmy asked, "Can I get a nice photograph of your mother? One you'd want to represent her in the paper?"

Bass nodded at Jimmy, then peered at me. "What else do you want to know?"

I racked my brain. "When was the last time you saw your mother before you found her?"

"Yesterday afternoon I was over here."

"When you arrived today, was she able to talk to you? To tell you what happened?"

He chewed a thumbnail, the corners of his mouth turned down. "She was unconscious. I checked her pulse. She was alive. The ambulance and cops got here a few minutes later. I'd untied her and laid her on the couch." He closed his eyes and softly shook his head again. "She was … so … battered." He averted his eyes, still shaking his head. "It was … awful."

"She wasn't assaulted—sexually?"

"No."

"Any weapon left lying around? Anything the police took?"

"The police dusted for fingerprints and took samples of blood on the table and floor around her. They even took the chair she was tied to, I think, for some kind of forensic analysis."

"I hate the question, but can you express how you feel? What do you want now?"

He sighed and ran his hand over his face, pressing against his eyes with his thumb and forefinger. "There are no words." He stared into space for a long moment, then looked directly into my eyes, and for the first time, I saw a frightening rage. "Come to think of it there are a lot of words. Horrified. Sick. Empty. Outraged. Livid. I want her killers found and sentenced to death. I'd like to kill them myself."

I stopped taking notes to reconnect with Bass. "Killers. Plural. You think there was more than one?"

He drew back. "Me personally? Yes. I don't know what the cops think. They don't tell me anything. But I think someone beat her while someone else went through this house."

"Was there a break-in?"

He lifted a shoulder. "That's just it. Not that we can find. She let someone in."

My heart hurt for him. "Someone she knew did that to her?"

His eyes darted about. "I don't know. But there are no broken windows, no doors jimmied. Police said there was no evidence of a forced entry."

"And what time do they think this happened?"

He raised his shoulder. "Middle of the night, I guess. My wife talked to Mom during the ten o'clock news. She said she was going to watch Johnny Carson and go to bed. So sometime after ten but before seven, when Miranda found her."

I had a thought. "Was she in her nightgown? Dressed for bed? Like she woke up and came downstairs?"

"No. She was wearing black slacks and a pink blouse, one of her favorites—the same thing she had on when I was here earlier." He paused for a long moment as he pressed against his eyelids, as he'd done earlier, as if he wanted to blot out the vision. They ripped her earrings out of her ears."

"Ripped?" It was Jimmy.

"Yes. Like I said, I was here yesterday afternoon. Mom had on new diamond hoop earrings. Pink diamonds that matched her blouse. She was so proud of them. And someone ripped them out of her ears."

Chapter 3

Suffice it to say I had one hell of a front-page story with a byline the following day. "Socialite Savagely Slain!" the headline screamed.

We ran the portrait photograph of Marilyn Bass Bennett that her son furnished. She was striking, with the same black hair and electric blue eyes I'd seen in her son. Marilyn Bennett was aristocratic in appearance with fine-chiseled features, a delicate chin, and nose. Along with the story, we printed an above-the-fold photo of the office with the portrait of Henry Bennett behind the desk. Beside it was the empty wall safe with its door hanging by one hinge. White fingerprint dust showed all around the desk and safe.

I used the direct quote from Abilene Police Detective T.J. Callahan. "It's one of the most sickening, violent crimes I've investigated and we will find the killer," the detective said.

I also used quotes from Bass about the housekeeper finding his mother. Well, I used most of what Bass told me. Why not?

Callahan didn't put anything usable in his police report. We included that a suspect was questioned and released. We did not print that suspect's name.

Jack had the business editor do a sidebar on Henry Bennett and Bennett Construction's legacy. Someone else did a companion piece profiling Marilyn Bennett's contribution to charity. She was a millionaire in her own right, heiress to some Western aristocrat's fortune.

The Bennett murder stories took up a big chunk of the front page, were carried inside, and were picked up by the Associated Press. I was looked upon with new respect in the newsroom.

Not so much at the cop shop.

I checked the jail logs. No arrests for murder and nothing else of interest, so I drove straight to the police station, asking to speak to Detective Callahan to check on the progress of the investigation.

"He's not available." Big Tits was more rabid than usual.

"May I leave a message? Ask him to call me?" I handed her my business card.

She snatched it from my hand and dropped it into her empty trash can without looking at it or me. "You wanna talk to Callahan? Crawl on your belly like the snake you are."

What a bimbo. "That's a little over the top, don't you think?"

"Hmph." She turned her back to me, pounding that brown Remington electric typewriter. Some report in triplicate. "You messed up everything." She ripped the report from the typewriter. It made a zipping noise. She crumpled carbon paper and chunked it into the trash. Still no eye contact. "They hold back details that only the killer knows. Now you've put everything out there."

"Well, maybe if someone told me that."

"I did tell you that." Callahan came through the detective division door. He didn't look at me as he walked past. "I told you all you needed to know." He called over his shoulder. "Prissy, I'm on beeper."

I watched him pass and darted after him. "There would be no news if all reporters did was swallow your crap. The people have the right to know."

He stopped and turned with a fry-in-hell glare. "The people also have the right to a properly conducted police investigation. You just blew the hell out of any chance of that."

They always overreact.

He stomped away, shoving the heavy glass lobby door with his open palm. It flew back, and I trailed after him, slipping through the door just before it shut. "How? How could my story hurt your investigation?"

He kept walking. Long strides.

I scurried to keep up. "Tell me, how did I hurt your investigation?"

He finally stopped and turned. I could feel the rage coming off of him. "Well, how about we start with the safe? Only the immediate family and the killer even knew it existed. That it was robbed. That the door was hanging by one hinge. That the friggin' Bierstadt was stolen! That we dusted for prints. That rifles were taken. And jewelry." His voice boomed as he swept his arm wide. "Now the whole damned world knows!"

He's still overreacting.

He stepped toward me, and I backed away, eyes wide. "Then let's move to the victim." He leaned in. "I didn't tell you she was tied to a chair. Now, did I?"

"No, Bass told me. Which means he also told everyone he knew, and they told everyone they knew." I was talking to his back. He'd turned mid-sentence and was walking across the parking lot toward a big black truck. "Things like that get out, Callahan, with or without a newspaper. You can't keep your thumb on everything."

He swung his right arm high. "Don't come back!"

I dashed after him again. "It's like a bad marriage, Buster. You're stuck with me!"

He tromped back, looming intimidatingly close. "I'll never talk to you again. I've had nothing but grief since I got up this morning." He actually jabbed his finger at me. "I told you, burn me and you'll never get another chance."

"I didn't burn you. I didn't print anything from you but the direct quote you gave me. You said, 'If you need any more, you'll have to get it somewhere else.'" I'd mocked him. "That's what I did. You left me no choice. I have a job to do, too, you know."

Damn, those eyes got big.

His brows climbed high, wrinkling his long forehead. "You have a job to do?" He glanced around the parking lot, standing as tall as he got—which was damned tall—his chin high. He sneered with an eviscerating glare. "You have a job to do? No! I have a job to do!"

Callahan's face flushed, and the veins on his neck bulged. I thought he might explode as he pointed at the police station. "We are sworn to protect and defend. We catch killers. We bring families justice." He stretched his arm toward me. "And what do you do? Fuck up our investigation, that's what."

He started to stomp off but turned back as if with an afterthought. "Tell me something. How does knowing the details of a murder improve anybody's life? How did showing that safe help anyone?"

"It's my job to inform the public. The public has the right—"

"To know. I heard."

Oh, Lord. He'd dip me in a vat of boiling oil if he thought he could get away with it.

He went on ranting. "Let me tell you something, Missy. Some things the public doesn't need to know, like exactly how a crime is committed. Nobody needs to know that. We keep details secret in case a suspect slips up and says something that proves he was there. Details make or break investigations."

"You two look like a married couple bickering in the parking lot." Red was approaching. Clearly not a nice guy.

We both turned our heads, glaring at him. "Butt out, Clancy!" Callahan growled.

I peered at the redheaded Clancy, who'd joined us, then focused back on Callahan. "Like it or not, you two are stuck with me. I'm the cop reporter. I'll be here every ... damned ...

day. And if you don't talk to me, you leave me no choice but to get my information from other sources." My gaze narrowed. "And make no mistake, Buster, I will, because, surprise, surprise, other people do talk to me. So maybe you'd be better served to treat me with some respect. Lay it out there. I won't print something if I know it will ruin a murder investigation."

I felt fire in my cheeks. My heart raced as I jabbed my finger back at him. "I used your direct quote. That's all I used from you. Everything else I got elsewhere like you told me to do."

They exchanged glances, mutually dismissing me, and each walked away without response. Clancy headed south down the parking lot; Callahan headed back toward that black truck. I followed him. Oh, man. He took big steps. "Where are you going?"

"Go find a quilting bee to cover!" He got into his truck and slammed the door, starting the engine and putting it in reverse. He began backing out.

I cupped my hands and yelled. "I'm going to follow you! And the only quilting bee I'll ever cover is the one where someone gets killed!"

He slammed his truck into park, got out, and marched to me, looming large. "I'll arrest you for obstructing justice."

I'd have laughed if I hadn't thought he might throttle me. "How am I obstructing justice? You're the detective in charge of the case I'm assigned to cover. That's not obstructing. What's the next step?"

"We're following up on leads."

"Do you have a suspect?"

He flailed his arm high. "You're worse than my mother. It's none of your friggin' business!"

"It's the public's business."

He roared, "Oh, Geez! Give me a fuckin' break!" His voice had gotten louder with each exchange. If I glanced over my shoulder, I'd see people inside the police station gawking out the lobby windows. I'm sure we made quite a show. I dared not look.

Callahan turned his back, taking big breaths, staring at the sky. He turned in a circle, glancing around the parking lot and back up at the sky. He took off his hat, wiped his forehead with his forearm, and slapped that hat against his thigh like cracking a whip.

Oh, shit! That man was good-looking. Damn!

That gaze came back to meet mine with a wicked slice. "If—and I mean if—I agree to talk to you, will you not go behind my back and print crap that hurts my investigation?"

"I'll make you a deal. Stop hiding stuff. Talk to me. I won't print anything unless you say it's on the record. And if I get information beyond what you give me, I'll run it by you to verify it and to find out if publishing it would screw you up. Scout's honor."

"And you won't print it?"

I lifted my hands in surrender. "If you swear to be honest. You can't say every crumb of information I get is going to ruin your investigation. Only what really will, if it's published."

He glared. I guess he was waiting for me to commit, so I did. "Then I won't print it."

His gaze narrowed, and he rubbed his thumbnail along his lower lip. He was studying me.

I stared back, waiting for an answer. I'd given all I was going to give. A stand-off in the parking lot of the Abilene Police Department no guns drawn.

Callahan glanced away and muttered under his breath. Finally, he growled, "Deal."

I offered my hand. "Shake on it."

He stared at it and finally shook it. His hand was twice the size of mine.

The stars must have been crossed. For some reason, it was a day for fights. I was barely back in the newsroom when a ruckus erupted between the sports guys and the education reporter. I heard the commotion when the elevator doors opened.

The sports guys—there were seven in all, but only four or five were in the newsroom at the time—huddled around a TV, cheering and jeering over some college basketball play-off game—March Madness. I was maybe three steps into the newsroom when they roared and high-fived each other over what had apparently been a stupendous shot on some college basketball court.

Like a Jack-in-the-Box, Carol VanMeter, who covered education, popped up from her desk chair and yelled. "Guys! Quiet down! I'm trying to work!" Carol was a tall woman with long auburn hair who was usually timid.

Being guys, the sports bunch shot her an obligatory glance and continued, glued to their TV.

Halfway to my desk, they erupted again, and Carol yelled louder. "I asked y'all nicely to quiet down!"

Nothing. The sports guys kept it up.

She stood again, turned in a circle, peering around the room for help. Everybody had their heads down. Carol cupped her hands around her mouth like a bullhorn and shouted. "Guys! Shut the fuck up!"

They did.

The sports guys gaped, jaws slack, all eyes wide and trained on Carol, not the TV.

She jabbed her finger at them. "Yeah, that's what I said. Shut. The. Fuck. Up!"

Everyone in the newsroom froze, silent for ten seconds or so, until the sports guys erupted with laughter.

The rest of the room joined in.

The copy desk and several reporters stood and applauded Carol, who peered at Jack with her hands held high as the sports guys kept cackling.

Jack stood at his desk and roared, "That's enough!" His voice was surprisingly big.

The sports guys all went mum, peering from one to the other, and Jack hollered again, sweeping his arm across the room. "Everybody! Back to work!"

I loved the newsroom.

I chortled all the way to my desk. I'd never heard Carol speak, much less swear. She was the mouse that roared. Fuck, on top of that. And the sports guys got spanked. Too funny.

Approaching my desk, my nearest neighbor, Al Nichols, winked. "I didn't know she had it in her." Al raised his big old hand and high-fived me. "If she hadn't done it, I was fixin' to."

Wow.

Newsrooms were naturally loud with the ubiquitous clacking of half a dozen teletype machines and babbling police scanners, but the sports guys apparently pushed it to an intolerable level. If Al had enough, you knew it was over the top. He was as unflappable as Molly Brown.

I was fortunate. I could tune it all out.

The teletypes were comforting to me—a proof-of-life sort of thing pounding away over there. We had a bunch of them: Associated Press (AP), United Press International (UPI), and several syndicated news services like the Washington Post, Knight-Ridder, and LA Times. Sports had their own teletype, and we had one dedicated to weather.

Those machines hammered out life in real time, and by virtue of sitting near them, I got to read what was happening before the rest of the world knew. There was something about knowing before anyone else that I liked. I guess that's why I chose that path in life. I liked knowing.

Each machine had a bell. Now and then, one or more would *Ding! Ding! Ding!* as an important news story broke. News flashes, they were called. Depending on the number of *dings*, we'd rush to the wall to see what happened.

I remembered the day Elvis died. August 16, 1977. The teletypes went ape shit.

Their constant racket bumfuzzled some staff members, who complained. Management discussed encasing them behind glass to muffle their sound. I loathed the idea. If you don't like noise, go work in advertising. News is life, and life is loud and messy, painful, and poignant all at the same time. Deal with it or get in another line of work. Whinny babies.

Speaking of noise. The bank of scanners behind the city editor's desk monitored emergency responder radio transmissions. We kept one scanner locked on each important frequency. Otherwise, you might miss something. Police dispatch and officers in the field, the sheriff's department and deputies, the Department of Public Safety dispatch and officers, the fire department, trucks, and EMTs. Now and then, we even heard something from Dyess Air Force Base.

Some people found them as distracting as the teletypes, hollering out, "Turn those damned scanners down!"

Oh, well. They didn't bother me, either. They were crucial to my beat. And I'd learned when to perk my ears for important transmissions and which ones to tune out. It was the level of excitement in a voice. A keyword.

Emergency responders used Ten Codes, which were developed in the 1930s. Law enforcement shorthand we learned in college. Ten-fifty was a major wreck. Listen up. Someone yells, "Ten-thirty-three!" Stop what you're doing. That was an emergency. You had to know their jargon. When someone said he was ten-forty-two, he was ending his shift. Ten-forty-one meant he was starting it.

I keep saying him because, in 1980, a mere five percent of the nation's police force was female, and none had found their way to West Texas. At least, not that I knew of.

I recalled Callahan telling me to find a quilting bee to cover. Sexist son of a horse's ass. Well, truthfully, I'd almost chortled at his quip, but had I done that, he really might have dipped me into a vat of boiling oil. But the point was: I was as impervious to their condescending, sexist remarks as I was to the noise.

My daddy preached to his daughters all of our lives: "Don't let anyone tell you that you can't do anything you want to do because you're a woman." I took his words to heart. Yes, I had breasts, and I could make babies, and the guy over there had a dick and a different role in baby-making, but our anatomical parts didn't have a damned thing to do with how good a reporter we were. What mattered was the mental acuity and the amount of gumption we brought to the game.

Five years in San Angelo, I'd won several awards from the Texas Press Association, just not as many as Jimmy. No one had. But I held my own in a man's world.

Al called over his shoulder, a cigarette dangling from his mouth, "By the way, kid. Hell of a story this morning."

I plunked my purse down on my desk. "Thanks."

"Damned smart snagging the Bennett kid. Good color."

"Appreciate it, Al." That meant a lot, coming from him. Al was a veteran, and he was right. Bass Bennett made that story.

What hair Al still had was gray. He had to be staring at sixty. He wasn't much taller than me but outweighed me by a hundred pounds, and he had thick, hairy arms. "Whatcha' got workin' today?" he asked.

"Not a lot so far." That sounded pretty whiny.

"Well, hang in there, kid. Take the good days with the bad." He lit one cigarette off the other from the time I got to work until he left at five. It didn't bother me. My dad smoked. I was used to it.

We all drank from the same cauldron of coffee in the back of the newsroom, relegated to a table just outside the photographers' dark room. It was a big metal barrel sitting on black plastic feet with a spigot at the bottom. I don't know how many gallons it held, but that coffee could grow hair on you by deadline.

As the newbie, I took obituaries by dictation over the telephone from all the funeral homes in the distribution area. I'd just finished the last obit and went for a fresh cup of coffee when Jimmy emerged from his dark room cave. "What's new on the Bennett murder?" he asked quietly.

"Not much." I sipped the bitter brew and grimaced. Nothing fresh about it, but it was warm. "I've been ostracized at the cop shop."

Jimmy snickered. His aquamarine eyes twinkled. "Boy, I bet they were pissed about the shots of the safe."

"You have no idea."

"Don't worry about it. Everyone knows Callahan's a hard ass."

"I'm working on him." I didn't remember anyone ever being that mad at me, but I'd convinced him, at least for now, to work with me. I guess I won round one.

Jimmy pulled the spigot and set his cup to catch the flow of black liquid. "They're either going to make this case pronto or never make it at all." He clenched his fingertips tightly in front of his face, Italian-style. "I feel it. It's one of those."

I watched him over my coffee cup. "My update sucks. Waiting on forensics, funeral day after tomorrow, blah blah."

Jimmy glanced both ways. "I was listening to her son yesterday. To Bass." He checked around as if being sure no one was nearby. "The way he described his mother. Nobody's a saint."

I peered at him over my cup of coffee. "She sounded like one to me, from everyone we talked to."

He whispered. "I overheard something."

The teletypes went nuts just around the corner, so I moved closer to hear better.

Jimmy nodded at Jack, way across the room, reading. "They'll never let you defame someone with her status and reputation but maybe, just maybe, she wasn't so lily white."

I was hooked like a wide-mouthed bass. "What did you hear?"

"I think maybe," he glanced around again. "Maybe she was having an affair. Maybe with somebody else's husband."

Reel me in. "You've got to be kidding me. Why do you think that?"

"Like I said, I overheard something."

"From who?"

Jimmy downed his coffee, tossed his Styrofoam cup in the trash, took me by the arm, and ushered me into the photographers' dark room. The name was fitting. One red lightbulb over a table with three trays of liquid illuminated it. I could barely see, but like a little mole, Jimmy was at home in the darkness. "Fred Beasley was whispering to someone on the telephone. Something like, 'What if it comes out about Marilyn and Tex?' Her husband's name was Hank, you know, so if Tex wasn't married, there'd be no cause for concern about people knowing she was seeing him. Right? She was a widow."

I'd been there long enough to know Fred Beasley was one of the newspaper's biggest advertisers. He owned two or three car dealerships. Jimmy not only worked for editorial, but he also took photos for the advertising department. He rubbed elbows with influential people.

"Tex who?" I asked.

"Hell if I know. Maybe we need to talk to that gardener. Or housekeeper."

"No. They won't talk to us." I was certain. Not based on the housekeeper's demeanor the day before. That old girl looked at me like I had smallpox. But then again, Bass said she wasn't the regular housekeeper.

"Housekeepers and gardeners hear plenty and see more," Jimmy said. "But they won't talk to just anyone. Let me see what I can do for you. Maybe somebody knows somebody who knows somebody." Jimmy was born and raised in Abilene. People whispered that the *Houston Chronicle* and *Dallas*

Morning-News had courted him, but Jimmy's roots ran too deep in the Big Country.

"What we really need is a source inside their circles," I said. "The country club set."

He snickered. "That ain't you or me, darlin.' I'm not tight with a solitary soul who's a member of the country club. Are you?"

Tossing back the last bit of my coffee, I grimaced, conceding defeat.

Jimmy winked. "I say, let's look in low places."

That was a thought. I added, "Like, who did her nails? Her hair? Those ladies hear lots, too."

Jimmy high-fived me. "We're on the same page."

I'd just taken her obituary and sent it to the city desk. "Her funeral is at ten o'clock, the day after tomorrow."

"What's the rush?"

"I had the same reaction when the funeral home told me, but they said the family just wanted to get it over with. Tomorrow's my day off. The service is the next day at First Baptist, burial at Woodlawn."

"Meet you at the church," Jimmy said. "Ten o'clock. Day after tomorrow.

I went back to my desk, stewed on it, and headed for the morgue—not the one with dead bodies, but the one with dead stories, located adjacent to the newsroom. All newspapers maintained libraries of published stories dating back Lord only knows how many years.

A librarian and her assistants clipped news stories from the newspaper daily. They filed them by name and category—yes, with scissors. What day did the tornado tear up Winters? Check with the morgue. They could find the answer under Winters or Tornado.

An older woman was on duty. I wasn't sure of her name, but she knew mine. "What do you need, Kat?" She smiled, standing at the Dutch door entrance to her department. Locked on the bottom, open on top. Nobody went back there but the archivists.

"Does the name Tex mean anything to you?"

Her face said, poor dear, what a stupid question. "Lots of men around here are named or nicknamed Tex."

I tweaked my mouth to one side.

She asked, "Why do you ask?"

I glanced at her name badge hanging on a lanyard around her neck, like our press badges. Maybelle was her name. I'd say she was about Al's age. "Maybelle, I heard a rumor. Something about Mrs. Bennett and someone named Tex."

Her eyes grew large. "Tex Gibson?"

I shifted my shoulders. "No idea."

"Well, those two run in the same social circles," Maybelle said, holding up her index finger. "Wait a minute."

She returned a few minutes later with a photograph of two smiling couples at the Cattle Baron's Ball. The caption listed the names of Hank and Marilyn Bennett standing with Tex and Roxanne Gibson, the men in tuxedos, and the women in long gowns. Maybelle tapped the clipping. "That's several years ago, but you can see they ran together."

I studied the photograph. The Bennetts were taller people than the Gibsons. Hank Bennett had an air of refinement, as did his wife. Both were statuesque, with salt and pepper hair. More pepper than salt. Standing in the photo beside Marilyn, Tex Gibson was a brawny man with gray hair and a thick mustache. He had his arm around his wife's waist. She was a petite, black-haired beauty, the smallest of the four.

In the photo, Tex and Marilyn appeared to be the same height. But she was probably wearing high heels, meaning Tex was a few inches taller but twice as thick as she was. He was built like James Billingsly, just older.

I whispered. "Don't repeat this, Maybelle. It's just a rumor."

"I understand." She had a kind smile. "Have you asked Mike about Tex?"

"Mike who?"

"My, you are new. Mike Tomlin covers oil and gas. He'd know more about Tex Gibson than anyone else."

Stunned, I asked, "We have someone who does nothing but cover oil and gas?"

She grinned and nodded.

I had a lot to learn about the *Reporter-News*. "I've never seen or heard of him."

"That's because Mike works dayside and mostly he's out in the field. Leave him a message. He's a good guy. Mike will talk to you."

"Where's his desk?"

"Over by sports."

I leaned over the Dutch door and hugged Maybelle. "Thank you."

"Tell the boss I deserve a raise." I think she was just glad to have company. I'd remember that. I turned around and gave her a thumbs-up.

Back at my desk, I debated with myself for a minute. Oh, what the hell?

I called the direct extension on his business card. I knew I was poking the bear. But I wondered.

The first ring, he answered in that low, slow drawl. "Detective Callahan."

"Callahan, this is Kat. Katherine. Coe."

I'm pretty sure I heard the f-word. His hand was probably over the mouthpiece. "Yeah?"

"Have you heard anything about Mrs. Bennett?"

He sighed heavily. "What about her?"

"I told you, if I got something, I'd run it past you. I'm doing what you wanted me to do."

"Okay."

I took a moment. How to phrase this? She was nobility in our part of the state, and per Jimmy's warning, I didn't want to smear her name just by asking the wrong question.

"So run it." He nudged.

"Have you heard anything about ... maybe ... she wasn't.... Maybe everything wasn't as perfect as it appeared at first?"

Silence.

"Callahan?" I asked.

Nothing.

"Are you there?"

"Yeah, I'm here." He sighed heavily, taking his time to speak. "No comment."

I snapped. "Seriously, how is this going to work? I have a tip that she's not as perfect as portrayed."

"So what? What could you do with that?" I pictured his glare.

"Nothing, unless I got it confirmed and learned it was relevant. Can you confirm she was seeing someone? And is it relevant?"

He guffawed. "Good luck with that."

"Fine. You leave me no choice but to go around the roadblock. And I will."

As I started to hang up the phone, his voice came across the line dangerously quiet. "Did you just threaten me?"

That sounded ominous.

"No, Detective Callahan, I'm trying to reason with you. Would it hurt your investigation if it came out that Marilyn Bennett was in the midst of an affair?"

After a long, irritating pause, "It might." No doubt, he swore. And this time, he didn't bother putting his hand over the mouthpiece. "Are you going to wart my ass constantly?" His voice got loud. "If you want to work this case, come on down. We'll switch places and I'll bug the hell out of you."

Okay, I was hounding stronger than usual, spurred by Jack's comment.

"We agreed if I found something I'd run it past you. So sorry for taking up your valuable time, detective." I slammed down the phone.

Horse's ass.

It rang right back. His go-to-hell glare traveled through the phone lines on his voice. "Let's get this bullshit between us ironed out. I'm trying to catch a killer and I don't have time to fight with you. It's distracting."

It took a second for that to soak in. So he threw down the gauntlet. You can't back down from a guy like that. One sign of weakness, and he'd eat you alive. My hands trembled, but my voice didn't. "When and where?"

"Have you ever been to Sambo's Barbecue?"

"No." He gave me the address. That voice. Something about him. I don't know. "I don't get off work until ten," I said.

"Neither do I. I'll buy you a beer. You and me, Miss Coe. We're going to have a meet and greet. And we're going to get some things straightened out."

"Fine. I'll meet you there."

Chapter 4

On first impression, Sambo's Barbecue was a dive. I mean a D-I-V-E dive off North Treadaway, not an upscale part of town. It was a shotgun-shaped cedar plank building with a metal roof and gravel parking lot. I heard the jukebox getting out of my car. *Mommas, don't let your babies grow up to be cowboys...*

I'd second that.

Only a few cars in the parking lot at almost ten-thirty on a weeknight. I took this to be one of those places where men brought women they weren't supposed to be with. That alone got my hackles up. Callahan's married, the secretary said. What'd he call her? Prissy? Had she said that as a warning? Did he think I was meeting him for a tryst?

I walked into the smokey joint. Well, it wasn't much smokier than the newsroom. A pool table and dart board were in the back. A few people congregated around both. That's also where the jukebox was. Ed Bruce's version of that song ended, and another had not begun. Things quietened a little.

Road signs, metal beer signs, and trophy deer were mounted on plank wood walls. Neon beer signs hung above the bar. Tables and chairs and booths. No dance floor.

Callahan was leaning against the bar over a mug of beer and what appeared to be an untouched barbecue sandwich, chatting up a blonde beside him when I walked in. Maybe his wife? She was taller than me, with straight blonde hair halfway down her back. Tight blue jeans. Skinny hips. Probably a barrel racer. I hated barrel racers. The whole damn bunch of them.

I hesitated to approach, but he was the one who said, 'Meet me there.' So I did ... approach, standing a few feet behind them. They didn't notice me.

I reached out and touched his back. "Callahan?"

He glanced over his shoulder, peered at the blonde, and tipped his hat. "Excuse me, darlin.' I've got to talk to this lady."

She shot me the evil eye, snatched her long-neck beer bottle, and moseyed down the bar.

"Do you want something to eat?" he asked.

"No thanks."

"Let's get a table." Callahan took his plate in one hand and his mug of beer in the other, calling over his shoulder. "Louisa! Two mugs in that corner," as he sauntered across the room with those long legs. I followed.

I'd seen enough of this guy's backside.

"Comin' up!" The bartender yelled back.

He stopped at a table tucked in the front corner of Sambo's and gestured. "Have a seat." It was dark back there.

He stood while I sat, then put his beer and plate down, taking the chair with his back to the wall. He tossed his hat in the chair beside him and said, "You'll excuse me. I haven't eaten since breakfast." Callahan chomped into that sloppy sandwich and washed it down with beer, his eyes on me the whole time. He wiped his mouth with a red cloth napkin. "Go ahead."

"Go ahead what?"

"You wanted to talk." He took another bite.

"No. You wanted to talk." I made an air quote with my fingers. "To straighten out the bullshit between us, I think were your words. We're going to have a meet and greet." I leaned in close. "What does that even mean? Were you trying to intimidate me, Detective Callahan? Because it certainly sounded like it."

He held up his hand while he chewed and swallowed, then said, "If you want to be a cop, take out an application. But you don't start out as a detective. You've got to work your way up."

I sighed and glanced away. "Okay." My gaze returned to meet his, which never seemed to let up. "Maybe I am pushing a little too hard."

"A little?"

My voice got loud. "Callahan, you hid crap from the start, not putting a name or address on that incident report. You know that's public record. I actually had to protect you from my boss, which I did, by the way. He was livid. He told me to find out everything. He said it'd be nice if I got everything before you did. I answer to him, Callahan, not to you."

He blinked. His face was blank for a second before he guffawed and choked, spitting his mouthful of food into his red napkin, covering his mouth as he sputtered. When he finally cleared his throat, he laughed so hard that his eyes watered. His friggin' shoulders shook. At last, he said, "You're going to find out everything before I do?"

And the arrogant ass went back to laughing.

He took another chomp, turning his head away as he chewed. I didn't know anyone could laugh and eat at the same time, but he was succeeding. What. A. Jerk.

He finished chewing, reached across the table, and grabbed my unused cloth napkin to wipe his mouth, but by then, it was impossible to wipe that smirk off his face.

He cleared his throat and said, "I filed a vague report because I wanted time to work before the media frenzy. If it wasn't for you, I might have had a day or two. Nobody else would've noticed. And if they did, they wouldn't have given a damn." His volume knob dialed up. "Do you think that's the first incident report filed like that? No reporter has ever stirred up as much trouble as you have already."

"I find that hard to believe."

"Well, believe it. Because I don't lie." That chilling tone again, but the amber in his eyes glistened with newfound amusement and a half-smile as he continued his supper. The man could eat.

A bite and swallow later, he said, "So, Katherine, if you find out who killed Mrs. Bennett before I do, what are you going to do? Are you going to print that Joe Blow killed Marilyn Bennett before I make an arrest?" His brows furrowed. "Let me do my frigging job. When it's done, you can report on it."

"Then I'm in the herd with every other reporter in town. I like to stay ahead of the pack."

The bartender brought two mugs of beer. "Thanks, Louisa." He nodded at me. "This is Katherine Coe." He paused, eyeing me. "A friend. Katherine, this is Louisa Hernandez, the proud owner of this joint."

"Nice to meet you." We said it at the same time, our gazes catching. Louisa had long black hair, beginning to gray around her temples, pulled into a loose ponytail at the nape of her neck. "Let me get you a chopped barbecue sandwich." She had a warm smile. I'd guess Louisa was fifty-ish. She was Hispanic or Native American, a tad on the heavy side, but an attractive woman. "You'll love it," she smiled.

I smiled back. "Thank you, Louisa. It does smell delicious. I'll take one to go, but I'll take a soda, please. If you have one."

"You don't drink beer?" Callahan asked with surprise.

"Sometimes. But I want a clear head tonight."

He raised one brow. "You can't keep a clear head with a couple of beers?"

I envied anyone who could raise one brow. It wasn't in my DNA. "I'm here on business."

He leaned back in his chair, taking a moment to appraise me like a horse at auction. He scratched that left brow. "Okay.

I get it. You want to be ahead of everyone, including me, on Marilyn Bennett's murder investigation." He glanced away and chortled again. He pressed his fingertips to his eyelids, his shoulders shaking as he tried to stifle the laugh.

If he was trying to make me feel foolish, he was doing one hell of a good job.

My sneer was strictly defensive. "No."

He wouldn't let up. "You just said it. Go ahead, admit it. You're trying to solve the crime and report on it at the same time."

Admit it over my dead body. I glanced away. "I don't have to solve it I just have to be on top of the developments. News is a competitive business. If you do something, Callahan, I need to know before anyone else."

He took a drink of his beer and aimed the mug at me. "You're the only one bugging me, so you probably will."

"Will you call me?"

He wagged his head, still with that grin, and those brown eyes glowed. "You are persistent."

That wasn't a no.

People cheered back in the game room. We both turned to see. At the dartboard, someone had an exceptionally good aim. A crowd gathered around the match between two guys who looked like they just got off a drilling rig. Both brawny and grimy, and all the darts were near the bullseye. Callahan's gaze lingered a bit longer, then returned to me. "Let's re-state the rules and start over. You ask questions." He touched his finger to his chest. "I'll be honest."

"Forthcoming," I said.

"No. I'm not volunteering a damned thing, but I'll be honest if you ask me about information that you find on your own." He aimed that index finger at me. "You don't print anything that I tell you will hurt my investigation. You swear."

Maybe I was a smidge snide. "We shook on it, remember?"

"Okay." He scratched that brow again and when he did, I was close enough to see a scar run diagonally through it. Somebody split that hard head open at one time. "So ask away."

I spoke quietly. "Have you heard anything ... interesting ... about Mrs. Bennett?"

"Define interesting."

And he thinks I'm frustrating? "I told you. I heard she was having an affair."

He lifted his shoulders.

"With a married man," I added.

He stared at me, silent, as Louisa brought my icy soda. I thanked her, and she left. As soon as she was out of earshot, I asked, "Yes or no. Was Marilyn Bennett seeing a married man?"

There went that lone brow again, his right, the one without the scar. "I can't say." He was onto his French fries.

"Can't or won't?"

He shook his head; his mouth was full again. "For the record, no comment."

"You said you'd be honest."

He sopped a fry in catsup. "I'm being honest. I cannot comment on that."

"Was she seeing a man named Tex?"

There it was. Something moved across his face and into those eyes.

I demanded, "Who is Tex?" Maybe a little too loud.

"Keep your voice down." He lowered his volume as he leaned in. "Tex Gibson is an oilman. You've heard of Gibson Oil. He's just as rich as she was. Only there are a lot of questions about," he paused, "the legality of his wealth."

"Why?"

He glanced around the room again. No one was near. "They say he was a slant-driller. At least in his younger years. Raises racehorses. Feds have been after Tex for one thing or another for as long as I can remember. Nothing's ever stuck."

"Were they having an affair?" I asked again. "Marilyn and Tex?"

He closed his eyes, shook his head, and opened them with a stabbing stare. "I … cannot … comment."

He's going to make this as hard as possible. "Is Tex married to someone named Roxanne?"

Our eyes were still locked on each other's. He swilled his beer. "She's Mafia." My eyes grew large. I felt them. "His wife is Angelo Marcelo's daughter. His kids are Marcelo's grandkids. Do you understand what that means?"

Marcelo. I knew the name. They ran New Orleans. Teamsters, drugs, prostitution. Louisiana Downs, the first horse racing track and casino in the South, was said to be Mafia-controlled, though I had no idea if that was true. But he just said Tex Gibson raises racehorses.

I leaned back in my chair, absorbing it. "Do you think they had anything to do with Marilyn's murder?"

His hands went high, and his voice got loud. "There you go again. You keep trying to solve the crime, not cover the investigation."

I sighed. "If I know which direction you're headed in, I can cover it better. Besides, I'm curious."

"So is the rest of the world."

We sat in silence for a moment, both staring.

"Dammit, Katherine. You've got to back off and let me do my job without worrying about you stumbling onto something that screws everything up. I'm serious. You're underfoot."

"I told you, if I find something, I'll ask you. I won't print anything that will mess you up."

He leaned in close, his voice quiet. "You don't get it. You're liable to bumble right into something that gets you killed. These are dangerous people."

I lifted my hands in surrender. "Okay. I'll back off. But just tell me, off the record, is Marcelo's revenge a possible motive?"

He shrugged. "I try not to get tunnel vision but off the record, it could explain the overkill."

"Over-kill?"

"Rage. Someone vented their rage on Marilyn Bennett." His jaw froze open. For that fleeting second, he forgot he was talking to a reporter. "That's off the record." He sat straight and tall, glaring. "Do you understand me?"

"Yes. I understand."

He tilted his head questioningly.

I lifted my right hand. "I swear. Do you think the pink diamond earrings being ripped out of her ears means something? That's pretty bizarre."

Callahan recoiled. He didn't know I knew that.

It felt too personal to print, and the story had plenty of detail without it. Callahan stared long and hard with an expression I couldn't read. Other than it was mean. "That piece of information does not need to come out."

"I didn't put it in my story. I won't use it."

"Go home and forget it." His jaw had hardened.

"Why?"

He glanced away, and as he did, I saw fire flash in his eyes, and I think, if we hadn't been sitting in a public place, T.J. Callahan would've pounded his fist on something the same way he slapped his hat on his thigh. Lord, that man had a temper. His gaze came back, meeting mine. "Will you just trust me, dammit? Keep that information to yourself. Who all knows that?"

I shrugged. "Bass told me and Jimmy. I don't know who else."

"Who have you told?"

"No one." But I had to gig him after the unmerciful way he'd laughed at me. "I also didn't put in my story that you think they tried to open the safe by removing the hinges, but when that failed, they forced Mrs. Bennett to give them the combination."

Oh, my. There was no brown left in those eyes. Just burning amber.

I said, "Bass told me. I didn't put that in my story either. See? I know some details are too intricate to print. If I think it is, I don't put it in the story. I had plenty of detail without those facts."

The irrepressible smile he'd worn earlier was long gone as he stared into some empty space high in the room. I'd bet Bass was going to get a phone call tomorrow.

I changed the subject. "Are you anywhere near making an arrest?"

That brought him back. He shoved his empty plate aside, took a long chug of that beer Louisa brought for me, and wiped his mouth. "No. But if I was, I wouldn't tell you."

"Let's talk in hypotheticals. If you were about to make an arrest, might a certain reporter get an anonymous phone call? So she could, let's say, have a photographer waiting?"

He chuckled. "In your dreams."

Maybe I got his mind off his mad.

I sighed. "Will you give me an exclusive?"

He lifted his hands. "If and when we make an arrest on the Bennett murder, the Chief will call a press conference and make sure everyone is there. That'll be way above my head."

"So what's in it for me to play along? Know stuff I can't report?"

He squinted at me. "Damned if I know." He rested his forearms on the table as was his habit. "We're in unchartered territory. I've never talked to a reporter in my life."

"So why now?"

That gaze narrowed even more. "Because you are a pain in my ass. You keep nipping at my heels like a little cow dog and I don't like it. But, I'll give you this. No one ever cared enough or had sand enough to do that before. And if you're going to be underfoot all the time, like apparently, you're going to be, we need to get on the same page." He leaned back in his chair, eyeing the whole of me. "Besides. Let's be honest. There's something about you ... I like."

"Are you married?"

He raised both hands and leaned back with a surprised snicker. "Woah, girl!"

"The first day I asked to talk to you about this case, Prissy said Callahan's married, like she thought I was after you. Let's be clear. I'm not after you. I don't do married men or cops. It's my job to ask you questions."

A part of me was lying to both of us. I'd damn sure be after him if he wasn't married and if he wasn't a cop.

Everything about Callahan was to drool over except for the fact that he was a smug, control freak, know-it-all cop.

He grinned, and I noticed a dimple. "No, I'm not married. I guess Prissy's just being protective." He scratched his cheek near where that dimple had shown. "Are you? Married?"

I glanced away, avoiding those eyes. But he didn't let up. "I was. Not anymore."

He asked, "Is Coe your married name or maiden name?"

"We didn't have children, so I took my maiden name back."

I don't think Callahan had taken his eyes off of me the whole time, but he wasn't ogling. I'd been visually undressed by men. Who hadn't? This was different. I'd felt it in his office—like he was trying to see behind my eyes to peer into my soul.

"Where are you from?" he asked.

"Brownwood. I went to Southwest Texas. Jake and I lived in San Angelo. I worked at the *Standard-Times*. You?"

"Grew up on a ranch south of Ballinger, off the Menard Highway. Do you ride?"

"I'm no barrel racer but yeah, I can stay on a horse."

He glanced at the bar. The tall blonde was still there, sidled up to a guy who wasn't near as good-looking as Callahan. He grinned. "What have you got against barrel racers? I saw the way you looked at Sheila."

I felt my face grow cold. "My ex was particularly fond of them."

His eyes widened. "I see. A rodeo man?"

"Yes."

"I rope." It was a pronouncement.

I leaned in with my elbows out, forearms crossed on the table. "Listen, Callahan. I got my heart tromped in a fucking rodeo arena, so if you don't mind, let's move along." I didn't even want to eat those words. He'd thrown out enough fucks of his own.

That dimple came back. "I can do that."

If I were after him, I'd have to stand in line. He had a disarming smile when he used it. And those eyes. Damn.

I asked, "So, yes or no? Are you getting anywhere in the investigation of the murder of Marilyn Bennett?"

He took another swallow of his beer. "Define anywhere."

My hands went high. "Geez-Louise. Now, you give me a break."

He chortled. It was plain to see he was having great fun toying with me. "We have interviewed, questioned, whatever word you want to use, almost everyone in her inner circle. We are waiting for the results of forensic tests on evidence seized at the scene of the crime. That's for the record. Off the record, I have some theories."

The game room erupted again, and his gaze whipped back there. He watched the group cheer a wide-shouldered rough-neck who must have won.

"What are you looking at back there?"

"Nothing for you to worry about."

"Roughnecks?"

His gaze came back to meet mine. "Known felons."

"What if I knock on Tex Gibson's door? Or find Mrs. Tex Gibson? Tell them I'm interviewing all of Mrs. Bennett's friends to get insight into her life and personality, for a profile. Just to shake the tree."

He clomped his empty beer mug on the table. I'd regained his undivided attention. "I'd say you were fixin' to step into deep horseshit."

"I've shoveled my share of horseshit. Would it mess up your case?"

Callahan's voice boomed. "Did you hear what I said?" He was so loud Louisa heard him way over by the bar. Their gazes met, and she flashed him a scolding stare. He took it down a notch. "Whoever killed Marilyn Bennett, whoever murdered her so viciously, do you think they'd think twice about making a reporter disappear? Listen, Katherine. You didn't see her. I did."

I hadn't thought about that.

He went on, a little loud again. "You're playing with fire. Now just cool your jets and let me do my job." He drew it out again. "Let ... me ... do ... my ... job."

"The paper's already been put to bed with a tiny shred of an update. A lot can happen before deadline tomorrow. Or I could write this update for the afternoon edition."

"Are you always this pushy?"

Not a tricky question. "When it comes to work? Yeah."

The moment had turned sour. "Suit yourself. Just don't use anything I said off the record. Do you understand?"

I nodded.

"And you asked me if it would hurt my case. Yeah. Hell, yeah, it could if that was the motive. Listen to me. No one needs to know we might be considering an affair as a motive. And I stress might be, because, like I said, I don't get tunnel vision. Got it?"

I sat straight and saluted with as smartass a smirk as I had in my repertoire. "Yessir."

He picked up his hat and settled it on his head. "Let's get out of here. Tomorrow's going to be a long day." He paid Louisa, who handed me my sandwich in a brown paper bag. I tried to pay, but she nodded at Callahan. "He got it. I hope you enjoy it," she said.

I smiled at Louisa. I liked her a lot. "I'm sure I will. It smells wonderful. Thank you."

And he walked me to my car. I didn't have to trail behind him. I had a little Buick he'd never be able to fold himself into. He opened my car door for me. Once I was situated, he closed the door, and I rolled down the window.

"You need to keep your doors locked," he said.

"Okay. Thank you for my sandwich and my soda. And the talk. I promise. I won't burn you."

Callahan leaned down, put his big hands on the open window, and said, "Did you hear me? Lock your car when you get out of it, and leave the Gibsons alone."

We stared at each other for a moment as I didn't commit. He slapped the bottom of the window frame, and I flinched. "Dammit, Katherine, you're smarter than that."

I nodded. "Okay."

Callahan straightened and started to turn but instead leaned down again, momentarily peering at me through the window. His voice was gentle as his eyes roamed my face. "You're a mighty pretty woman, Katherine Coe. It would break my heart to work a missing persons case on you." He tapped the roof of the car lightly. "Go get some sleep."

Now, how am I going to sleep after that?

Forget what an arrogant ass he could be. T.J. Callahan was the best-looking man I'd laid eyes on in—I didn't know how long. Maybe ever. And he wasn't married, and he just said I was pretty. He said there was something about me he liked.

I wanted to tell him how handsome he was. But nothing came out. His compliment was too unexpected. "Thank you," was the best I could muster as he strode away. "Be careful!"

He stopped and turned around one more time. "You be careful." He raised his arm goodbye and strode to that big black truck, got in, and we pulled out of the parking lot together.

I went to bed thinking of him. Reliving Callahan standing in the moonlight. Leaning into my car window, our faces close, saying in that smooth drawl, "You're a mighty pretty woman, Katherine Coe." I never expected that.

Men have no idea what hearing something like that means to a woman, especially hearing it from someone like him. Or did he? Was it merely flirtatious manipulation?

His warnings to keep my doors locked, to leave the Gibsons alone. Protective. Or controlling?

"It would break my heart to work a missing person's investigation on you." Now, why did he choose those words? Break my heart? He could've simply said he didn't want to. Break my heart. That made mine pitter-pat.

I had no idea how to get inside a man's head, but Callahan had crawled inside mine with those honey-brown eyes. He was in there, and I couldn't get him out. Him staring at me that way with his face so near, I had butterflies. Several times, I'd wanted to touch it. What was it?

Our rivalry. The way we sparred with each other. That was fun. Kind of exciting. Something I'd never done before, certainly not with so much passion. Which of us could hold the upper hand? Maybe that was it.

I fell asleep thinking about him, not understanding why, and he came into my dreams sometime in the night. I watched T.J. Callahan walk through a field of gold. The sun shone like a small golden orb in an empty cerulean sky as Callahan moved with outstretched arms, running his palms across heads of ripe grain. He glanced over his shoulder, smiled, waved high, and disappeared onto the horizon.

Chapter 5

Maybe I was obsessive-compulsive. I'd gone to sleep thinking about him, and he was the first thing on my mind when my eyes opened the next day. Why?

Callahan was a handsome man, yes. But Jake was handsome, too.

They couldn't have been more different.

Callahan was larger than most men with hair the color of rich, dark chocolate and those beautiful honey-brown eyes.

Jake was five-ten with caramel brown hair and eyes the color of a glacier-fed lake.

Both men were solid muscle, but the thing about Jake was he could move. Limber like a wildcat.

In the beginning, when Jake smiled at me, those blue eyes glistened like sunshine bouncing off a high mountain lake. But the more Jake won in the arena, the more luster I lost in his eyes. In the end, all the glimmer was gone.

Brown eyes and blue eyes. Both could be mesmerizing.

Callahan's eyes broadcast his every emotion, sometimes warm and welcoming, other times flaming and fierce. Whatever he felt shone through those burnt umber eyes, and I shrugged, conceding the truth to myself: I didn't have to call him last night. I wanted to. I was drawn to that man like a paperclip to a magnet and had neither the strength nor the will to resist the force.

Thinking of Callahan made me think about Marilyn Bennett, imagining what happened inside that house. What a beautiful woman. What a horrifying fate. What had her final moments been like?

I did that sometimes. Pondered obsessively over the victims of my most recent stories. It's another commonality between reporters and first responders. We see things we wish we hadn't. We think about what we saw; we just don't talk about it.

Usually, I neatly expunged ugliness the same way I tuned out noise. I was surprisingly good at it. When a horrid recollection crept out, I moved—physically moved—and got busy doing something else, somewhere else.

Get away from it. It will go back from where it came.

But that morning, thinking about Marilyn Bennett, for some reason, other disturbing on-the-job experiences began rising from their graves.

Take a cop like Callahan. He worked on his own cases. He didn't realize or care—none of them did—that I not only covered their cases but also the sheriff's department's murder cases, deadly fires, drownings, fatal highway collisions, and plane crashes. If you do it for any length of time, a cop reporter sees it all.

High-speed crashes could be some of the most sleep-depriving. You don't forget what it looks like or smells like when an eighteen-wheeler crosses the median, traveling seventy miles an hour, plowing into oncoming traffic. Once you've choked on the caustic fumes of burning diesel as it melts metal, plastic, rubber, and human flesh, you don't forget it.

You don't forget hearing the cries of the trapped and the dying. I pressed my fingertips to my eyelids against another incoming image.

The driver's side front tire of a van carrying a youth baseball team to Midland blew out. Even at seventy miles an hour, that might not have been so bad had the van not been traveling side-by-side with a semi-tractor-trailer rig when the tire blew.

The driver lost control; the van flipped onto its side, sliding underneath the big rig. They finally stopped in the median, the baseball van and all inside crushed under the heavy trailer. I saw it under there like a crumpled soda can, and the hair on my arms stood on end, hearing little muffled pleas for help coming from inside.

We got there right behind DPS.

The troopers discussed trying to dig to reach the children but feared anything they did to the ground might shift the trajectory of the eighteen-wheeler, worsening the situation. They called for cranes to lift the truck off of the van, the only safe way to reach the victims.

It felt like we waited for hours. I'm sure it wasn't that long, but minutes crept by as we listened to children scream for help, unable to reach them. Their frightened voices grew fainter and fewer as we waited.

How do you write that agony? How do you convey to a reader the excruciating terror in their voices or the sickened expressions on the faces of stymied state troopers who wanted to help but had no way?

Words can't do it justice; I don't care how good a writer you are.

That's where news photographers prove they are worth more than they'll ever be paid.

A picture of the driver of that eighteen-wheeler, who thought he'd found a private spot to get on his knees, his anguished face turned to the sky with tears rolling off of his chin, the wreck behind him—that one photograph summed it up better than I could.

But not even a photograph can convey what it does to your soul to hear the pleas of trapped and dying children, knowing no one could get to them to help them. Only those who live it can understand it.

Once in a blue moon, I'd still hear their voices. Seven children and the van driver died that day.

Now, you can swallow that, bury it, or try to suffocate it by refusing it oxygen, but you can never kill that memory. It's branded into your brain. Part of who you are from that day forward.

I covered an axe murder once. I'd worked in San Angelo long enough for the cops to trust me. I was on deadline when the call came over the scanner. I just needed enough to make the morning edition. When I got to the remote location, the sheriff's deputies acting as crime scene guards were cracking jokes about pizza sauce. I remember that. Macabre. Somehow, their way of coping. They radioed the Texas Ranger in charge of the case that I was there.

"Let her come back," he said. "Tell her to stay on the path. I'll meet her." It was mid-summer. The sun was setting. The deputies parted the barbed wire fence to let me crawl through, but the path wasn't clear at twilight.

I walked right up to a headless corpse. The victim's head rested on the ground a foot or so away from his torso. The mouth and eyes were open, a head full of brown hair. The headless neck looked like stewed beets spilled out, and the earth was soaked in the same sickening color.

My hands clamped over my mouth as I froze. Paralyzed. Staring.

"Dammit, Kat, I said stay on the trail. You don't need to see that. Plus, you mess up my crime scene." The Ranger in charge was Norman Giddings, a kind, older officer nearing retirement.

I closed my eyes. "I got lost. You're right. I didn't need to see that." I glanced at it again. Morbid curiosity, I guess. I turned away, got my information from Norm, and got the hell out of there.

Leaving, I glanced over my shoulder to see him knee-deep, elbow-deep in that sickening slice of life. Norman Giddings couldn't glance at it and run away. And as if on cue, over his shoulder, the western sky glowed the color of the blood-soaked earth as the sun sank into the horizon, taking with it all of my self-importance.

There, in that mesquite thicket, I saw clearly: I was a mere observer of the game. Cops, firefighters, EMTs, emergency room doctors, and nurses—they were the real deal. It was the difference between watching a football from the sidelines and taking the hits on the field. I might fuss with them, but I respected the hell out of them.

My Dad had a border collie named Sancho who delighted in all things dead. Sancho would lay on his back, feet in the air, and wiggle around on whatever decaying creature he found, rolling, rubbing his neck in the stench of death.

I guess something inside me was like Sancho that morning. Like I said, it didn't happen often, but that particular day, I couldn't seem to get five years' worth of appalling images out of my head. So, I wallowed in them.

They'd started with the vision of her, Marilyn Bennett, tied to a chair. She couldn't flee or defend herself. Terror must have frozen her mind. She gave them the combination for the safe. Why rip out her earrings? Her face was unrecognizable, her son said. Callahan said, "You didn't see her. I did."

Like Texas Ranger Norman Giddings, Callahan had been elbow-deep in that crime scene, staring into the unrecogniz-able face of a defenseless woman. How many nightmarish visions crowded that man's brain? I wanted him to catch her killer. I resolved to respect Callahan's wishes, back off, and let him do his job.

I checked in with Jack late that afternoon, asking about updates on the Bennett murder. Nothing new, he assured me. "Is Mike Tomlin in?" I asked.

"Yeah."

"May I speak to him?"

"You're lucky you caught him. Hold on. I'll transfer you," Jack said.

Mike Tomlin answered with a gravelly voice. I introduced myself. "I understand you cover oil and gas?"

"Yes, ma'am. For ten years."

"Can you talk to me about Tex Gibson?"

There was no response, just the sounds of the sports teletype clacking behind him. "Mike?"

He coughed. "I don't have much truck with Tex."

"Why not?"

"I don't know. Just don't. Why are you asking about him? I understand you cover cops. Nightside."

"I heard a rumor."

He groaned. "Oh, shit." His voice got quiet. I think his hand was cupped around the mouthpiece. "About him and Mrs. Bennett?"

"Yes. You've heard it too?" I asked.

"Yeah." He took a drag on a cigarette. "I never could see it. Mrs. Bennett was like Jackie O. Way too classy for someone like Tex." He exhaled heavily.

"Is Gibson Oil a big company?"

He snorted. "Gibco? Yeah."

"Okay, thanks. I just wondered. Maybelle thought you'd know more."

He cleared his throat. "Listen, that rumor's been around a while. Even before old man Bennett died. If I were you, I'd leave it alone."

I sucked in my air involuntarily. "Before he died?"

"Yes, ma'am."

"And how'd he die?" I'd forgotten what Bass told us.

Another drag on his cigarette, and this time, Mike exhaled before answering. "Keeled over from a massive heart attack. Out of the blue."

"Was foul play ever suspected?" I wondered aloud.

"Not that I ever heard. But you've got to wonder." Mike cleared his throat again.

I wondered what he looked like. How old he was? I knew nothing about him. Fifty-some-odd of us worked in the newsroom.

Mike's voice brought me back. "I'm telling you. I wouldn't be asking around town about Tex Gibson if I were you. Just cover what the cops do. That's one story you don't want to break."

Why did men feel the need to tell me what to do, as if I needed protecting? I was capable of taking care of myself, thank you. But I stifled it. "Thanks, Mike. I hope to meet you someday."

"You, too," he said. Then, "Kat? Seriously. I hope you heard what I said. Leave. It. Alone."

Chapter 6

That following day, I met Jimmy as planned at First Baptist Church. My shift hadn't begun. I was on my own time. It seemed the Bennetts were in a terrible hurry to get their mother in the ground. Why? The funeral home director said Bass told him because of the horrific nature of his mother's death, the few survivors wanted it over with. His mother's casket would be closed.

With the church parking lot packed, Jimmy and I realized even if we got inside, we'd be standing at the back door, neither of us able to see anything. So he set up across the street for a wide-angle view of the comings and goings. He'd get a shot of the pallbearers carrying her casket.

Seeing the overwhelming crowd, not knowing who was who, I left Jimmy and drove to Woodlawn Memorial Cemetery, where I spotted the open gravesite.

I waited in my car, watching from a distance. Hopefully, I'd see something there.

The early March wind swayed bare trees, and I idled my car to keep the heater running, burning my gasoline. My car, my fuel, not the newspaper's.

I'd almost given up when I spotted the funeral procession coming slowly, led by two police cars with flashing lights. Then, the black hearse was followed by a black limousine that carried the family. Then, relatives and friends. Lots of friends. All the cars pulled into the cemetery grounds, parked, and people gathered under and around that big green tent.

Those mourners had to be doubly miserable. Grieving and shivering. The temperature plummeted from the previous day, and the northwest wind howled relentlessly. The valences of the funeral tent fluttered and flapped.

The sky was gray, as if laden with snow.

I exited my car and moved closer, still keeping my distance. I was an objective, third-person observer; I tried to persuade myself. But Callahan nailed it. I was playing detective, driven by Jack's directive. After our meet and greet and my visions of poor Mrs. Bennett tied to a chair, I'd decided to ease off. I just needed to be on top of whatever he did.

My newness in town thwarted my reporting efforts. I didn't recognize any mourners other than Bass. I assumed the auburn-haired woman on his arm was his wife. There were two small children with them. A second woman at his side had his black hair. Had to be the sister. Bass escorted the group, a hand on each woman's shoulder, while the auburn-haired woman guided the children.

Bundling my gray wool coat around me and pulling up the collar, I hunkered from the wind behind a wide-trunked live oak. Attending a funeral, I'd worn a dress. Big mistake. My bare legs were popsicles, my freezing hands were tucked into my coat pockets, and my face was chapped by the wind as my long hair whipped uncontrollably. I should've worn it in a ponytail. Too late now.

"Why are you standin' way back here?" The woman's voice came from behind me. It was slow and Southern, maybe even Cajun. "Who are you?"

Startled, I turned. A raven-haired woman stood just behind me—a little too close. I responded to her question, "Who are you?"

Her thin black brows knitted together as she demanded. "An'suh my question furst."

She couldn't pronounce her r's. That voice crawled off the pages of a William Faulkner novel. Her gaze sizzled, eyes narrow, as if she'd just caught a slave eating donuts with his bare feet on her polished dining room table.

"My name is Kat Coe. I'm a reporter."

She lifted her chin haughtily. "Why are you skulkin' back here?" She tilted her head toward the gravesite service underway. "Why aren't you up there where you can hear?" Again, she couldn't pronounce the r's.

"Another reporter's covering the service. I'm covering her murder."

Her round, dark eyes spit darts. She was exactly my height. Our gazes were level. She had plump, red lips and diamond teardrop earrings.

She sneered. "You people make me sick."

My skin must have been getting a little thin. Insults usually rolled off, but I snapped back quickly, leaning my face close to hers. Why not? She intruded into my space. "The woman was murdered. You don't think that's a news story?"

"You already made her death a news story. I saw what you wrote, Kat Coe." She said my name snidely. "What do you think you're going to find here?"

"Honestly, I don't know." I lifted my hands in exasperation at her questions and the circumstances. "I don't know what I'm looking for until I see it." Maybe I'm looking at it. Something sinister hung around her. "You didn't tell me your name. I'd like to quote you for the newspaper."

"Go to hell." Her pronunciation was perfect. No r's in that sentence.

She dismissed me, lifting that delicate chin, her little scoop nose in the air, as she walked past me toward the tent. She wasn't as tall as me. She was wearing three-inch heels. A long, soft leather trench coat draped just above her ankles. That coat cost more than I earned in a month. There's no telling the cost of those earrings. Her espresso-colored hair fell below her chin, and she tied it down with a scarf. Her hair wasn't blowing about.

I cupped my hands around my mouth, calling after her. "Are you a friend or relative?" I'd seen the picture. I knew who she was. I just wanted to gig the uppity witch.

She either didn't hear the question or ignored it.

I began to study others in attendance. I couldn't judge who was a hairdresser, manicurist, or gardener from a banker or real estate tycoon. It was ludicrous to think I'd learn something here.

No. Wait. A lone black woman. Not the woman I saw at the Bennett mansion. Could she be Miranda? The woman who found Mrs. Bennett?

I watched her dabbing her eyes as she stood in the wind, listening to the preacher, uninvited to sit with the family. She had to stand alone in what had become blowing sleet while people who knew Marilyn Bennett less well got to sit under the canopy. Something about that made my hackles rise.

Thirty or so shivering minutes later, the crowd began to disperse. I moved to the black woman as she departed alone. She was a small woman with white hair and a coat too thin for the weather. "Ma'am?"

She turned to the sound of my voice. The whites of her eyes were red, and her ebony face pruned. The corners of her eyes were still moist from tears.

"Are you Miranda?" I asked.

She nodded slowly, curiosity in those weary eyes.

"I'm so sorry for your loss." I introduced myself, explaining I was from the paper.

She said, "I've read your stories, Miss Kat. Mr. Bass spoke well of you."

"Miranda, can you tell me? Was Mrs. Bennett involved with someone? Seeing a man?"

Miranda raised her hand. A thin, tiny hand. "You never get me to say a word against Miss Marilyn. I been with that woman for twenty-five years. She treat me like family."

Maybe she did, but the rest of them didn't. Having worked for his mother that long, Miranda should have been asked to sit with Bass and his family, and her coat should've been much thicker. It made the Bennetts seem much less to me.

"I just thought since you were so close, you could help me understand. When you found her, was she conscious? Could she talk?" I asked.

She shook her head softly, closing her eyes. "No, ma'am. It was the awfulest thing I ever did see."

"Was she seeing someone?"

Miranda pulled her coat tightly around her; the collar was already up around her ears, and she shivered as she spoke, her arms folded across her chest. "She was lonely after Mr. Henry passed. I think it was just something to pass the time. Them being friends and all."

"Them?"

"Her and Mr. Tex. They just friends. Old, lonely people passin' time together. Miss Marilyn, she loved Mr. Henry way too long. There'd never be another man in her bed."

"But Tex is married. Why would he be lonely?"

Miranda smiled sympathetically. "You don't have to be alone to be lonely."

I couldn't help myself. I hugged her tightly. "Thank you, Miranda. God bless you. I won't repeat our conversation."

She lifted her hand, nodded, and toddled on. I wondered what would happen to her, with her employer having been murdered. Out of a job. Too old to start a new one. Maybe things hadn't changed as much as people thought. I still wasn't over her not being offered a seat at her age, having served that family for so long. I was disgusted all over again, watching her walk away.

Bass and his family were the last to leave. I waited to approach. I felt comfortable with Bass. I offered my hand in sympathy. "I hope you get justice."

He took my hand gently. "Kat, meet my wife, Audra." Bass placed his hand on the heads of his children. "Our son and daughter, Little Hank and Melissa." He nodded at the other woman. "And this is my sister, Mary Beth."

She was as beautiful as I imagined her mother must have been at that age. Mid-thirties, if I had to guess, tall and slender. "Mary Beth, I am so sorry for your loss. If any of you have anything you want to say, Bass has my phone number. I won't trouble you any longer. I just wanted to extend my sympathy."

Her blue eyes were severely swollen and red. "Thank you," she dabbed at them. "We just can't imagine how something like this could happen."

"Well, again, I am sorry to meet you under these circumstances. Audra, nice to meet you. I'll leave you all."

"Thanks for coming," Bass said.

Audra never opened her mouth. Never looked straight at me. Nor did the children.

Back in my car, I started the engine, turned on the heater, and grabbed my notepad, jotting down names and descriptions before I forgot them.

A hard rap on my driver's side window surprised me. A man I'd never seen had his face near the glass, rolling his wrist as a directive for me to open it. He wore a low-crowned silverbelly Stetson, which he held to his head lest it be whipped off by the gusting wind.

My window halfway down, he growled. "Who the hell are you?" A heavy-set man with a big, square red face.

I rubbed my hands together and blew into them. The heater hadn't been on long enough to warm the car. "Who's asking?"

"I'm Tex Gibson." With snapping, light blue eyes, gray hair, and that heavy mustache, he looked differently than he did in the newspaper clipping—more walrus-like. "Now answer my question. Roxanne said you've been lurking around like a vulture."

I'm a cow dog, a pushy one at that. Then a snake. Now I'm a vulture. "I'm a reporter, Mr. Gibson. Kat Coe with the *Reporter-News*. Who is Roxanne? Are you a friend of the family?"

"Damned straight, I'm a friend of the family. Roxanne's my wife. She's a friend, too." He waved his arm at Bass and the other Bennetts getting into the limousine. "You leave those poor kids alone, you hear me? They've got enough to deal with. They don't need a good-for-nothing reporter prying into their business. Cops are doing enough of that already."

Good-for-nothing, too. So this is the guy she was having an affair with? Surely not. He had to have something special going on if she was because he was nothing to look at.

"I'm sorry, sir. I meant no harm. Another reporter covered the service. I'm covering Mrs. Bennett's murder."

"There's no murder here." He had gravel in his throat.

"But Marilyn is here. I just … wanted to see her service, that's all. Would you like to make a comment for the paper about your friend?"

He waved his hand, his face scrunched. "Git outta' here!" He sounded like my father did when raccoons turned over the trash can.

"It's a free country, Mr. Gibson."

He squinted and glared. "I'm going to give your publisher a call."

"Like I said, sir. It's a free country."

Gibson tromped away, keeping his hat smushed to his head.

As I rolled up my window, I glimpsed something even more surprising than Mr. and Mrs. Tex Gibson.

James Billingsly drove by. He saw me see him. Our gazes latched for that fleeting instant, and something inside me quivered.

A few weeks earlier, I'd covered the US Marshals arresting a federal fugitive in Cisco. Callahan said the feds had investigated Tex Gibson for years. Federal marshals probably knew something about him that they would share, at least on background.

Calling the FBI was a waste of time. I'd never gotten one of those snotty bastards to return a phone call in San Angelo or Abilene. They were either too good or too busy to acknowledge the local press. Local reporter questions were funneled to the Dallas headquarters. If Dallas deigned to call back, the answer was always, "The FBI does not comment on investigations."

Even the cops hated the FBI.

More than one had told me the feds always wanted local cops to share what information they had on a case while refusing to share what they had. One detective told me the FBI once asked to look at his case notes, promising to return them, then refused to give them back.

The FBI? Useless to anyone but the FBI.

The US Marshals might help if you could catch one of them. I missed them on that trip. The door was locked and the lights were off inside their office.

I also wanted to know more about James Billingsly. What, exactly, had been his original crime? Who, what, where, and when? My shift had yet to start; I was still on my own time, so I drove from the federal building to the Taylor County Courthouse, District Clerk's Office, asking to see all court records for James Billingsly.

Like the newspaper morgue, court records were on paper and filed in manilla folders.

People were much more accommodating and friendly in the courthouse than at the police station. Martha Henderson brought me two file folders with a smile. Martha had helped me before, and we'd become friends. That is to say, we ate lunch together once.

A tiny little woman, just a tad over five feet tall. On tiptoes, she leaned her elbows on the counter and whispered, "You know, James is always a suspect in something. Ever since he got out of prison."

I didn't include his name in my story or tell her I was investigating him in connection with the Bennett case.

Cops worked with the district attorney's office. People in the DA's office overheard lots of juicy tidbits about crimes and investigations, and you can bet they whispered their juicy gossip to courthouse friends like Martha. And the courthouse friends whispered it to others like Martha just did. Information is power. A status symbol. Nothing stays secret for long.

Assuming from her remark she knew, I said, "They questioned him that first day but released him."

Martha glanced over her shoulder. No one was near. "That's because his wife gave him an alibi. That's a hard nut to crack."

Now, how'd she know that? Who in the DA's office was running their head about privileged information? That's the person Callahan should be mad at.

I asked, "Who did he rape? Billingsly told me it was consensual, that he just didn't know she was sixteen. He was just eighteen."

Martha snickered. "You know that's sealed. You'll never know the name of a sexual assault victim officially, but rumors were that he raped Mary Beth Bennett. And it wasn't consensual. They say Mary Beth was beaten. That's why the jury gave him five years."

Involuntarily, my hand clamped across my mouth. Oh, man. Mary Beth Bennett. Was that why he drove past the funeral? To get a glimpse of her? Or was he checking out the funeral of the second Bennett woman? Were they both his victims?

Martha was ten years my senior, at least. Married with three kids in school, she liked to talk about. "Are your kids doing well?" I asked.

"Oh, they're all going every which way." She waved her hand. "Jeanie's playing tennis."

"I bet she's good."

Taking Martha's files, I studied the mugshot of eighteen-year-old James Billingsly, with his blond hair and blue-green eyes. "He was a good-looking kid, wasn't he?" It hit me. Martha probably went to school with him.

"That he was. James was quite the sought-after football star for Abilene High." She tapped the file folder. "That arrest ruined whatever dreams he had of going to college and having a football career. He always swore it wasn't rape."

A bitter man. Motive. Callahan said someone vented their rage on Marilyn Bennett. Five years in prison for something you didn't do. That could evoke rage. But why now? He'd been free for years.

Callahan never told me anything about that. But if Martha knew it, he did, too. My cheeks flushed, and I felt like a fool all over again. No wonder he laughed.

"Thanks, Martha." I touched her hand. "I owe you lunch."

"I'll hold you to it.

Try to think like Callahan.

You've got two people with possible motives. A jealous wife from a Mafia family and a bitter ex-con who had convinced himself he was wrongfully imprisoned for having consensual sex with a rich man's daughter. But here's the thing: Marilyn Bennett wouldn't open her door to James Billingsly, certainly not late at night. And there was no break-in.

Would she open her door to Tex's wife? And why would anyone rip those earrings out of her ears? In my amateurish mind, that single act of cruelty meant something significant. Callahan's reaction to my mentioning them gave credence to my hunch.

"You're in over your head," I chided myself out loud, driving to the newspaper office downtown. My shift was beginning. I had brought jeans, boots, and a turtleneck sweater to wear after the funeral, and I couldn't wait to get into them. Miserably chilled, I changed in the women's room at work.

At my desk, I asked myself: What can you report? For all my time and effort, all I had were suspicions—nothing printable. There was no update other than the measly crumbs Callahan shared two nights ago that he'd talked to the inner circle and was waiting for forensics. Forensics. Maybe they're in.

Forensics labs could determine blood types, fingerprints, and footprints. They could match ballistics and analyze material, like fabric, to determine its composition and whether a victim's or suspect's blood type was on a sheet towel or weapon. Even with semen, the best forensic scientists could do was determine blood type, and any defense attorney would argue that at least a fourth of the population had that blood type.

On the way to the cop shop, I had an idea and pulled into an Allsup's convenience store. Reaching Prissy's desk, I made a peace offering, holding out a package of Juicy Fruit gum. "I thought we might try to start over," I said. "Peace."

She eyed it as if I offered her a rattlesnake. After inspecting the gum suspiciously, she finally reached out and took it. "Thanks." She laid the pack on her desk.

"Is Callahan in?" I was my most pleasant self, though still shivering.

"No."

"Really?" I rubbed my arms as I peered at the big door to their inner sanctum.

"Yeah, really. Him and Clancy have been out most of the day."

"Do you know where they are?"

She lifted those perfectly plucked brows and gradually cracked a grin. "If I did, I couldn't tell you."

I sighed heavily and glanced around the lobby. "Okay. Will you please tell him I stopped by?"

Reluctantly, she muttered, "I can do that."

"Thank you, Prissy." I remembered something Jack told me a while back. The sweetest sound to anyone's ears is their own name. Use it.

The US Marshal's Office was a few blocks away, on the second floor of the federal building. I checked there again. The office, with its frosted glass door, was still locked and dark inside.

Jimmy's voice was in my head. 'They're going to make this case pronto, or they won't make it at all.' He said that the day before yesterday. Dammit! They're making this case right now, and I'm groping in the dark.

Chapter 7

Staring at my terminal, trying to create a follow-up with not a shred of new information, the phone rang at my desk. *"Reporter-News.* This is Kat Coe."

His voice was hushed, as if his hand was cupped around the mouthpiece. "You've got about thirty minutes to get a photographer to the Sally port if you want a picture of our suspect. Be discreet. You never heard from me." *Click.*

It took a second to recover from the shock of his call. I yelled across the newsroom above the scanners and teletypes. "Jack! Where's Jimmy?"

Jack peered up, hollering back. "Not sure."

"Beep him! Urgent!"

The city editor strode across the room to stand in front of me. "Why?"

People were looking. I lowered my voice, peering around. Al was nowhere to be seen. "They're bringing a suspect to the jail in the Bennett murder. We can get a shot at the Sally port if we can get there in twenty minutes."

Jack stepped back, his eyes a little wide, chewing on the earpiece of his glasses. He levied a long stare at me. "Now how in the Sam Hill would you know that?" He glanced at his desk, aiming the eyeglasses at the bank of scanners. "There's been no traffic about that."

I smiled. I was proud. "I'm developing sources. That's what you pay me to do." Snatching my purse and keys, I bolted toward the door. "No time to waste. Tell Jimmy I'll meet him there."

Who did he have? My money was on Roxanne Gibson.

I beat Jimmy to the Taylor County Jail. "Be discreet," Callahan had warned. I went inside, ostensibly to check the jail logs. That was feasible. I hadn't been by today. Speak to whoever was on duty. Make it look as if I innocently stopped by at the same time they brought in a suspect. Just keeping to my daily routine. "Afternoon, George. Anything interesting today?"

George Wimberley was a retired sheriff's deputy who passed the time working as a jailer because he couldn't stand to be at home alone. His wife of fifty years died two years before. I learned in San Angelo that a friendly jailer could be an invaluable asset and George was living proof. He volunteered quietly. "Narcs made a big bust this morning."

I ran my finger down the list of inmates, the time of incarceration, the names of the inmates, the charges, the arresting officer, and the arresting agency.

Domestic abuse, parole violations, burglary, possession. This had to be it: 5:30 a.m./ Dickey, Frederick/ 35 yoa/Merkel/M&D/ Scott DPS.

"What's M&D.?"

"Manufacture and distribution of narcotics." George tapped the log sheet. "Their shorthand. Sometimes they do that when they're tired or lazy but sometimes they do that hoping you reporters will miss it. I've had 'em put people in here for capital murder and all they write on the log is C.M. Gets mistaken for criminal mischief."

I cut my eyes at George. "They don't jail people for criminal mischief."

He grinned. "Most reporters don't know that, Kat."

Wow. Abilene police were way sneakier than Angelo cops. I pointed to the name on the clipboard log. "Do you know this officer? Scott? DPS?"

George had white hair and kind, blue-gray eyes. "One of 'em that works for Russo."

I lifted my gaze, meeting his. "Russo?"

"Lieutenant John Russo. Heads DPS Narcotics. Heads the West Central Texas Drug Task Force."

"So they busted a drug lab this morning?"

George swilled from his white ceramic coffee mug, grinning at me and holding the cup in a toast. "Big one, I hear."

Unusual. I brushed my wild, windblown hair out of my eyes. "I need to talk to them."

"What you need is something to tame that mane. A rubber band?" George appeared amused, his eyes on my wild hair.

With the sleet and humidity, my hair was curlier than usual. I didn't have a mirror, but I must have looked like a wild woman. "Do you have one? Big enough?"

He rustled through a drawer and held up a big, wide rubber band with an even wider grin.

I took it, tying my hair in a ponytail. I twisted it into a knot and pulled a pencil from my purse, using it to hold the bun in place. "Thanks."

George scratched his head, grinning at my makeshift hairdo. "The narcotics boys are all in bed." He tapped the jail log clipboard again. "They booked Freddy in around 5:30 a.m. Means they worked all night and most of the morning."

"Any rumors on the Bennett case?"

George winked and leaned in, his coffee mug shielding his whisper. "You're in luck. I hear they're bringing someone in."

I feigned surprise, opening my eyes wide. "Really? Who? When?"

"Don't know who but they're 10-76. If you want a peak, mosey around, and hang out at the Sally port." Ten-seventy-six meant cops were en route to the jail.

"Who's 10-76?" I asked.

"Callahan and Clancy."

I rushed out of the lobby toward the Sally port, the entrance to the jail garage. It was a long jog to the far side of the jail.

The police unit would pull up and stop while someone inside opened the big metal door. The cop car would pull into the garage. The garage door would close. But in those twenty or thirty seconds while the vehicle was idle, waiting for the wide garage door to open, Jimmy could get his shot of the suspect in the back seat.

A lot of times, suspects would duck and turn their backs to the camera, so all you got was a shot of their back, but Jimmy would get some kind of shot that nobody else would have. News is a competitive business. It was all about one-upmanship. This was a feather in my cap. Thanks, Callahan.

Jimmy stood with his hands thrust into his coat pockets, camera around his neck. He wore a toboggan tucked over his ears. Shivering and waiting. His cheeks were fiery red. Windburned. "What have you got? Why am I out here freezing my ass off?" That wind had not let up all day. Sleet had turned to a dusting of snow.

"P.D.'s bringing in their suspect in the Bennett murder."

Jimmy's face froze with the same expression Jack had earlier. His eyes were wide, and he looked a little aghast. "How do you know that?" Jimmy peered left and right, leaning in, his tone accusing. "No reporter's ever gotten a heads-up that the cops were bringing in a suspect."

"Maybe no one ever asked quite as nicely as I did."

He backed away from me warily as if I was contagious.

I shrugged with my hands in the air. "What do you want me to say, Jimmy? I'm developing sources. It's what good reporters do."

He hung his head and scuffed the toe of his leather hiking boot in the frozen grass. His narrowed gaze met mine. "Tell me you didn't crawl into bed with that Nazi Callahan for a news story."

My cheeks flushed, and I controlled the reflex to slap him. "How dare you? No, I don't sleep with men for news stories." And he's not a Nazi.

He cocked his head. "Not like it doesn't happen."

"It doesn't happen with me." He turned my stomach sour. I hope people don't think that.

Obviously, I didn't have a poker face. He said, "Listen, Kat. People always suspect reporters who are five steps in front of everybody else of doing something underhanded to get ahead."

"Nobody ever accused me of that in San Angelo and I kicked plenty of ass there. It's not like I started covering cops yesterday, Jimmy. I've done it for years, just not here." I jabbed my finger at him. "That accusation is just your dirty mind."

"No, it's not. I don't know what happened in San Angelo, but no one has ever worked cops here the way you're working them, so you might as well get ready for it. There will be plenty of rumors and innuendos and suspicions." Jimmy took a step closer. "Because, frankly, some reporters do get—too close—to their sources. It never ends well."

I was still in shock. My mind was off-kelter.

Swapping sex for news never once occurred to me. He made my skin crawl. I couldn't concentrate. But I wanted to see who they brought in. So I told a white lie. "For your information

George, the jailer, told me." He did, just not first. I sneered. "No. I'm not screwing George. And while you're at it after you get this shot of the Bennett suspect, will you go inside and shoot the mug shot of Frederick Dickey? Narcs busted his lab. When I leave here, I'll go to DPS for that story." I glared at him again. "No, Jimmy. I'm not doing the narcs, either."

I stormed away. I couldn't stand the sight of him. Not right now.

He yelled at me through cupped hands. "Jack just beeped! See what he wants!"

I slid a dime into the pay phone inside the jail lobby. Jack answered. "City desk." Did he think of me that way? Is that the reason he looked at me so suspiciously earlier?

"Jack?"

"Speaking."

"It's Kat." My voice was flat. "Jimmy asked me to call you. Said you paged."

"Head to the police department. They called a news conference in thirty minutes. I'm sure it's about this arrest. Have Jimmy call me when he leaves."

"Okay. Narcs busted a big drug lab overnight. I was going to get that story, too. I asked Jimmy to get a mug shot."

"Good work, Kat. I'll leave it a few inches."

"Thanks."

I went back to Jimmy. "Police called a news conference. I'm headed over there. Jack wants you to call him as soon as you get this shot." I couldn't ask questions there anyway. I just wanted to see who they arrested. "Don't forget the mug shot. I told Jack to be expecting it."

Jimmy's voice was apologetic. "I'm sorry I offended you."

My heart pounded faster than Prissy could type. I didn't want to look at him, but I did. My claws were out. "Guess I'll have to get used to it, Jimmy, because I intend to be the best cop reporter Abilene ever had."

It was a cluster when I arrived at police headquarters, a two-story brick building downtown. TV station live vans crowded the parking lot; their masts raised high.

The Abilene Police Department building had as much personality as a cardboard box, like most municipal buildings built with taxpayer funds. A plain, basic structure. No frills. Tan brick.

Patrol, detectives, and narcotics were on the first floor. I think all the brass and records were upstairs. That's where the wood-paneled conference room was.

The three television stations, the local ABC, NBC, and CBS affiliates, were set up, crowding the room with tripods and lights, photographers, and reporters when I arrived. The main news anchors of ABC, NBC, and CBS were reality TV stars, locally and nationally.

TV cameras were big outfits with heavy, clunky decks with a three-quarter-inch videotape. A long cord ran from the camera to the deck, and people occasionally tripped over them. Sometimes, their photographers—videographers, as they liked to be called—would turn off their camera, eject one tape and put in another, then go back to rolling tape. Always noisy.

I guess I looked at TV people the same way cops looked at me: pain in the asses.

Half the time, none of them had a clue what was going on. They regurgitated whatever news crumbs government officials sprinkled out, just happy to have it. They didn't seem to know much about cultivating sources, knocking on doors, or digging deep. And really, not a lot about the law. Or procedure. I wasn't sure if broadcast majors had to take press law like journalism majors.

None of them tracked down James Billingsly. None of them had an interview with Bass Bennett. Shots of the safe. And none of them got an anonymous tip about an arrest. I didn't think.

Entering the conference room, the podium still empty, Brett Davis smiled. "Hey, Kat. Where ya been?" She reported for the ABC affiliate.

I cut her a sideways glare. Didn't answer.

"Wow. Who pissed in your Post Toasties?" Her skin was porcelain.

I tweaked my mouth to one side, chewing on my now-chapped lips. I didn't answer. I wasn't in the mood for anyone or anything, and Jimmy's insinuation would take a while to get over.

"Come on, Kat. What's the matter with you?" Brett seemed genuinely concerned. We didn't have much of a relationship, but there was no reason she'd gig me. We'd always been respectful to each other.

"Nothing. Just got a lot going on." I glanced at the door, eager to see Jimmy.

"Do you know who they arrested?" Brett Davis was an attractive woman, as almost all television news reporters were. Television stations didn't hire ugly men and women for on-air positions.

"Not a clue." That was the truth. I wished Jimmy would get there and tell me. "Do you know who it is?"

"No idea. Guess we'll find out soon enough." Despite having dark brows, Brett's smooth, chin-length hair was the color of wheat, parted on the side and turned under. Deep blue eyes. Young. Abilene was probably her first job out of college. Brett checked her watch. "What are they waiting on?" She glanced around the room. "I've got a deadline."

Brett reported for the six o'clock newscast and the ten. Local TV stations didn't do five o'clock news back then. Their morning news was a regurgitation of the ten o'clock news from the night before. Their noon newscast covered what happened that morning, like the city council meeting, county commissioner's court, and any breaking news. TV reporters ran around like chickens with their heads cut off compared to print reporters with one deadline a day. Mine wasn't until ten.

"They are pushing you." I offered her a teaspoon of sympathy. I could get over myself long enough to do that. She was nice. "I guess you can go live from here."

"That or do a set piece. I won't have time to put a package together."

Whatever that meant.

Brett and I had snagged front-row seats. I chanced to peer over my shoulder as Jimmy came through the conference room door, summoning me with a wave. "Save my place," I whispered. "I'll be right back." I left my purse in the chair as double insurance.

"Billingsly," Jimmy whispered.

My shoulders drooped. "You're kidding me." I'd hoped it wouldn't be him. I'd rather have seen that snotty mush-mouth Mafia princess in handcuffs.

"So much for his wife's alibi," Jimmy said. "I got the shot. And I got your druggie mug. Jack wants a high and wide of the news conference from back here. Then I'm out."

I was still processing Billingsly. Well, he had driven past the funeral. Was he akin to the arsonist who returns to watch his fire burn? Made my skin crawl a little.

Jimmy called me back to reality. "Here's the Chief."

I glanced over my shoulder, nodded, and scurried to my seat as Abilene Police Chief Marvin Bates, dressed in uniform, took the podium. A heavy-set older man, maybe in his mid-fifties, and I think the Chief might have been attractive in his younger years, but a big purple burn scar across his right cheek was hard not to see.

"Ladies and gentlemen, I'll be brief. This is an ongoing investigation so the information we can share is limited." Chief

Bates turned his head and cleared his throat. He wasn't speaking into a microphone. The room wasn't that big.

"This afternoon, Abilene Police detectives arrested James Edward Billingsly, age 38, in connection with the murder of Marilyn Bass Bennett. Billingsly is in the Taylor County Jail, being held without bond, on one count of capital murder, one count of murder, one count of aggravated assault, and one count of robbery. Mr. Billingsly surrendered to police at his place of business on South First Street in Abilene, shortly before 3 p.m. Questions?"

My hand shot up. "Chief, have you recovered any of the items missing from the Bennett residence?"

"No comment."

Here we go again. "What's the evidence then? On what grounds did you arrest him?" I followed up. "He was taken into custody initially then released. What changed?"

He hesitated before answering, glanced at the District Attorney beside him, who nodded, then said, "A witness placed Mr. Billingsly at the scene of the crime at the time of the murder."

"How?" I kept firing my questions. "That house is way off the road. How did a witness see him? Was he in a vehicle, walking—"

At once, everyone began yelling questions.

Chief Bates raised both hands high, quelling the room. "The time of death has been established between 11 p.m. and midnight. A witness came forward and placed Mr. Billingsly at the Bennett house a little before midnight."

Who saw him? And how? I raised my hand. "Can we get the identity of the witness?" I knew it was exempt from disclosure, but it was worth a try.

Chief shook his head. "We will not release that information."

"Did the witness say Mr. Billingsly was carrying weapons? A sack of stolen property?"

"No comment."

"Was he on foot or in a vehicle?" It was all me. The TV reporters were taking their notes, cameras running.

Chief Bates said, "Miss Coe, we're not divulging details of our investigation at this time. Everything will come out in a court of law at the appropriate time. I turn the podium over to the District Attorney Alvin Doss."

Compared to Chief Bates, Doss was a slight man. Middle-aged. He'd been the assistant when the previous DA died of a heart attack in office a year earlier, so Alvin was appointed. He hadn't had to run for election yet.

Doss cleared his throat and spoke into the microphone. "The District Attorney's office will pursue a speedy trial to bring justice for the family in this most brutal slaying. We will seek the death penalty."

The death penalty. James Billingsly, who claimed he was innocent of the original rape twenty years ago, who claimed he was locked up for a crime he didn't commit, who said he didn't harm Marilyn Bennett, now faced the electric chair.

There weren't a lot more questions to ask. They weren't going to answer them anyway. Nobody else was chiming in.

They all looked at me. "Mr. Doss, your investigators had to file a probable cause affidavit. Will you release it?"

He shook his head with a smirk. "I will not."

I peered up from my notes. "It's public record."

"Not at this stage of an investigation." I wasn't sure about that. But there was no point in arguing. They could legally drag their feet filing it for several days but once filed, a probable cause affidavit was damned sure public record. Unless they could get a judge to seal it. Come to think of it, they would probably do that in this town.

"While we're at it," Doss said. "I'm asking the judge for a gag order in this case, which prohibits investigators, attorneys, and witnesses from making any statements regarding the trial, evidence, or investigation."

That was bullshit. My incredulity was in my voice. "You're going to ask for a gag order before the trial even starts?"

"Yes, ma'am. We're not going to let this get out of hand and give the defense an argument for a change of venue. That's a needless expense to the taxpayers."

Brett whispered. "Close your mouth."

What do you do? I shifted back to the Police Chief. "Chief Bates, can you at least say if there is any evidence beyond the witness to support this arrest? You don't have to say what it is, but do you have anything besides this unnamed eyewitness? Fingerprints? Forensics? Recovered property? Is there any physical evidence tying James Billingsly to the murder of Marilyn Bennett?"

He chortled with a wide grin. "Keep trying, Ms. Coe. You get an A for effort."

The room laughed.

There you had it. Stonewalled. A frigging gag order. I wanted to walk out in protest, but it was almost over anyway.

"Last question?" It was Chief Bates.

Some television reporter, a dark-headed guy who appeared to be just out of college, asked, "Who were the arresting officers?"

"Police Detectives T.J. Callahan and Art Clancy."

Doss said, "Arraignment is 10 a.m. in Abilene's 42nd District Court. Thank you, ladies, and gentlemen."

"Can we get a mugshot?" Someone yelled.

"Talk to the jail."

In the newsroom, I filled Jack in on the news conference. Then I called Bass Bennett.

"I know," he said. "Detective Callahan was here. Said he didn't want us to hear it on the news."

"Can I get a comment from you, Bass?"

"The family is relieved at the swift justice in this case. We dread the trial phase, but we want our mother's killer to pay for what he did."

I had to ask. I spoke quietly so no one in the newsroom could hear. "Bass, did James Billingsly assault Mary Beth years ago? Could that have anything to do with this?"

Silence.

I waited for what felt like a long time before I tried again. "Come on, Bass. That's motive. He says he was innocent—"

"Don't cross a line." His tone had changed. Cold and hard. Maybe even threatening. "We don't go there." This wasn't the same guy I talked to before.

"Fair enough." I didn't want to lose him as a source.

He said, "What happened twenty years ago needs to stay twenty years ago." Still, the tone was cold and threatening.

"Even if it was the motive for murdering your mother?" He heard the disbelief in my voice.

"Yes. Even if it was motive. That incident ..." He paused. "Tore up our family. Mary Beth's never really been the same since."

"Does she know?"

"No. She flew back to Sante Fe after the service." He paused again. "Kat, don't drag that stuff up in your story."

"I can't. She was a juvenile and juvenile records are sealed. I was just told ... that the rumor at the time was ... Mary Beth was his victim."

More silence. Maybe that rumor was news to him. After a long pause, Bass said, "Thanks for calling. You can say the family is thankful for the swift justice. We appreciate the efforts of the detectives. Leave it at that."

What an air of superiority. I missed it on the earlier encounters. Bass Bennett had dismissed me like a bondservant.

I said, "Thank you, Mr. Bennett."

I slammed that story out in record time. It just rolled off my fingertips. Another front-page byline with Jimmy's shot of

Billingsly handcuffed in the backseat of the cop car at the Sally port. He didn't turn his face away but didn't look at the camera either. A close-up profile of James Billingsly, his hands cuffed behind his back, riding in the back seat of the police unit.

They also had his mugshot from the jail, and Jack had Jimmy's high, wide shot of the crowded news conference. They'd run the abbreviated re-write covering the funeral from the afternoon paper. Jack even had a thumbnail of her nice portrait picture. The Bennett story would dominate the news again tomorrow.

I glanced at my watch and went to Jack's desk. "I need to put together the drug bust story."

He nodded and waved me on. This was crunch time for him. "Four inches. We're full."

Back at my desk, I called the Department of Public Safety, asking for Narcotics Lieutenant John Russo. He answered on the first ring. So, they did work nights. It was nine.

"Lieutenant Russo? This is Kat Coe, with the paper. Can I get information on the arrest of Frederick Dickey early this morning?"

"Well, hello, Kat Coe. I've been reading your stories. What do you want to know?" Surprising. A welcoming tone from a cop.

"Anything you'll tell me." I was typing notes at my terminal as he spoke, the same way Al did, with my phone receiver cradled against my shoulder. Sometimes, that made my neck ache, especially when I was taking obits that took forever.

"I can tell you, our agents took Frederick Charles Dickey into custody around 4 a.m. at his residence outside Merkel, where we seized a working methamphetamine lab along with more than five pounds of illegal product. Agents of the West Central Texas Drug Task Force dismantled the lab. The product was sent for analysis to determine its exact chemical make-up. We estimate, stepped on, we seized between forty-five and six-five-thousand dollars' worth of crystal meth. Like I said, depending on its purity." Russo had an unusually deep voice. Not a Texas drawl, but a more guttural sound than most.

"Stepped on?" I asked.

"Diluted. By the time it hits the streets, pure crystal methamphetamine has been cut with something, sometimes several times over."

"Cut?"

"Combined with something. Like I said, we got up to six-ty-five thousand dollars' worth, depending on its degree of purity. I'll know that in a few days."

Now, this guy was easy to talk to.

"For the reader, what's the difference between amphetamine and methamphetamine?" I asked, my fingers flying across the keyboard.

"They're both synthetic drugs that speed up the central nervous system. Amphetamine is legal. Prescribed by a doctor. It's made in FDA-approved laboratories, mostly as diet pills. But it can be abused." He sounded like a college professor. "Meth isn't made in any FDA-approved lab or prescribed by any doctor. Meth is injected or snorted. It's amphetamine on steroids."

"Any chance I can get a photo of the lab or seized equipment?"

"Sure. I'll let your photographer get a shot of this stuff. I can give you Dickey's address. Y'all can shoot from the road, but we can't take you to where the lab was. That's private property."

This was exciting. "Hold on a second, can you? Let me see if I can get a photographer there tonight."

I ran to Jack's desk. "DPS will let us take a photo of a meth lab they seized if we can get a photog there."

Jack held up his palm. "Hold it for tomorrow." Then he peered up. "No one else has it, do they?"

I held up my index finger and ran back to my phone. "Lt. Russo, does anyone else have this story?"

He snickered. "Are you kidding me? Reporters never call me."

I nodded at Jack, giving him a thumbs up, mouthing "Tomorrow."

"My editor wants me to hold this story and do it tomorrow so we can get photographs and give it more space. He can't get a photog this late."

"Fair enough," Russo replied. He read off the address. "It's between Merkel and View."

"Anyone else taken into custody?"

"Not yet."

"Was Dickey working for someone bigger?"

"No comment. This is part of an ongoing investigation."

I was used to the runaround. "Does Dickey have any priors?"

I think he lit a cigarette. I could've sworn I heard the flicking of a lighter. "His sheet's longer than my arm." Russo exhaled. Yes, he was smoking. "Drug possession. Drug delivery. Burglary. He's done two stints in TDC."

"How long did your people work on this investigation? I mean, was it a six-month or yearlong investigation—"

He interrupted. "Let's not go there."

"Okay." He was a new source, so I wasn't going to push too hard. "Thank you, Lieutenant. Is there anything else you want to say?"

"This arrest was made in cooperation with the Abilene Police Narcotics division, Taylor County Sheriff's Office, the West Central Texas Drug Task Force, and DPS Narcotics. Off-the-record? Do you want a good story? Look into how many crimes can be traced back to illegal drugs. How many robberies and burglaries are committed so these addicts can get money for their next fix? Look into how many rapes and murders are committed while these idiots are high. We've got a drug problem in this part of Texas and for some reason, people aren't willing to see it."

"And methamphetamine is the main problem?"

"Mostly. Some heroin, some downers, acid, and PCP, but not a lot. It's the need for speed. And they're making it with all kinds of crap. They cut it with drain cleaner, battery acid, and paint thinner. They fry their brains and ruin their insides.

Take a look at Freddy Dickey's mugshot and tell me how old you think he looks. I guarantee he's twenty years younger than you'd guess. But Freddy's one hell of a cook. Made a name for himself. That's what got him."

"Can I quote you on all that?"

Long pause. I think he took a long drag off that cigarette and exhaled. "No, better not. You can report all I said about the difference in amphetamine and meth, what it's made of, that stuff. If you treat me right, I'll talk to you. Burn me once, I'm done."

"What do you mean 'treat you right'?" Jimmy was back inside my head.

"Just what I said. I'll talk to you as long as you don't print anything I say off the record. Don't print anything unless I tell you this is for the record. And never let your photographer get a picture of me or my men. You'll get us killed."

Now, why wouldn't Callahan be that open and trust me like Russo did?

"I won't, I promise. But wait. I didn't ask. How big is this drug bust, comparatively?"

"Biggest we've ever made."

"Ever?" Yes, my voice went up an octave.

"Ever." He repeated.

"You buried the lead, Russo. DPS narcotics agents made the largest drug seizure in Taylor County history. That's the story."

"Don't say DPS narcotics agents. We had people from other agencies helping and they'll get their feelings hurt if DPS takes the credit. Maybe just say law enforcement and list all the agencies involved somewhere in that story. And call it West Central Texas, because we haven't made a bust this big anywhere in the district."

"Wow. Thanks, Russo. I appreciate it. I'll call back tomorrow, find out if you have new information before the deadline, and set up a time for my photographer to take pictures."

I called them all by their last names because that's how they referred to each other and to themselves. If Art Clancy answered his telephone, he didn't say "Art." He said, "Clancy." T.J. Callahan wasn't T.J. He was Callahan. And John Russo was never John. Always Russo.

Billingsly's arraignment was tomorrow at 10 a.m., but my shift wouldn't start until two. I asked Jack for permission to come in early and cover it. He peered at me over those reading glasses. "It's your story. You've earned it."

Chapter 8

The following day, my stories dominated the front page again with my byline. This time, Jack even ran a thumbnail picture of me with the story—the same one on my press ID. That never happened before.

All of Abilene's news photographers-slash-videographers were waiting in front of the Taylor County Courthouse as sheriff's deputies escorted James Billingsly, wearing an orange jail jumpsuit, handcuffed and shackled, to court. Mikey Jergenson was our dayside photographer, assigned to get the all-important shot. Mikey was younger, bigger, slower, and less experienced than Jimmy. But he was solid. He'd grow with experience.

His shot of Billingsly would be used every time anything happened in his case from that day forward, all the way up to his execution, if and when that came.

Some TV reporter shouted, "James! Why'd you do it? Why'd you kill Mrs. Bennett?" as he shuffled by in ankle bracelets. I knew their TV tricks. They shouted out a question using his name, hoping Billingsly would react by facing their camera. But Billingsly didn't. He kept his eyes straight ahead, walking with those thick, broad shoulders held back proudly. I wouldn't describe his appearance as defiant, nor did he appear defeated. His face was blank, like the cops, as he mechanically shuffled through the motions.

District Judge Alejandro Chavez presided over the hearing. He was a nice-looking, square-faced Hispanic man who read and explained the charges to Billingsly, asking him first if he understood what he was being charged with. Chavez had been DA before running for judge.

"Yes, sir." The accused met the judge's gaze, his head high, his shoulders back.

"How do you plead to these charges?" the judge asked.

"Not guilty." The answer was loud and emphatic.

"If you cannot afford an attorney, one will be appointed for you. Can you afford an attorney, Mr. Billingsly?"

"No, sir. I cannot."

"One will be appointed."

The DA requested no bail. The judge granted the motion, citing the heinous nature of the crime.

There were no cameras in the courtroom, just reporters. But Billingsly would be paraded by all the TV cameras on his way out. If Mikey felt he got a good shot coming in, he was off to his next stop. Otherwise, he'd be out there, too.

Brett grabbed my elbow and whispered after the hearing. "How did you get his picture being brought into the jail yesterday?"

I smiled at her and winked. "No comment."

She'd have to learn things like that on her own.

∞

Billingsly's arraignment was played below the fold the next morning since there wasn't much new information, just that full-frontal photo. He pleaded innocent, and the judge denied him bond.

But I still had the lead story with a banner headline on the seizure of the largest illegal drug lab in the history of West Central Texas. "Busted! Massive Meth Lab Seized" was the headline.

Reporters didn't write headlines. All that happened after we hit 'Send.'

Jack got our stories first, reading them for content, quizzing us sometimes, and adding details we left out. Then, he sent them to one of several copy editors who checked for spelling, typos, and grammatical errors. The news editor double-checked everything, laid out the paper, and assigned column width and headline size. I can't say which editor wrote which headline or if one wrote them all.

Jimmy got shots of Dickey's place between Merkel and View. A double-wide mobile home with a large barn. I figured the lab was in the barn, but Russo didn't specify.

At DPS headquarters, Russo laid out wrapped packages of the seized methamphetamine on a scale, along with the cooking utensils. Jimmy went, not me. Russo refused to be in the picture, of course. He issued Jimmy the same warning he gave me: never publish a photograph of him or one of his agents.

We also used Freddy Dickey's mugshot. Russo was right. Freddy looked fifty-five years old, not thirty-five, with a narrow, drawn, leathery face, long, scraggly hair, and beard. His light eyes were lifeless.

For the Sunday paper, I pitched the bigger story, the news feature about how the growing drug problem in West Central Texas translated to increased crime. Jack bought the pitch. I did an in-depth feature, interviewing Russo many times, always getting information I'd forgotten to ask. He was forthcoming, unguarded, and kind of a friend even though he was in law enforcement. He was so much more open and trusting than anyone at Abilene PD.

But it was a delicate relationship. I needed Russo's information to do my job. He didn't need me. But my stories stroked his ego. Ego or not, if I burned Lt. John Russo, our relationship would end.

For the Sunday feature, I interviewed sheriffs from each county in the West Central Texas Drug Task Force realm and Chief Bates about how drugs are related to crime. The story included interviews with burglary victims whose assailants were determined to be looking for money to buy drugs. We even did a graph showing how crime increased proportionately as drug use increased. All in all, I was making my bones with the paper.

Time rolled on. With Billingsly jailed, awaiting trial, and Marilyn Bennett buried, there wasn't a lot of follow-up to do on that story.

News slowed down. Life and work went back to routine as March rolled by.

Did boredom, curiosity, or daring drive me to the library on my day off? I spent the morning searching old newspapers and magazines for anything on the Marcelo crime family. Their power dated back to the 1920s, spreading from New Orleans to Biloxi to Shreveport, with tentacles as far west as Houston and Dallas.

I found a newspaper photo of Angelo Marcelo entering federal court in New Orleans a decade earlier. He was a handsome but small Italian man, born in 1918. He had five sons and one daughter.

Leaving the library, I headed back to the US Marshal's office. This time, I was in luck. The lights were on. Entering the office, I saw no one. An empty receptionist's desk with a typewriter.

"Hello?" I called. "Yoo-hoo!"

Nothing. Lights were on in a room off the lobby.

I waited a minute or so. My ears perked. Someone was on the telephone, speaking quietly.

"Hello? Is anyone here?"

"Have a seat!" A man called from the adjoining room. "I'll be with you in a second."

I did, waiting in a straight-back wooden chair against the lobby wall. The office was old. Nothing modern about it except the Remington electric typewriter. I think the Federal Courthouse in Abilene was built in the 1930s. Three stories of that same cream-colored brick used in the municipal buildings.

The federal building didn't appear to have ever been modernized. The big office door had 'United States Marshal's Office' hand-painted in gold on antique-looking frosted glass. A few minutes after answering my yoo-hoo, Dan Jones, a federal marshal I met in Cisco, peered around the door.

I smiled, relieved to see a friendly face I knew. "Hey, Dan."

"Kat. What can I do for you?" he asked. "It's been a minute."

Dan was a middle-aged man, not much bigger than me. His brown hair was parted on the side and cut up over his ears. When I'd seen him in Cisco, he wore a white, wide-brimmed cowboy hat with a low crown. I think they called it a cattleman's cut. He wasn't wearing it in the office.

"I'm poking my nose into places it doesn't belong. I thought you might give me some advice. Steer me in the right direction."

He nodded. "If I can."

"It has to do with a story I covered a few weeks ago. What can you tell me about a man named Tex Gibson? I understand he's been on the feds' radar for years."

His eyes flashed steely. "Where did you hear that?"

I mustered my sweetest, most manipulative smile. "You know I can't tell you that. Reporters have good ears, and we don't burn sources."

He clenched his lips together, his gaze a bit narrow. "Why do you want to know about Tex?"

"I heard a rumor he might have been involved with Marilyn Bennett and I wondered—"

He cut me off, palm raised. "You need to stop right there." His face was stern. All the friendly had washed out.

"Why?"

"Because you're right. You're poking your nose into places where it doesn't belong. Dangerous places."

"Off the record, Dan. For background. I'm just trying to understand."

He wagged his head. "On the record, understand this. You don't need to go there. You don't want to go there." His forehead furrowed. "Do you understand?"

My hands went up in frustration. "Not really. Why can't I at least know his background? How is that dangerous?"

He stood silent for a moment, peering first at me and then at the ancient hardwood floor. His eyes came back to meet mine. "People who get cross with Tex have a way of disappearing." He clenched his fingers together in front of his face, the way Jimmy had before, kind of Italian style, and then he flicked them wide, saying, "Poof. They disappear."

"Like who?"

Dan sighed and groaned. "Come in and sit down." He turned into his office, sitting behind his desk as I took the chair in front of it. He said, "Dammit, don't poke the bear. Let law enforcement do their jobs."

"Who disappeared, Dan? How many?" I asked. "I'm not quoting you. Not on the record. I just want background."

His face scrunched; the corners of his mouth turned down as he appeared to ponder. A moment later, "Over the years, I can think of a few competitors who conveniently had car wrecks or heart attacks. One drowned."

Drowned. For some reason, that word took me somewhere I didn't want to go, covering the drowning of a four-year-old boy. I shoved the memory away and stood. "I met Tex and his wife at Mrs. Bennett's funeral. She made my skin crawl with that syrupy Southern drawl."

He replied, "It's real. Born and raised on Lake Pontchartrain. Roxanne Marcelo Gibson is as deadly as she is pretty. Nobody's ever proved anything on any of them, but people who get crossways with the Marcelos never come out on top. Did she threaten you?"

I'd walked to the windows, peering outside. "No. She just snarled."

"And Tex?" Dan asked.

I detected concern in his tone. I turned to face him. "Same."

"If you're as smart as I think you are, you won't gig Tex or his wife. Let the detectives do their jobs."

"Are the detectives looking into them?"

There it came, plain as day. Dan pulled out his blank cop mask. I have to say, the Abilene law enforcement guys had cornered the market. Maybe they took some training course in it because, in my years working in Angelo, I'd never seen the blank face used as often as I'd seen it in my first two months here.

"Dan? Are Abilene police investigating the Gibsons in connection with Mrs. Bennett's murder? Yes or no. Off the record."

He stared. Didn't answer my question.

I took a different tactic. "Do you think Roxanne Gibson would kill a woman for having an affair with her husband?"

He laughed. Snorted, really. "What do you think?"

I was serious, "I don't have the faintest idea."

He lifted a hand in frustration. "I just told you, she's a Marcelo. Any Marcelo is capable of murder or ordering murder."

"Darnit, Dan. You guys are experts at avoiding questions. Are Abilene cops looking into Roxanne Gibson as the killer?"

"I can't tell you about another agency's investigation, even if I knew. You know that."

I opened my mouth, but Dan raised his hand, his palm facing me. "Now, I've said too much already. No. Comment. Period." He shuffled some papers on his desk, avoiding my eyes, and grumbled. "Take my advice, Kat. Quit digging."

"You honestly think I could get hurt?"

He raised his head quickly, those gray-blue eyes piercing mine. "Why don't you call the New Orleans newspaper? What's it called? The *Times-Picayune*, yeah. Ask about a reporter named Larence Zandt. Investigative reporter. He got too close to Marcelo a while back. Call down there and ask

what happened to Larence Zandt." Dan clenched his fingertips in front of his face again and flicked them wide, like before.
"Poof. Probably alligator bait."

There it came again: Callahan in the moonlight saying, 'It
would break my heart to work a missing persons case on you.'
He knew then that a reporter disappeared. He was always three
steps ahead. No wonder he laughed.

Chapter 9

A few weeks after Callahan's call and Billingsly's arrest, I felt a little guilty. Well, that's an understatement. It gnawed at me that I took Callahan's information, got a photo no one else had, a professional coup, and dropped him like a hot rock after what Jimmy said. I never extended the man the courtesy of saying thank you, nor did I explain why I stopped bugging him on his investigation.

That didn't keep the big man from stalking my dreams, almost like misty memories, which were never clear; they were just swatches of Callahan, sometimes Callahan and me. I watched him work with livestock. In one, I stood on a porch watching him play with children and a dog. In another, we walked hand in hand along the ocean's edge with waves washing over our bare feet, sucking sand from beneath them as waves retreated. And we laughed.

One dream in particular was jolting. Callahan was fighting alongside other men in knee-high grass. The men were not in uniform. Some had rifles. Others had swords. Out of nowhere, a man ran a long blade through Callahan's side. Our gazes locked as he fell to his knees.

I bolted upright in bed, gasping, my heart racing.

Turning on the bedside lamp, I went to the bathroom and splashed cold water on my face, staring at my image in the mirror, trying to understand. Why? Why had that man invaded my dreams? I didn't know him. He was a chauvinist, a know-it-all, but also a gentleman. He wouldn't sit until I did. Considerate. Opened my car door. Protective, warning me to lock my doors, to leave the Gibsons alone. He'd given me a news tip. I never said thank you. And he said I was pretty.

I never dreamed of a man as I did him.

It was the guilt. I'd accepted his token of friendship and disappeared. I needed to fix that. It was wrong of me. Sitting on my couch in the early morning lamplight, I leaned my head back. Admit it. It was more than what Jimmy said.

You're afraid of having a crush. You're afraid of making a fool of yourself over a man every woman wants. That night in his company at Sambo's, he made me feel so alive. Just his hushed voice on the phone that day tingled through me. I was so excited that he did that. Then Jimmy ruined everything.

Oh, well. It was a hopeless infatuation, anyway. He was a cop, and I was a cop reporter, and never the twain shall meet.

I was back to my usual runs. There were no big crime stories, no big arrests, and only piddly three- or five-inch stories on burglaries and car wrecks. Scanning the jail log, I asked George, "Has anyone been appointed to represent James Billingsly?"

"Culpepper," he replied.

Still bent over the clipboard, I peered up. "Is that a last name or first?"

George smiled out of the side of his mouth. Some people can do that, as some can raise one brow. "You never heard of Culpepper Hayes?" I think George was as big a man as Callahan, just older. Not as powerfully built.

I straightened. "Doesn't ring a bell."

He took a sip from his coffee mug. "How long have you been here, Kat?"

"Almost the end of my second month in Abilene." I grinned. I was settling into things.

He cocked his head. "Seems like you've been here longer than that. Where'd you work before?"

"*San Angelo Standard-Times.*"

"What brought you here?"

I'd finished perusing the log. "I don't know. A year or so after a divorce and you keep running into the same old crowd, your ex with his new girlfriends. Angelo felt a little crowded. This position was open, and they wanted someone who had experience covering cops."

George smiled sweetly. "I didn't think this was your first rodeo."

"Most reporters hate this beat. I'm the odd one who loves it."

He set his coffee mug on the counter. "Well, Culpepper's as big as they come around here."

Surprising. Pro bono attorneys were usually young and hungry, scratching for clients and trying to make a name. The county didn't pay pro bono attorneys much, but at least they paid. Pro bono work offered young newcomers a steady income and a chance to build a practice.

"Really?" I asked. "Judge Alvarez gave him a good attorney?"

George lowered his voice. I think he had radar ears, over-hearing a lot, and he didn't want others to know how much he knew. "Word is, Culpepper asked for it. Lots of publicity on a case like this."

"Why would he need publicity if he's so big?"

George twisted his neck. "There's never too much publicity for Culpepper Hayes. He's a firecracker."

I'm not sure why, but that gave me a thought. "What would it take to get an interview with Billingsly? Can he talk to me?"

George lifted his shoulders. "Never heard of a jailhouse interview with the newspaper, but if he wants to, you'd go to the visitor's window and talk to him just like any other visitor."

"Has anyone been to see him?"

George shook his head. His eyes seemed sad.

"Not even his wife?"

George rubbed his chin. "Not to my knowledge."

"Poor guy. Culpepper?"

"Culpepper just got appointed." He cocked his head. "I'd bet Culpepper would advise him not to talk to you. So if you're going to do it, now's the time."

"Can you ask him if he will? Talk to me?"

George tilted his head to the side, those soft gray eyes fixed on mine. "You know if you do this, you're going piss off the cops."

This time, I laughed loudly. "Walking across the room, I piss off the cops."

He laughed, too. "Wait here. I'll see."

He came back several minutes later with a smile. "His visiting hours are over today. It'll be ten o'clock the day after tomorrow before he can see visitors."

"But he'll see me?"

"Apparently so."

As I walked away, George hollered out. "You're the first reporter I've ever had ask to interview a jail inmate."

I returned to the counter. "There are two sides to every story, George. Thank you for always being so nice to me and for not being mean like so many people in law enforcement."

"They're not mean, Kat. They've just been burned."

Nobody batted a thousand. Since I'd come up short, I was working on a story Jack assigned, localizing a national story on the sudden increase in the number of criminal gangs in rural areas, including West Texas. There was talk of creating a gang task force that would function like the drug task force, with several entities pooling resources under one commander.

This one would be managed through Abilene PD since gangs tended to be more of an inner-city problem. But they would also coordinate with Russo's drug task force since drugs and gangs went hand in hand. So did gangs and illegal weapons.

I was interviewing the mother of a girl believed to have been the innocent victim of a drive-by shooting, which was thought to be gang-relate, when a call came over the scanner that no one ignored.

"Ten-thirty-three!" The officer was breathless. We could hear gunfire. "Shots fired!" A moment later. "Officers under fire! Request backup!" Then, "Twenty-eleven North Tenth!"

At once, several frequencies talked on top of each other. Police dispatch and officers in the field responded. Fire and ambulance.

Everyone in the newsroom stopped what we were doing to listen. Even the teletypes ceased their clacking courteously, allowing us to hear. Then, another frantic transmission. "Unknown number of hostages!"

Jimmy waved from the elevator. "Dammit, Kat! Come on!"

I got off the phone, grabbed my purse and reporter's notepad, and ran.

As he started the news car, the police dispatcher came over Jimmy's handheld scanner. Her voice was smooth and reassuring. "All officers, all stations, be advised, hostage negotiator en route. Hostage negotiator en route 2011 North Tenth."

North Tenth Street was as close to the inner city as Abilene had, just ten blocks from the railroad tracks running through downtown. Old, modest, low-income homes. The street was full of police cars and gawkers when we arrived. Jimmy parked a couple of blocks away, and we ran to what was obviously the scene.

Police cars stopped in the street in front of a 1930s-era shotgun house. My grandmother lived in one like it, but this one had scraggly, high grass—no shrubs. An old Ford pickup truck was in the old-fashioned driveway, which consisted of two strips of concrete with grass growing in the middle. There were more weeds than grass.

A patrolman stopped us at the far edge of the adjacent property. The neighboring house had been evacuated.

The young, uniformed officer held out his arms, standing in front of yellow crime scene tape. "This is as far as you go."

Several people lingered near the officer, who was tall and young. One of a handful of Black police officers on the force. Jimmy and I held our press badges hanging on lanyards around our necks. Lots of times, the press got to go where onlookers could not. The officer shook his head and said, "Gunman inside. You get shot, it's on me. Stay where you are."

The television live crews were coming into sight behind crime scene tape on the far side of the house where the gunman was held up. They were bustling down there, raising the masts of their live vans. I spotted Brett standing near the crime scene tape, three houses away.

"Can you at least give us the basics? What happened here?" I asked.

"I can't say anything, ma'am. Someone from the department will be here to brief the press." Cops didn't break ranks. You had to respect that, whether you liked it or not.

A voice nearby said, "I can tell you what happened."

I whirled to the voice belonging to an older, heavy-set Hispanic woman.

The woman pointed to the cedar shingle house as the young officer scowled at her. "They're always fighting. I was afraid this day would come. I told my husband, someday, he was going to kill her. Or she'll get sick enough of his abuse and kill him." She was a short, plump, silver-headed woman. Round face, thick neck. Pleasant black eyes.

"You know the people?" I asked.

The patrolman shook his head, warning her to keep quiet, but the little lady kept talking, glancing at the man beside her, who I took to be her husband. "He came back this morning."

I cut her off. "Who came back?"

"Raul. They'd been yelling ever since. We called the police when we heard Elizabeth scream. A few minutes later, we heard a gunshot."

"Elizabeth who?" I asked.

"Landeros," she answered.

"Spell it for me, will you? To make sure I get it right?"

"L-A-N-D-E-R-O-S."

"How old is Elizabeth? And Raul?" I scribbled my short-hand on my reporter's notepad.

She exchanged glances with the man. "I'm not sure. Thirty? Thirty-five? They have three children in school."

I peered at the woman questioningly, then at the police officer, and raised my hands questioningly. "If the kids are in school, who's he holding hostage?"

"Her parents, I guess. They're staying there," the woman said.

"He's a Vietnam vet." The man offered.

"Raul Landeros?" I wanted to be sure.

She nodded.

The old man with thick, white hair jumped in. "The kid's been messed up ever since he got back from 'Nam. He works. He gets depressed. Goes on a bender. Loses his job for not showing up. Disappears for a week or so then comes back home mad." He gazed at the Landeros house. "It's not the first time."

Still scribbling, I asked, "Can I have your names?"

"Oh, no." The woman's eyes showed fear. "I don't want my name in the newspaper." She waved her hands back and forth in front of her, which surprised me. She'd been so forthcoming. And she saw me taking notes.

I pleaded. "This is an important story. Your neighbor Elizabeth, she may be dead."

The patrolman sneered. "Raul may be dead before long. He fired on the first officers on the scene. They're lucky to be alive."

I turned to her. "Did you see that? Did you see him shooting at police?"

"Oh, yes." She nodded, glancing at her husband. "We saw it all." She touched her chest. "I called the police. When they arrived, someone, I guess Raul, started shooting out the front windows at them. The officers took cover behind their police cars. One ducked into his front seat. They yelled for Raul to put his weapon down, but he hollered, 'I killed her. I'll kill them if you don't leave!'"

She lifted her hands high again with her eyes on her husband. "But they couldn't leave. They couldn't pull their cars back, either, because he kept shooting at them. Their cars are right where they were when they first got here."

One Abilene Police patrol unit was stopped in front of the house, and the other was in the Landeros driveway.

She gripped her husband's arm and buried her head against it. "It makes my blood run cold to think of Elizabeth in there. Shot. Maybe dead. She's a good mother. She put up with him."

I coaxed. "Those children just lost their mom. They're going to lose their dad, one way or another. Jail or a bullet. Please," I begged. "Let me quote you. I mean, I can say a neighbor said, but it's a better story if I can use your name. What were you doing at the time?"

"Cooking tamales." The couple exchanged glances again. "Had to shut everything down. They're ruined now."

I gave her my most pleading stare.

She nodded reluctantly. "Okay. Isabel. Isabel Gomez. We live there." She pointed to the neat frame house next door to the Landeros house, just behind the crime scene tape.

"How long have you lived here?" I asked.

The two exchanged glances. "Thirty years," the man said.

"And your name, sir?"

"Alberto."

"Gomez?"

"Yes." Alberto and Isabel were small people. He was no taller than me, and Isabel was several inches shorter. If I had to guess, they were in their sixties. "Alberto, do you know Raul well?" I asked.

He nodded. His thick neck had several folds. "When he's in his right mind, he's a good kid. He's helped me with my car. He climbed up on my roof for me to get rid of a tree limb that fell, and to see if the roof was damaged. But sometimes, something triggers him." He spun his forefinger near his temple. "And he just goes loco." He shrugged. "The police have come here many times."

As Alberto spoke, Callahan walked into view, stopping beside the patrol officer. He cocked his head toward the crowd. "Marcus, clear the block." He nodded at the Landeros house. "I don't want anyone in that house to see anyone but me. Tell the guys on the other side."

He spotted me, maybe in his peripheral vision, or maybe he'd seen me as he walked up, I don't know, but Callahan turned from the patrolman and faced me squarely. I was stunned. I had no idea he was a hostage negotiator. I'm sure my shock showed. I never expected to see him here. Our gazes held. I couldn't read him, but his eyes locked onto mine and didn't let go for a moment.

With neither expression nor acknowledgment, he turned, ducked under the yellow crime scene tape, and strode toward the house, yelling through his cupped hands as he neared the house. "Raul! It's T.J. Callahan! Let's talk!" He kept walking and spread his arms wide as he stepped in front of the Landeros house. "Raul! It's TJ! I'm unarmed!"

The patrolman began ushering us back. "You heard him. Everyone back up to the end of the block." He keyed his radio. "Hostage negotiator says get everyone off this block. No line of sight from the house."

Jimmy and I exchanged glances. We both knew better than to argue. He kept snapping shots as we walked backward, but my mind was on Callahan. My heart quickened. Raul Landeros just killed his wife. He shot at the patrol officers. He's threatening to kill people inside. Why wouldn't he shoot Police Detective Callahan?

I had to snap out of it. "Isabel, one of you said, you heard Elizabeth scream. Did she say anything or just scream?"

"She yelled, 'No, Raul. No!' And then we heard the shot—a loud boom!" Isabel was excited and animated.

Alberto appeared heartsick. I saw sadness in those round, dark eyes. "Those poor kids." He kept shaking his head, and his thick, soft white hair wafted as he did.

"How old are they? The children?" I fought to focus on the interview. My mind kept wandering to Callahan.

"I don't know. Middle school and elementary school," Alberto said, his brows white and thick.

"Boys? Girls?" I asked.

Isabel said, "The oldest, Junior, is a boy. A daughter, Elena. The youngest is Miguel."

"And Isabel's parents are inside?"

Alberto replied, "I guess. They live in Veracruz, I think, but they've been here for months. I think their being here so long is what set Raul off this time." He rubbed the back of his neck. He griped about them a lot." He lifted his shoulders. "But if it wasn't them, it would be something else. Every so often, something sets him off."

"Tell me about Raul." I was writing and flipping pages, fighting to focus on the interview.

"He's a rock mason. He can always find work. He's a good hand. He would make good money if he could stay sober and keep a job."

My attention drifted from them altogether. My gaze traveled to Callahan and stayed there. He stood in front of the Landeros house, near the porch, bareheaded and without a weapon. I couldn't hear anything being said. He still held his arms outstretched at his sides, I guess to prove he was no threat.

I knew that voice. It could be soothing, as he sounded when he said I was a pretty woman. If anyone could calm a crazy man, it would be him, but that man just killed his wife. He didn't have much reason to go on.

It felt a long, grating time before two people emerged from the house. An older man and woman, similar in size and age to the Gomezes, hurried out. Callahan pointed them toward the police tape and ushered them away. He raised his hands, clasping them behind his head with his elbows out, and disappeared onto the porch or inside the house. I couldn't see. I'd never witnessed a hostage negotiation, and we were so far back we couldn't hear.

Tedious minutes eked into half an hour. The neighborhood waited silently, with no idea what was going on inside.

I flinched. We all did at the roar of gunfire. One shot.

I sucked in my air. Callahan didn't have a gun. He didn't fire that weapon.

Long seconds passed—he hadn't come out—and armed officers rushed to the house. Callahan emerged, his hands in the air, his head hanging low, his gaze on the ground.

His shirt front, his arms, soaked in blood. Was he hit?

Patrolmen and plainclothes officers surrounded him as he lowered his arms, shook his head, and spoke to them.

He trudged to a man who I took to be in charge. Who was he? Not the chief. Maybe his sergeant? Anyway, an older guy. They spoke for a moment. The older man gripped Callahan's shoulder, and I watched as he plodded toward his big black truck.

I ran to him.

As he glanced over his shoulder to pull away from the curb, he saw me standing in the street and rolled down his window. He shook his head softly, the eyes empty. "Not now."

"I just wanted to tell you I'm sorry."

He stared at me with a blank expression. And drove away. He hated me now. Whatever chance I might have had with him was gone. I saw it in his lifeless eyes. I stood frozen, watching that black truck disappear.

Jimmy was by my side. "What was that about?"

"Nothing. I just felt sorry for him." I turned to Jimmy. "Did you see his face? He was sick over that guy killing himself."

"No, but I saw the way he looked at you before he went in."

"What does that mean?" My hackles were up, the claws out. He wasn't going to insult me or him again.

Jimmy snickered, his gaze narrow. "You seem to forget I'm a guy. I know the look."

"What the hell does that mean?"

"It means he's got a thing for you, Kat, whether you can see it or not."

Oh, how I wished that were true. But that's not what I saw in those eyes. Jimmy didn't know about the favor, which was never acknowledged or appreciated. He couldn't know. "No. He hates me."

"Whatever." Jimmy scoffed. "He got that nut job to release his in-laws and didn't get shot himself. I'd call that a successful day." He pointed at the Landeros house. "We're missing the gang bang."

Gang bang. That's what we called a news conference.

Jimmy and I headed for it. The patrol sergeant was briefing a cluster of TV cameras. He didn't give them anything I didn't already have except to confirm that the assailant's wife was, indeed, deceased. Her name was Elizabeth Landeros. Age 34.

The assailant, Raul Landeros, aged 38, died of a self-inflicted gunshot wound.

I don't know if the TV people got neighbor interviews on the other side, but none talked to the Gómezes. They would make that story with their insights from years of overhearing fights between the couple.

I spotted Elizabeth's parents huddled with Clancy behind big arborvitaes between the Landeros and Gomez houses. I approached, keeping my distance. "Clancy?"

His gaze met my voice. Clancy was round-faced, with a button nose and lots of freckles.

I asked him, "Can I get their names and where they're from?"

"I don't know their names. No habla Ingles."

"Thanks. Well," I hung my head and hum-hawed. "Tell Callahan I'm sorry."

"For what?" I saw surprise in Clancy's eyes, his bushy red brows pulled together.

"I saw his face when he came out."

Clancy nodded. "Yeah, he takes it hard sometimes. I'll tell him."

I nodded at the couple clinging to each other. They didn't notice us, too consumed by the loss of their child. The woman wept into her husband's shoulder as he stared dumbfounded at the ground. That couple watched their daughter murdered. Her body was still inside. They'd been held at gunpoint all that time, wondering which one of them was next.

I gestured to the couple. "He saved them."

It's impossible to put yourself in their place, and I found it equally impossible to crawl inside Callahan's skin, him trying to save their lives with nothing but his ability to calm and persuade. Then, he tried to convince a desperate man with nothing left to live for not to kill himself. But Raul ended his own life, anyway, right in front of Callahan's eyes.

The fresh blood that soaked Callahan's shirt was that of Raul Landeros. He'd clutched him as he died. How gut-wrenching does it get?

I told Clancy, "He's been here before, judging from how he acted when he went in."

Clancy scoffed and rubbed the back of his neck. "We've been coming to this house since we were on patrol." Clancy was talking to me like a human being. I couldn't believe it.

"How many years?" I asked.

He gazed at the sky for a moment. "We both made detective what? Six, seven years ago? Let me tell you, if Callahan couldn't talk Raul out of it, no one else could have."

"Will someone investigate Elizabeth Landeros' murder?"

"Sure. But I don't know who's doing what. Murder-suicide. Not a lot of investigating to do." He nodded at the traumatized couple. "I've got to get them to an interpreter. You can call me later. I'll give you their names if the big guys let me. They're victims themselves, you know. I can at least tell you where they're from and their ages."

I offered my hand, and he took it. "Thank you, Clancy. Don't worry. You've said nothing on the record. I'll give you a call later."

One more time, at the loss of life, I had a hell of a front-page story. Jimmy's pictures told it better than any words. Thanks to his telephoto lens, he captured the expressions on the faces of Elizabeth Landeros' parents as they emerged from the house. Terror and relief.

I'd been too absorbed worrying about Callahan to notice Jimmy climb a tree across the street from the Landeros' front door to get that shot. He snuck beyond the police tape. Always, Jimmy King was the man to trust to get the shot that told the story.

Plus, we had my interview with Isabel and Alberto. I used the good things Alberto shared about how helpful Raul was when sober. His military record. It helped humanize him. Bad as he was, there was good inside Raul Landeros, as in all of us.

Some stories write themselves. That one had to because my mind would not leave that tall man who walked into that house with no weapon, his arms outstretched, trusting that the man who murdered his wife, fired on patrol officers, and held an old man and woman hostage, would not shoot him. Audacious faith if you think about it.

Callahan. Such sadness in those brown eyes, on that long face, as he left. Defeated. That's the word. I saw defeat in Callahan's eyes as he drove away.

I wanted to know that man—fiercely. Having witnessed his selflessness in trying to secure the safe release of a little old couple—people he didn't know—I wanted it even more, awash with shame for having treated him so rudely. I'd never even said thank you when it might have meant something. Now, it was too late.

My story finished and filed; I debated with myself and finally picked up my desk phone to call his direct extension.

It went to voice mail. That smooth voice. "This is Detective T.J. Callahan. Leave a message ... *Beep.*"

"Callahan, it's Katherine Coe." I sighed. "I just wanted to say I'm so sorry. I know it broke your heart. What happened. But you saved two lives. Remember that. He could've shot you. You were so brave. Don't beat yourself up. Please ... Okay. I just ... wanted to say I'm sorry."

When I left work, my car steered itself to Sambo's, and all the way, I wondered if he was there, would I have the guts to go in? I wasn't sure. He might be drowning his sorrows in the arms of a barrel racer.

I was thankful his truck wasn't there.

Chapter 10

The narcotics guys were working overtime. That next day, I was back at the jail, checking logs, surprised to see several fresh drug arrests, one for felony possession with intent to distribute. Ben Sims, twenty-nine years old, from Clyde, was pulled over by a DPS trooper for speeding on Interstate 20. Drugs were found during the traffic stop.

Now, wasn't that a convenient coincidence? Russo had an undercover officer or a snitch who tipped them off. I knew how that worked.

I couldn't remember seeing any arrests for manufacture and delivery or possession with intent to distribute before they busted Freddy Dickey. What was the connection? All of the recent arrests had to be related, somehow. I'd call Russo from my desk.

When I did, there was no answer. I left a message. I also needed Russo's information for a story Jack assigned. The FBI released its Uniform Crime Report for 1979, confirming Russo's theory that crime increased across the board nationwide the past year, corresponding with increased use of illicit drugs. Across the nation, murder, forcible rape, and aggravated robbery incidents had increased markedly.

The Uniform Crime Report listed national and state statistics, but I needed local statistics. I knew they had them because the feds compiled state reports using them. I left messages with the Abilene Police Chief and Russo, asking for calls back.

It wasn't long before my phone rang. I was expecting Russo or Chief Bates to return my call. "This is Kat."

Silence.

"Hello? This is Kat Coe."

No one was there. I started to hang up.

"I appreciate your phone call last night." My heart halted. I knew that voice. He said, "Your message was ... nice."

Somehow, he brought out the femaleness in me. The cynical, cryptic reporter went mum. I wanted to stroke his face, to assuage his unmistakable melancholy of yesterday. My voice was soft. "I saw the hurt in your eyes. It broke my heart."

"Yeah?"

"Yes." I sighed. "One more time. I'm so sorry, Callahan."

"What exactly are you sorry for?"

"For everything. For what happened yesterday." I paused. Say it. "And for never thanking you for your favor. Truly. I apologize."

"You threw me away like an empty sack of potato chips."

I chuckled nervously. "I did not."

"Yeah, you did. Before that, I couldn't get you out from under my feet. After that, you disappeared."

"That's not true." I felt like a schoolgirl.

"Yeah, it is. You know it is."

I ran my fingers through the hair hanging in my eyes. "I'll explain someday."

"What's wrong with today? I did something for you I've never done for another human being. I gave you a heads-up on something we were doing, because it seemed so important to you, and you work so much harder than anyone else. I didn't see any harm in you getting a picture the others didn't have. But not so much as an acknowledgment. No thumbs up. Nothing."

"Callahan, please. I'm sorry. There was a reason. Let me buy you a barbecue sandwich and a beer. My treat. And I'll explain. Honest."

There was a long pause. "I'm not that easy."

He always said the unexpected. When I stopped chuckling, I asked, "What would you like in return for your news tip, sir?"

"A dance."

Was that code for something? "A dance? I don't under-stand."

"What's not to understand? I asked you to dance. With me."

"You mean, like a real dance?"

I certainly entertained him because he laughed heartily. "That's the only kind I know of."

"You mean, like a date dance? You'd be seen with me in public?"

"Why not? You got the cooties?"

I giggled, remembering his grin as he'd toyed with me at Sambo's. I was almost giddy.

Almost? Hell, I was giddy. I heard it in my voice. He must have heard it, too.

"Let me buy you a sandwich and beer and we'll discuss the dance," I replied.

"When?"

"I get off at ten."

"Where?" He asked.

"I guess, back at Sambo's?"

"I'll see you there. I'll be the pretty one in the corner."

I kept smiling and chuckling even after he hung up. My heart raced. I couldn't deny it.

It wasn't long before Jack came to stand at my terminal. I peered up from my story.

"We're losing Al," he said. "He wants to retire in June."

My chin dropped. "Oh, no. I love Al."

Jack shrugged. "They're talking about banning smoking in the newsroom."

"His smoking doesn't bother me."

"It does some." Jack shrugged. "I don't think it'll happen anytime soon, but someday smoking will be banned every-where." He glanced over his shoulder and nodded at the tele-types. "They'll put them behind sound-proof glass before they ban smoking."

Undeniable melancholy clouded Jack's face, maybe because of losing Al. Perhaps realizing how fast things were changing in our business. When I started in San Angelo, we composed news stories on typewriters, not at connected terminals. The methods of gathering news and newsroom technology were evolving at an alarming speed. We had to adapt or die.

Jack cleared his throat. "Anyway, Al said he'd just go ahead and retire if people were bitching about him smoking. He's old enough. But it's one hell of a loss." He stood there, hum-haw-ing, twirling those glasses. "I need to ask you something, Kat. When I replace Al, traditionally the newest nightside person takes the cop shop. You worked cops in Angelo and you're doing a great job here. Do you want to keep it? Or hand it off?"

"Are you kidding me? I'll fight to keep this beat."

"Okay. I'll shift the dayside guy to cover courts and the DA's office. You stay on cops solo. I'll have the new person pick up obits."

"I'd love it. Thank you, Jack." I wanted to hug him, but I wasn't sure how he'd take it.

"You're damned good at it, Kat. You'll work a floating shift depending on what's happening."

So that was it. That's how I became the official cop reporter. Not a temporary or shared assignment. Those guys really were stuck with me long-term. It was like a bad marriage.

Chapter 11

I t's true what they say about March, at least in Texas. It sweeps in ferocious as a lion but waves goodbye with a gentle hand. The month was all but done. I welcomed a soft breeze caressing my face, rustling my hair as I walked into Sambo's that night. There's something about the smell of spring air. I had a bounce in my step. The permanent assignment to cover the criminal justice system boosted my spirits, not to mention Callahan's call.

I was on top of the world, and even though I worried this liaison was a conflict of interest, I didn't let it stop me. Anytime I was around him, I felt more alive than, well, maybe ever; even if the emotion was anger—his and mine—just being in his presence brought me to life.

Approaching the building, I realized I'd never seen it in the daylight. For some reason, Sambo's didn't seem as dilapidated as it had that first night. I didn't see Callahan when I got inside, which was no surprise. His truck hadn't been in the parking lot.

Louisa was behind the bar. With only a handful of customers, she took advantage of her slow time, wiping down the bar with a big rag as I approached. "Good evening, Louisa. Has Callahan been in?" I smelled bleach.

She glanced up. "Hey, Kathrine. Haven't seen him."

"I'm supposed to meet him here." I pointed. "I'll wait for him in that corner."

"Do you want a beer?" she asked.

I couldn't stop smiling. "Not until he gets here. I'll take a soda while I wait. When Callahan gets here, will you bring him whatever he drinks? It's my treat tonight."

She stopped her bar-mopping and lifted her head. "You think?"

I took my place in that dark corner again, where I could see the door, watching customers in the dining room and others around the pool table. I waited. Checked my watch a couple of times. No Callahan.

Louisa came to the table with my soda and set her free hand on her hip. I still smelled bleach. "He's not going to let you pay, you know that."

I smiled at her, so happy to see him again. Yesterday, I was certain he hated me. I'm sure I gushed, "I'll make him."

She tilted her head toward the bar. "He just called. Said to tell you, he's tied up at work."

My face fell. Louisa saw it. "He said for me to tell you to wait. He'll be here as soon as he can. Maybe twenty minutes."

My revived smile could not be erased. "I'll wait. I owe him a sandwich and a beer."

She was a pleasant woman with a gentle way, and she peered directly at me through coal-black eyes. It was a beautiful face when she was young, I was sure. Heavy now. "You really don't know him very well if you think he'll let you pay."

"I owe him."

"For what?" she asked.

"Well, I can't say. But I do."

She grinned. "You may owe him hon, but Thomas Jefferson Callahan's never gonna' let you pay."

Thomas Jefferson Callahan. You had to love it.

I went to the ladies' room a bit later, checking myself in the mirror. Newspaper reporters were lucky. We could dress comfortably for work. I wore a deep green, long-sleeved, satiny button-up blouse with a collar and blue jeans. Loafers.

Those poor TV reporters like Brett had to dress in high heels, pantyhose, and suits. Ugh.

I wasn't tall, but I wasn't short. On the slim side. Not overly endowed up top, like Prissy. I wore my hair longer than most. People said it was chestnut brown. Wavy, with a mind of its own. My best friend used to iron it, to straighten it, when we were in high school, but I'd given that up. It was what it was. Thank goodness I lived in the western half of the state because I could be mistaken for Little Orphan Annie when it rained or sleeted, like the day of Mrs. Bennett's funeral.

He said I was pretty. Hearing that from a man like Callahan did a lot for a woman's ego. I'd put on lipstick, mascara, and perfume in the women's room at work, knowing I would see him. Like I said, Callahan made me feel like a woman, not just a reporter.

I was back, sitting alone in my corner, nursing a second soda, when a man who'd been shooting pool as I walked by to the restroom approached.

It looked like he just left the drilling rig or closed the sale barn. He wore a dirty plaid cowboy shirt with a yolk and white snaps instead of buttons, oil-grimy faded jeans tucked inside worn leather boots, and, of course, a hat, which he tipped. "If you don't mind me saying so, ma'am, you're way too pretty to be sitting back here all alone." He set that hat back down onto sandy brown hair. He might not have been a bad-looking guy if his clothes hadn't been so soiled.

I smiled back. "Thank you. But I'm not alone. I'm waiting for someone. He'll be here soon."

He grinned. Terrible teeth. "Well, if he stands you up, we're right over there." He pointed toward the pool table, his shirt sleeves rolled up tight around bulging biceps as Callahan came through the front door.

Callahan was the kind of man who turned heads. Not just mine. "That your feller?" The roughneck asked.

I glanced from Callahan to the roughneck. "He's who I'm meeting."

He nodded and ambled back to his pool group, but not before Callahan spotted him. He went to the bar, said something to Louisa, stopped at a booth, spoke briefly with a man and woman, then headed my way.

They should've made him the Marlboro man. I'd guarantee there wasn't a woman in the place who wasn't looking at him in that dark blue pinstriped shirt with those broad shoulders, the black hat, and that silver belt buckle. He stopped before me, smiled, and motioned with his hand. "Hop up."

"Excuse me?" I was looking up.

He aimed his finger. "You got my seat."

I had to smile. "Why's it your seat?"

"Because I don't sit with my back to the door." He lifted his chin with a grin. "Hop up."

I had never noticed the scar under his left jawline. "Really?"

There came that dimple. "Yeah, really." His palm facing up, he waved his fingers again, coaxing me.

So I got up, moved my drink to the other side of the table, and Callahan sat where I'd been sitting for what felt like a long time, with his back to the wall, where he surveilled the room from front to back. "I don't put my back to the door," he said, peering into the game area, "or the room, for that matter." Someone back there has his undivided attention.

I couldn't suppress my schoolgirl smile. "You came just in time to save me."

His gaze was still on the game room. "Yeah, I saw that. That was Danny Dickey. Narcs busted his older brother a while back."

"Well, he saw you come in. Do you think he knows you're a cop?"

His eyes came back to me, and he smirked. "What do you think?"

I just kept smiling at him. "So how are you, Callahan?"

"I'm okay."

"I'm—"

He showed his palm. "We're not talking about yesterday."

I nodded.

He took off his hat, set it in the chair beside him, and raked his fingers through his hair, as I'd seen him do before. He crossed his forearms as he leaned on the table, those umber eyes near mine for the first time in what felt like forever. I had his full attention. "Now, are you sorry?"

I played coy. "For what?"

Those eyes snapped. "For treating me like a worn-out shoe." He used that Hank Williams line so perfectly I tilted my head back and laughed so hard my eyes watered. I wiped them with my fingertips. "I can explain."

"You better."

Louisa brought two mugs of beer. He smiled at her. "Thanks, Louisa."

She tilted her head at me though her eyes were on him. "Kathrine says tonight's on her."

He cut his eyes at me and left them there. "She can think what she wants."

Louisa smiled at me mockingly. "I told you so."

"No, Louisa, don't take his money. I'm buying tonight."

She aimed her thumb at Callahan. "You think I'm bucking that one?"

I told him, "I want to do this for you. To make amends."

He held up his mug. "And I appreciate that. But you're going to have to do it some other way. I don't let ladies buy my meals."

Louisa walked away, chuckling.

Is he even from this century? No point in arguing.

We each took a long sip of our beers, and Callahan raised that lone brow. "So you don't have to keep a clear head tonight?"

I giggled, remembering, and glanced away.

He deserved to know, but this wasn't going to be easy. I cleared my throat, took another swallow of the icy beer, avoided his eyes, and said, "Okay. That day, when you called me, and I sent Jimmy to the jail to get the picture..." I met his unyielding gaze. "My city editor and Jimmy both looked at me like—I can't even say it. Let's just say they were suspicious. How could I possibly know that?"

His brows shifted high.

"Don't worry, I didn't tell a soul. I wouldn't. But Jimmy actually said it."

"Said what?"

I took a deep breath and exhaled. "He said, 'Tell me that you haven't crawled into bed with T.J. Callahan for a news story.'" I left out the Nazi part, for Jimmy's sake.

He shoved back his chair. "Why, I'll beat the shit out of—"

I showed him my palm. "No, Callahan, it infuriated me, too. And it hurt my feelings. But I guess Jimmy was just warning me that reporters who get too close to sources get accused of things."

I peered into my mug and took another hefty drink of beer. "So, I thought it would be best, I guess for my good name, if I stayed away. From you." I leaned over the table, whispering. "I don't want people to think I'd have sex with you for a news story, or that you would give me news tips because I did."

He was already way into that first beer. He chugged it and clomped the empty mug on the table, loud, motioning Louisa at the bar. "Someone insinuated the same thing to me."

"And?"

It seemed the room quietened as he answered in his angry voice. "I told him to fuck himself."

Ooh ... that traveled.

He cut his eyes at Louisa, who glowered like a schoolmarm as she crossed the room with two beers. The couple he'd spoken with earlier turned to peer at him.

Callahan lowered his volume. "I wouldn't touch a woman who would sleep with me for a news story, and I didn't like him insinuating that about you."

"Thank you."

Louisa clomped our beers on the table, put her hands on her hips, and glared at Callahan as if he was her kid.

He peered at her. "Sorry."

She wagged her finger and shook her head, and as she walked away, I was sure I heard her chuckling.

I watched her to avoid his gaze, but it never let up. My eyes met his, and I couldn't know if he could tell from my face, but my heart was yearning. "Why do you have to be a cop?"

His was more of a snicker. "Why do you have to be a reporter?" He took a long drink of his new beer, watching me.

I leaned back, avoiding his gaze again, and inhaled deeply. Total honesty. I hadn't given it. But how do you say it? I took another long gulp of my beer and leaned toward him. "To use your words, Callahan, let's be honest. It's more than just what Jimmy said." I shrugged. "I like you. Maybe too much. Even if you are a sexist pig."

Mid-swallow, he inhaled some brew, laughing, choking, hacking.

My eyes wide, I stood to slap his back, but he held up his hand and finally got the beer out of his windpipe—then went back to cackling. "Why would you say that? I'm not sexist."

The fact that he doesn't realize it is hilarious. "Really? Find a quilting bee to cover?"

His head tilted back as he chortled. His eyes twinkled like lights on a Christmas tree. "I was mad."

"I remember." My gaze shifted back to my beer mug as I took another long drink. I glanced at the bar, holding tight to my mug, avoiding eye contact. "I don't want to make a fool out of myself, Callahan."

"You know I like you, too," he said.

My gaze beelined back, meeting his.

His voice was honey. "There's something about you, Katherine. I can't ... quite put my finger on it. You can make me so damned mad I want to tear up the town and the next thing I know, I hear your voice. You bat those eyes. And here I am."

My heart jumped into my throat. It took a moment before I could find my voice. "So what now?"

"Let the chips fall where they may." Callahan had never taken his eyes from me except when he was choking, which had actually scared me. He leaned close. "Let's dispense with the bullshit, Katherine. You're a beautiful woman and I'm attracted to you. Very much."

He touched his fingers to his chest. "I'm a man. You say you're attracted to me. So, what's the problem?"

I lifted a shoulder, rubbing my fingertips over the condensation on my mug. "The conflict of interest between your job and mine. It's not like you're a welder and I'm a secretary. We're on opposing teams and both of us pretty much live what we do."

"Speak for yourself." He glanced at the bar. With all the customers, you couldn't see Louisa. "I'll be right back. Do you need a refresh?"

"Yes. Thank you." I was guzzling my beer like he was only I wasn't as big as him. He took both mugs and strode to the bar, chatting with guys ahead of him.

I watched, admiring, not ogling. It was my turn to appraise him like a horse at auction. No slouching. His back was straight, his chin high. Self-assured.

When he returned and set my fresh mug on the table before me, I blurted it out. "I dream about you."

One beer, and you're spilling your guts. Don't be a ninny!

What a lovely, surprised smile. "Yeah? What kind of dreams?"

I ran my fingertips idly over the rim of my icy mug, again avoiding his eyes because if I looked up, they would surely be fixed on me.

"They don't make sense. Just dreams with you in them, doing stuff. Different times and places. You've just, I don't know. You've invaded my dreams. I can't understand it." My cheeks burned, and I covered my face with my hands. "I'm sorry. I'm an idiot. I'm so embarrassed."

He reached across the table and took my hands from my face—our first real touch. He tilted my chin, forcing me to see him, and my heart raced. "Funny thing. I dream about you."

My eyes grew wide. I felt them. "What kind of dreams?"

That grin was sheepish. "I think you really would be embarrassed."

We both sighed, and he put his hand on the table, palm up. I placed my hand in his, and he folded it around mine.

He was holding my hand, and mine felt tiny. My heart thumped like a rabbit's.

"Here's how it's gonna work. We agree, we don't talk about work."

I snickered. "So, what do we talk about?"

That lone brow arched high again. "Really? You don't have a life outside of work?"

Now that I thought about it, "Honestly, not much. Work is how we know each other. It's the reason we're here, isn't it?"

He let go of my hand, drawing back. "I'm not here about work." Those eyes narrowed. "Are you?"

"I hurt you and I wanted to make up for it."

"That was personal. The favor was personal." He leaned in. "Listen, Katherine, my interest in you hasn't got a damned thing to do with work." He retook my hand, gently rubbing his thumb across my wrist as I stared, almost in shock. Mute like a ninny. Heart pounding.

His eyes had already melted me. "Our work isn't who we are. It's just what we do. If work's all we've got, we'll be mighty lonely people."

I ducked my head.

I never thought about it like that. I always defined myself as a reporter, Callahan as a cop, and Jake as a bull rider. Maybe that's what ruined my marriage. I was always all about work. Jake needed more, and I didn't give it.

Maybe Callahan read my thoughts. "You've got to know when to leave it at the door, Babe. I had to go home last night and deal with yesterday. By myself. I got up this morning and did my damnedest to leave it behind. You can't carry it with you. If you do, you'll end up like Raul."

I nodded my understanding. "He could have killed you," I whispered.

The corners of his mouth turned down as he let go of my hand again and took ahold of his mug. "I had on a vest."

"He could've shot you in the head."

Quickly, his gaze met mine. "When it's my time, Babe, it's my time."

"Do you even know how brave you are?"

He lifted the mug. "That wasn't brave. I knew him." He took a drink. "Raul wasn't going to shoot me as long as he saw I didn't have a weapon. If I'd pulled one on him, he would've."

"That's still brave."

He took a long drink and clomped the mug on the table. "Leave it."

I toyed with my mug, imagining what he went through with Raul, remembering the things I'd seen. "How? How do you ever really leave it?"

It was a sincere question.

He gripped his mug tight. "You look it in the eye and accept it for what it is. Death is part of life." He took a long drink. "I learned that when I was young."

I tilted my head questioningly.

"'Nam."

I don't know why that surprised me, but it did. "You were in Vietnam?"

He nodded gently, that mouth hard. "I did my eighteen months. And I left it over there. Guys like Raul brought it back with 'em."

"How old were you?"

"Nineteen when I went in." After a long pause, staring into his mug, Callahan shrugged. "Babe, we live, and we die. The sun rises and the sun sets. You can't have one without the other. You accept. It is what it is."

That's the difference between us.

Good or horrible, Callahan stared at life unflinchingly and accepted it. I glanced at it, closed my eyes tight, and denied it, dug a hole and buried bad memories like bones.

Callahan's voice brought me back. "I don't want to think about or talk about the past. I want to think about you. About us. I want to know you, Katherine. And I want you to know me."

He took my breath. "I want the same. But I'm a cop reporter. You'd really be seen with me in public?"

He glanced around the room and whispered mockingly, "We're in public, and it looks to me like we're together—alone at a corner table—just like before."

Stone-faced for a second, my face froze as I glanced around the room. "I thought all along this was a place not to be seen."

His head dropped down, and he laughed. I'd say he almost giggled. His shoulders shook. When I wasn't making him mad, I amused the hell out of him. He collected himself, wiped one eye with the back of a knuckle, and said, "Come with me."

He stood with a smile and tilted his head to one side. "Come on," he said, holding out his hand.

I took it, and Callahan led me to the booth where he'd stopped to visit with the couple when he first arrived. They were ten or fifteen years older than us. A heavy-set man with short-cropped salt and pepper hair. The woman was attractive. She wore her graying hair stylishly short.

Callahan said, "Sorry to interrupt, Judge, Pat. This won't take but a second. Katherine Coe, meet Taylor County Judge

William Riley and his wife, Patricia—Pat. Bill and I team rope together."

To say I was surprised would be an understatement. I'm sure it showed. "Nice to meet you both," I said.

They said the same.

"Katherine's afraid to go out with me. She thinks it'll create a scandal for a cop to date a reporter."

I interjected. "Not any reporter. The cop reporter."

"Well, Judge, what do you think? Is that some kind of scandal?" Callahan sounded like he was questioning someone on the witness stand.

The judge swallowed his food, wiped his mouth, and peered at me. "No more than a judge and a detective roping together. Callahan and I don't talk business." He read the surprise in my eyes and shook his index finger. "We don't do it."

"That's what I told her."

Pat Riley smiled at me with kind blue eyes, nodding at Callahan. "You two go out and have a good time. Don't worry about what people say."

"Thank you," I muttered. "Do you come here often?"

Pat gushed, "Louisa makes the best barbecue in town. We're here almost every Wednesday. She has a special. But we went to the movie tonight and decided we wanted barbecue on the way home."

Callahan nodded. "Enjoy your meal. See you Saturday." He'd never let go of my hand as we stood before them. He led me back to our table, and we sat back down—as always, he stood until I sat. "Now, is that behind us?" he asked.

"What happens if I need to call you on a story? Legitimately, for a news story on one of your cases?"

"I'll treat you like any other reporter. Just like yesterday. No more news tips, Katherine. That one bit us both in the ass. I won't let anyone question our integrity again."

"What if I get information on my own that hurts your case?"

"If you think it might, ask me. I'll be honest. Nothing changes. You do your job and I'll do mine."

I gave it a moment, letting it sink in. "Yes, I can live with that." I sipped my beer, my eyes on him, smiling. "So, does this mean we're dating?"

Why are you such a fucking schoolgirl around him?

His head dipped down again as he chuckled. "Well, I don't know." He crossed his forearms on the table again. "Do you want to go out with me?"

"I do."

His eyes were sparklers on the Fourth of July. "Okay, then, Miss Coe, would you accompany me to the roping in Coleman on Saturday? There's a dance afterward. Can you dance?"

"I most certainly can." It was the one thing Jake and I did really well together—the only time we'd been truly in sync. That limber rodeo cowboy could move across a dance floor like no one else, waltzing me in circles, twirling, and two-stepping.

Chances were, Callahan couldn't hold a candle to Jake on the dance floor. Big men just didn't move like that. I didn't care. He wanted to dance with me, and I could only imagine those arms holding me, whether he could twirl or not.

Jake. It hit me. My gut did a somersault. Maybe I misunderstood. "I need to know the rules going in. Is it just me? Or do you date other women, too? I want to know upfront."

He tucked his chin; his brows went high. "Are you seeing someone?"

"I haven't had a date since I moved here. You?"

"I'm not seeing anyone. Haven't for a while." His face inched closer, and his eyes roamed my face. "Katherine, you're the prettiest thing I've ever seen. It's high time we got to know each other. Now, I just told you, I'm not seeing anyone. I've got no desire to see anyone but you." Unflinching, unapologetic honesty.

My hand went to my heart. He was so direct he took my breath. I never dreamed of this. "Thomas Jefferson Callahan, you have no idea. I want to know you, too. Just you."

He lifted his mug. "So, I guess that means we're dating. And no one else is invited to our party. If anybody has an issue with that—little Mr. Jimmy or your editor, you tell 'em to take it up with me."

Louisa brought our sandwiches. "So, tell me about your family," he said. "Let's start with the parents. You go first then I'll tell you about mine."

I did. And he did.

Callahan and I sat at our dark corner table and visited until closing time, learning about each other. Beer took a backseat to barbecue and conversation. We didn't talk about work but about family, friends, and growing up. He was the oldest of three children. His brother lived outside Ballinger, and his sister was in Germany with her Air Force husband and family. He told me about his home, his horses, and roping. He liked archery and skeet shooting, and he loved deep-sea fishing.

When he left the service, he entered the police academy in Abilene and has been there since. Callahan was almost five years older than me. When he went to Vietnam, I was a freshman in high school.

I told him about growing up in Brownwood and my family. There were six of us kids. I was the middle child. I told him about my close friends and college. Not my former marriage. I explained a little about the newsroom. He didn't speak of the war or his job.

I told him about my dreams. The ones I could remember, and his eyes danced around the room above me as I did. I did not tell him about the one that woke me up. I couldn't.

He never detailed any of his. When I asked again, he shook his head.

"Can I kiss you?"

We stood by my car at closing time, and his question surprised me. He didn't seem the kind to ask. But then again, this man was as old-fashioned as I'd ever known. *Oh.* Just look at him in the moonlight. With unmistakable yearning, I said, "I wish you would."

Never taking his eyes off of mine, Callahan took off his hat, set it upside down on the roof of my car, and softly ran his fingertips across my cheeks. That touch penetrated the core of me as I anticipated his kiss. His fingers found my hair, and he held it back, those eyes studying my face. He rubbed his thumb softly along the ridge of my cheekbones and across my lips. He leaned down, holding my face with both hands and touched his lips to mine—just barely, lingering on them feather soft.

I wanted more. Yes, it was me.

My lips parted, and I kissed him deeply, driven by what had become uncontrolled desire. When I did, Callahan lifted me off the ground with apparent ease. He wasn't leaning anymore.

The animal in each of us was unleashed.

One big hand enveloped my thigh, lifting, and I clasped my legs tightly around him, lost in an inexplicably familiar kiss. It wasn't like kissing someone new. He was the man in my dreams, and I felt I was back in the arms of a long-lost love, intoxicated by his touch.

My blouse was untucked. His hands caressed my skin, exploring, and I let him. He lifted me higher, his mouth, his tongue on my neck as he unbuttoned the top of my blouse. His hand was on my breast, and I knew where his mouth was going—"Oh, T.J."

Bright headlights brought sobriety. A passing car.

"Wait." I was breathless.

His hands were firm, his voice as smooth as his tongue on my skin. "No, Katherine. Let's go home together."

"No." My hands pressed against his chest. "We have to stop."

Callahan stilled. His heart pounded. I heart it. I felt it.

He removed his hand from under my blouse and eased his grip as I unwrapped my legs. He lowered me to the ground, pressing the side of my face to his chest with one hand. His heart was a thundering jackhammer.

Mine was that of a racing rabbit.

We stood still for a long moment before he picked me up again with the ease of lifting a feed sack. His arms enfolded me, holding me to him, face to face, those eyes probing. He kissed me sweetly, gently, but there was no mistaking the want in his eyes. "Come home with me, Katherine."

His heart still drummed loudly. I wanted him. Surely, he knew that. But I whispered. "I can't. Not yet."

Slowly, reluctantly, he set me back on the ground. "I sure wish you would."

My knees were mush as my hands rested on his chest, and I marveled at the firmness of his body. I peered up at him. "It's too soon."

I saw his dimple in the blue hue of moonlight and neon. "Speak for yourself. It's not too soon for me."

I stroked his cheek softly. "I can't. Not yet."

"Okay."

"Someday." I kissed the back of his hand. I dared not touch his lips again with mine. If I did, nothing would stop us. I placed his hand on my heart, yes against my breast, to be sure he felt my heart pounding too, and I whispered. "Thank you. For tonight."

He reached, found his hat, and settled it on his head as I straightened myself and buttoned my blouse. He grabbed my car door handle, and it opened. "Dammit, Katherine. You didn't lock it. I told you. You've got to lock your doors when you get out."

"I will."

"Someone could be hiding in your backseat. Promise me."

"I promise."

He shut the door after I got in and leaned in the window that I rolled down. "I mean it. You don't seem to get how dangerous the world can be, especially for a woman."

No one had ever been protective of me.

"I promise. I'll be more careful."

Callahan ran his fingers through my hair, raking it back from my face, and rested his thumb on my cheek. "Now, when you get home and you're lying in that bed all alone, you just remember, I would've held you all night."

I took his hand and kissed it. I didn't want to leave him, but I couldn't live with myself if I didn't. It was too soon.

As I pulled onto the road, I looked in my rearview mirror.

T.J. Callahan stood alone in the parking lot, a tall, broad-shouldered silhouette, watching me drive away.

Sleep eluded me as I lay in bed alone, reliving that kiss. I ached inside with the vision of being in bed with him, making love, and falling asleep in his arms.

Desire. Desire was the forbidden fruit that Eve tasted. I never wanted anything the way I wanted Thomas Jefferson Callahan. I was falling in love with him, I was sure.

Yes, sleep eluded me.

Chapter 12

My alarm failed to wake me. I overslept. I opened my eyes with Callahan on my mind. I guess he'd been there all night. I stared at the wall, alone in my bed, curled up on my side. I'd never known anything like his kiss. And I'd been married, for heaven's sake.

Yes, I knew sex. I enjoyed sex. But I never experienced passion like that. I melted in that man's arms. He aroused feelings in me that I never knew existed. Such a sensuous touch—his hands, his lips, his tongue. Heaven help me. With his hand on my breast, had his tongue touched it—if those headlights hadn't hit me in the eyes, I might have begged him to carry me to his truck, and I was too damned old for that. I would've been ashamed.

Be honest with yourself if no one else. Was it morality that stopped you? Or fear? Fear of what that man could do to your heart if he changed his mind. What if I gave myself to him, and he walked away?

I was way over my head, way too fast. I had to slow down, get to know him, go to the roping, go to the dance, and give it time. That's what my common sense said.

My heart didn't hear it. I couldn't get enough of Thomas Jefferson Callahan. I craved everything about him. Yes, crave was the right word. And it made no sense. Jake and I dated a year before he proposed, and when he did, I wasn't expecting it. Callahan and I had two evenings together, and I was head over heels.

But then, the first time I tasted ice cream, I knew I loved it. There was no debate. No hesitancy. I peered at the clock. Oh, man. You've got to chop-chop.

I was at the Taylor County Jail at ten o'clock sharp. The parking lot and lobby were full, so I assumed everyone there was doing the same thing as me: visiting a jail inmate.

I asked to speak to James Billingsly.

"He's with a visitor," the jailer said. It was a female deputy I didn't know.

Dammit. His lawyer got here before I did. George was right. Any lawyer would advise his client not to talk to me. Earlybird gets the worm. That's what you get for lying in bed daydreaming.

I had time to kill, so I asked to look at the jail logs. Scanning down the clipboard, I caught two more arrests for drug distribution.

Arrests for possession are a daily thing. Not distribution. What is going on?

Russo had yet to return my call from the night before. I took down the new information. I needed to call him, but he'd be asleep now.

Maybe thirty minutes later, a man sharply dressed in a gray suit approached me as I sat in a line of chairs along the lobby wall. People on either side of me were waiting to visit their inmates. "Are you Kat Coe?" he asked. His light brown hair was graying at the temples.

"I am."

His white dress shirt was stiffly starched, the top two buttons open, and he wore no tie. "I'm Culpepper Hayes." He offered his business card, not his hand. "I represent James Billingsly. I advised him not to speak with you." He tilted his head toward the visiting area with an expression of disgust. "But for some reason, he wants to see you. So we agreed: nothing he says to you can be published."

"I know. There's a gag order."

His gaze narrowed accusingly. Culpepper had sharp features. His nose was a beak, his face angular with a pointed chin. He wasn't anything to look at, but self-assurance radiated from that man. "So why do you want to talk to my client?"

"It just helps me understand. Put things into perspective."

He nodded slowly, assessing me. "Okay. But let's understand each other: Nothing James Billingsly says to you can be published and shouldn't be repeated." His flat stare wasn't one to mess with.

Boy, that was getting old: men telling me what I could and couldn't do. I tucked his card in my purse. "It's a free country, you know."

Culpepper glanced over his shoulder toward the visiting area. "Might be. But my client isn't. If he hopes to ever be free again, he better follow my advice." He cocked his head. "They've got a thin case and a lot of gall charging him with nothing but the word of an eyewitness, seen at a distance in the dark. I can get this dismissed if you two don't screw it up." Culpepper's gaze narrowed again; his clear intent was to threaten. "His life is on the line, Miss Coe. Keep that in mind." Straight-backed, shoulders wide, Culpepper Hayes strode out of the jail lobby, briefcase in hand.

I kind of wanted to shove it up his ass. Talk about an air of superiority. Some lawyers were like that.

Minutes later, a jailer called over the intercom. "Coe. Visitor's Window Two."

The visiting area was down a hall and around a corner from the lobby. One wall was made of cement blocks, maybe three feet up, with solid double-pane glass above that. Embedded in the glass were rectangular metal plates with slats, spaced maybe five or six feet apart. Visitors sat on round metal seats protruding from the wall in front of the metal plates through which you conversed with the inmate.

I sat at the second window, dug out my notepad and pen, and waited. Several minutes later, a deputy escorted Billingsly, handcuffed, to the window. His thick shoulders were back, his stance proud, as it had been each time I'd seen him before.

He was clean. No grease.

"Thank you for seeing me," I said through the slats in the metal plate. "Your lawyer told me you can't say anything on the record."

He nodded and leaned to the window, his mouth near the speaker. "I want you to know the truth about me and the Bennetts."

"Okay."

"Those people sent me to prison for something I didn't do. Mary Beth wanted me. She thought she was in love with me and maybe I thought the same. We'd been flirting with each other since the summer. I was a senior. She was a junior. How in the hell was I supposed to know she was promoted up a grade? That she was just sixteen? After a ballgame, we went out. Went parking at Lake Kirby. One thing led to another. Her father found us. I guess he'd been suspicious, I don't know. Anyway, old man Bennett yanked her out of my car."

"After you had sex?"

"It didn't take long. Next day the cops knocked on my door, took me into custody for rape and assault." He raised his right hand in an oath. "I never hurt her. And I did not rape her."

"How'd she get beaten up?" I asked.

"I told you. Old man Bennett. She was scared to death of him. Said he hit all of 'em sometimes. You should have seen the fear in her eyes when he jerked that door open and dragged her out. He backhanded her right there in front of me and when I went for him he aimed a pistol in my face. I told the cops all of that. You think they took my word over his?"

"He hit them?"

He lifted his shoulders. "That's what Mary Beth told me."

My mind flashed to the funeral. Bass and his silent, subservient wife. Did that gentle-looking man hit his wife? She'd seemed so submissive. Households that hit. That's something that gets passed down. "Did Mr. Bennett threaten you?"

He sneered. "What do you call a gun in your face? But, no, he never spoke to me. I wasn't important enough for him to acknowledge. He just sicced the cops on me."

I recalled Bass's authoritarian tone when I stepped on his toes, how he'd dismissed me like a chambermaid. I understood what Billingsly was saying. "Look at me, James."

His eyes met mine. "Did you go inside the Bennett house that night? A witness placed you there. Will they find your prints inside that house?"

He shook his head slowly, his chin defiant. "No ma'am. I did not rape Mary Beth and I never laid a hand on her mother."

"So what were you doing at the Bennett house that night?"

He stared at me silently.

"Why, James?" I asked again. "Why would you go there late at night?"

His gaze flashed his anger. "She came into my shop that morning for an oil change. When she recognized me, she backed out, screeching her tires like a scalded dog." He lifted one shoulder. "Pissed me off." He peered at his hands and then returned his eyes to meet mine. Hate was in them. "They lied." His voice got loud. "They sent me to prison because their daughter wanted a poor boy. I had scouts looking at me.

I could've played college ball and had a career. The more I thought about it, the madder I got."

This wasn't the time to ask questions. It was a time to listen. Billingsly went on. "I was going to knock on her door and tell that hypocritical bitch what I thought of her. The queen of society, hiding her dirty secrets inside a white castle. They knew they sent an innocent man to prison to protect their image. If something's wrong with Mary Beth, like people say, it's not because of what I did to her. It's because she kept her mouth shut and let me spend five years in prison for doing something she wanted."

He paused, taking a few seconds. "Anyway, that night, when I got there, it hit me, that lyin' bitch might call the cops and accuse me of doing something, again, that I didn't do. So I left. I never knocked on the door. Never stepped inside."

Of course, I was taking notes. I didn't have a tape recorder. "And you swear?"

Billingsly raised his wide right hand again. "On the lives of my children."

James Billingsley was still a nice-looking man. After weeks in jail, his broad face combined with his heavy blond beard to make him look like a Viking—at least, my image of a Viking warrior.

"Why did you drive by the funeral?" I asked.

He took a deep breath, scratching the back of his neck as the corners of his mouth turned down. "Hell, I don't know. Morbid curiosity I guess."

Morbid curiosity. I knew something about that, too.

I just didn't see him as a killer. My heart hurt for him. "James, did you ever think that maybe Mary Beth tried to defend you to her parents, but they wouldn't listen?"

He shrugged. "Doesn't make any difference now, does it?"

"Do you have any idea how to prove your innocence?"

He recoiled, a stunned expression on his face. "Isn't that the deal? About America?" Billingsly squinted, and I saw naked fear in his eyes for the first time. "Isn't it supposed to be the other way around? Don't they have to prove my guilt?"

Chapter 13

I drove home, showered, and dressed for work, calling Callahan. He wasn't in his office. I left a message. I wanted him to know I interviewed Billingsly, even if I couldn't use it. I hadn't thought about telling him about the interview last night. I chuckled to myself. I didn't think about much of anything last night except him and those eyes and... Enough. You're not in high school anymore.

Once at work, I called Russo. No answer from him, either. I left a voicemail asking him to call about the new arrests and asking why he didn't return yesterday's call.

I returned to the jail and rechecked the logs at my routine time. Dammit!

Since I was there earlier, another man was booked for manufacture and delivery. Jerry Stubblefield. Age 35. Address: 545 Stubblefield Road, Tye. It was time to get to the bottom of all these drug arrests.

Since I hadn't heard from Callahan, I drove from the jail to the police station with a fresh package of Juicy Fruit. I'd decided to be Prissy's supplier. Offering it, I asked, "Is T.J. in?"

She snatched the gum and sneered. "So it's T.J. now?"

I was bold. He said don't hide it. "You know, it's none of your business. But yes. He and I are dating."

She shot me the stink eye. "He told us." Then, another full-frontal sneer. "I don't know how it's gonna' work."

"It'll work because I like him, and he likes me, and we agreed we wouldn't discuss work unless it's here and for the record. By the way." I leaned on her desk, my weight on my hands. "Why did you tell me he was married?"

She rose from her chair and stuck her face in mine. "What if I tell you he is married."

"He is not."

"You don't deserve him."

My voice went loud. "He'll decide that."

She whispered hideously, "Maybe Mrs. Callahan will decide that."

I caught myself with my hand in the air. "Tell him I stopped by."

She leaned across her desk. "Kiss my ass."

"Bitches first."

I hated her. If he was married, he would never have introduced me to the Rileys or talked to them about us dating. So why did part of me feel so sick?

Was it possible? Could Callahan be married? Maybe his wife was an invalid or something. Was he separated but not divorced? Was the divorce not final?

No. I refused to believe any of that.

Driving to the newsroom, I realized Prissy said, 'He told us.' He wouldn't do that if he were married. She's such a liar. I needed to do the same. Jack was in his afternoon meeting with the other editors.

Seeing Jimmy, I said, "I need to talk to you." I tilted my head toward the coffee pot.

He followed. "Yes ma'am."

I opened the spigot and poured a cup of coffee, the freshest I'd get that shift. "About Callahan. We're dating." I had to laugh at the size of those eyes. "I thought you should know we've seen each other a couple of times. He told people at his work, so I'm telling you and Jack."

Jimmy snickered. "I knew. The way he looked at you and you running after him." He fiddled with his coffee cup. "Jack says you're staying on cops. How are you two going to make that work?"

"We agreed. We won't talk about work anywhere but in his office. He treats me like any other reporter. I don't need news tips from Callahan to kick ass."

"Congratulations, I guess." His voice let me know it was insincere. "I never knew of a reporter dating a cop. Especially not a cop reporter dating a cop."

I tipped my coffee cup at him. "Callahan said to tell you, that if you have a problem with it, take it up with him." Jimmy shrugged that off like a pro. "The narcs are on the move. I left a message for Russo, but he's not answering. I'm going to DPS to see if I can get a story. You want to come?"

"Are we friends again?"

"As long as you don't accuse me of sleeping with someone for a news story. If I sleep with him, it'll be because I'm crazy about him—not for a friggin' story, Jimmy. Understood?"

"So you haven't slept with him?"

I had to guffaw. "It's none of your business, Jimmy. But no."

The newspaper and police headquarters were downtown, not far apart, but the Department of Public Safety headquarters was located on U.S. Highway 277 South, which was known locally as the Coleman Highway.

We pulled into the parking lot to a sea of cop cars. Callahan's black truck was among them.

"Oh, man. Something big is going on." I jumped out of the news car, racing for the lobby.

"I'd say so." Jimmy was behind me with his gear.

In the lobby, I handed the secretary my card. "May we see Lt. Russo?" As often as I'd interviewed him, I'd never seen him. Jimmy took the photos. I'd never even asked Jimmy what Russo looked like.

She studied my card and smiled. "Sorry, Kat. He's tied up. Those stories you've done lately, they're real good." She glanced around the room and whispered. "We've all enjoyed them. Nobody ever writes about what we do over here."

A nice secretary. How refreshing.

"Thank you. I've enjoyed writing them." I nudged my head toward Jimmy at my side. "May we wait?"

"I think you'd wait a whole lot longer than you'd like."

I glanced around the reception area. Judging by the number of desks, several secretaries worked at DPS but she was the only one there at the time. An older woman. "Will you let him know I came by, and ask him to call me when he can?"

"Yes, ma'am." She winked. "I have a feeling he'll be calling you anyway when he can."

Jimmy and I walked outside.

Callahan and Russo. What's up?

I remembered my story about all the robberies and burglaries that could be tied to drugs. "Do you think, in your wildest dreams, that the motive in the Bennett murder was drug-related?" Jimmy and I stopped in the parking lot on our walk back to the news car. "Maybe to get money and rifles to buy drugs? I mean, everyone knew how rich they were. Could it be that simple? And James Billingsly is the wrong man?"

"No idea," Jimmy said. "I've never been in lockstep with the cops like you are. Every time they do something you're up their asses. Uncanny, when you think about it."

"Not really. You've just got to know how to read them. All these drug arrests. It's pretty clear something big is up. Now we see Callahan's truck here. That's no coincidence."

Jimmy made a 360-degree turn in the parking lot. "There are cop cars here from Nolan, Coleman, Eastland, Brown, Jones, Shackelford, and Callahan counties."

"They're all in the West Central Texas Drug Task Force. Maybe it's just a meeting."

He snickered. "No, your boy's not in the drug task force."

I shot him a nasty glare. "You might as well accept it."

Jimmy shrugged.

This had something to do with one of Callahan's cases, but the Bennett murder wasn't his only case. "Dammit, I don't know what to do. If we leave, we can miss Russo."

"She said, they're not coming out any time soon."

True.

It was early in our shift. We had time. I said, "Let's check the jail logs again. I've got a feeling with this many cars, they're still bringing people in."

As we neared the news car, I heard my name called. "Katherine!"

We turned to see Callahan coming out of DPS Headquarters. Look at him. He was wearing a tan shirt today. He also wore a wide, wonderful, surprised smile. "What are you doing here?"

He came close as I peered up, beaming back at him. "They've made a bunch of drug arrests. We came to interview Russo but he's busy. What are you doing here?"

"No comment." He tried to suppress that smile but couldn't.

Neither could I. "What's Russo got going on?"

He aimed his thumb at the building. "You'll have to get it from them." He lifted his hands with a sheepish grin that showed the dimple. "Sorry, Babe. You know the rules."

"Babe?"

Oooh ... That snark slipped from Jimmy's subconscious mind right out of his mouth. It was one of those things you wished you could grab and shove back in. But it was too late. Lightning had flashed in Callahan's eyes. I knew that temper.

I closed my eyes. *Don't hit him.* I held my breath, eyes frozen wide, as Callahan took a big step toward my photographer, towering over him. He seemed poised to snatch Jimmy up, lift him off the pavement by his shirt—I knew he could do it—but he didn't. He just loomed large with that glare. "You got a problem with that?" He aimed his thumb at me, his eyes eating Jimmy alive. "You got a problem with me and her?"

Jimmy was unprepared. He stammered, "No. Just ... unusual."

Callahan stared hard and long enough to convey his message. "Well get used to it." He glanced back at me. "I'll see you after work?"

I nodded, smiling, and he got into his truck and drove away.

"Damn," Jimmy said. "You weren't kidding."

I'd come to feel like my heart was one of those little red rubber balls attached to a wooden paddle—the kind you played with as a kid, seeing how long you could keep it bouncing.

My little rubber ball heart was sky high on Callahan last night and this morning, and then *Blam!* Prissy slapped it hard, making me doubt him.

That smile he wore seeing me, witnessing how he intimidated Jimmy—and *Whop!* My faith in Thomas Jefferson Callahan flew sky-high.

Yes, when it came to him, my heart was a red rubber ball being whacked from high to low, and right then, I was riding the high.

∞

When we arrived back at the jail—my third trip of the day—George was on duty, but it was the first time I'd seen my favorite jailer. "What have we got this afternoon?" I asked.

He shoved the clipboard at me and aimed his thumb at the back of the jail. "Narcotics boys are rounding 'em up left and right. We can't keep up."

Since my last check, there had been six more drug arrests—everything from manufacture and distribution of a controlled substance to delivery, possession, possession with intent to distribute, and even possession of drug paraphernalia. I peered at George wide-eyed. "Is this for real?" I began jotting down names, ages, addresses, and charges. "What's going on?"

"Not for me to say, Kat."

"Can we get all these mug shots?"

"When they're processed." He rubbed the back of his neck. "Seriously. They're having trouble keeping up in back." George cut his eyes at Jimmy. "I've got your number. I'll call you when."

"Thanks," Jimmy and I said together.

"Anything else?" I asked.

George leaned close. "Callahan and Clancy have been around more than normal."

Jimmy and I exchanged glances.

I scanned the list of names on the clipboard: five white males and one white female. "Callahan's not here about drugs. Who did he question?" I asked. "And what about?"

George snickered. "Even if I knew, I couldn't say."

I winked at him. "Can't or won't? You boys can sure be hard on us."

He grinned out the side of his mouth. "Can't and won't." As he spoke, I spotted Callahan walk by, way back on the far side of a half-glass wall that separated the reception area where George worked from the cell area. Callahan was right in the middle of whatever was happening.

Jimmy snarked. "Does this new arrangement with Callahan mean you can't do a run-around?

"I'll do my job. He'll do his." I replied.

He took his eyes off the road. "So, you wrote down everything off that log?"

"I did."

He lifted a shoulder. "Let's backtrack them. Let's knock doors of the people arrested, like we did with Billingsly. Someone will talk to us."

I tapped him on the shoulder with the back of my hand. "Good idea, Jimmy. But I need to check in with Jack, first. He doesn't know what we're doing."

"Are you still going to tell him?"

"Who, Jack? About Callahan? Yeah, I have to. He stepped up and told his people. He told you. I need to do the same."

Jimmy always drove, which was fine. I could study notes while being chauffeured. He took his eyes off the road long enough to meet mine. "Has it crossed your love-addled brain that Jack may say you can't cover cops if you're involved with one? What if Jack flat-out gives you a choice: Callahan or the cop beat?"

My face sagged. I felt it, and I was certain Jimmy caught it before I turned my face to the window.

"I'm telling you, Kat. You can work this beat better than anyone we've ever had. You've got the nose for it. It's like you sense what they're doing as they do it. But you and Callahan? You might not last two weeks. You may have to make a tough choice pretty soon."

Somebody tell me: Why does this have to be so complicated?

Chapter 14

"Where's Jack?"

"Sick," the News Editor Rhonda said. I wasn't sure of her last name. Rhonda and I rarely crossed paths. Editors had their own sphere. She peered up from reading copy. "They said he has a stomach bug. He left after the editorial meeting."

I glanced around the room. "Who do I report to in Jack's absence?"

She raised her brows with a quirky smile. "Me."

"I'm sorry, Rhonda. I'm just stupid. I think DPS has a big story. Jimmy and I went by. Tons of cars and six new drug arrests. We were going to knock doors. Talk to the neighbors near where the arrests were made. Is that okay?"

"Sure. I'll leave a hole. City council meets tonight, and the President is speaking. I'm sure they'll take most of the front page. Council's talking about a bond election for new streets that'll cost taxpayers a fortune, and Carter's talking about the Soviets invading Afghanistan."

I tilted my head at Jimmy. "Can he come with me?"

"Until council starts." She nodded at him. "I'll page you if something else comes up."

∞

"They've made eight drug arrests today," I told Jimmy as we walked to the news car.

He cut his eyes at me, expressionless. He didn't get it.

"Eight," I repeated. "Today."

Nothing. He was clueless.

"Why were you at the jail this morning?" he asked.

"I interviewed James Billingsly."

Now, there was the Jimmy smile I loved. "You go, girl!" His eyes twinkled, and he high-fived me.

"I can't use it, though. I forgot about the damned gag order when I asked for the interview. Then his lawyer came out and said anything Billingsly told me was off the record, even if there wasn't a gag order."

"He can't do that."

"It's okay. At least it gives me background information I can use down the road."

"Who's his lawyer?" Jimmy asked.

"Culpepper Hayes."

"Oh, man. The hits just keep coming."

"So where do we start?" he asked.

I scanned my list of jail inmates. "We've got arrests in Tye, Lawn, Ovalo, Tuscola, Potosi, Merkel—"

"Tye." Jimmy put the car in gear. "It's closest."

"Jerry Stubblefield. Manufacture and delivery. Thirty-five-years-old. They got him at 9:30 this morning."

We headed that way. Tye was a tiny crossroads farming community between Abilene and Merkel, off Interstate 20. Jimmy pulled into the Dairy Queen. We both went in, and I asked if anyone knew where Jerry Stubblefield lived.

Everyone there did. Stubblefield Road, duh. They told us how to get there.

Stubblefield Road implied the family owned all the land along either side of the caliche road that led to a white frame house, which was surprisingly tidy for someone accused of manufacturing meth. Those places usually looked like Freddy Dickey's place. Trashy, overgrown, rundown.

This house had a nice yard and nice flowerbeds. My guess? A woman's handiwork. I never knew men who worked in flowerbeds.

The shotgun-style house was back from the road and faced east. I'd bet they caught some beautiful sunrises from that porch because the pasture in front of the house and across the road was wide open. They could drink coffee and watch the sunrise sitting on a front porch swing.

"Here goes nothing," Jimmy said, pulling into the long white caliche drive, narrower than the road.

Several rundown cars and trucks were parked in and around a detached garage by the rear corner of the house but otherwise, this place was as tidy as my grandmother's.

Well, except for the pit bull on a chain in the front yard. He was already barking and frothing, and chickens were clucking and scratching in the yard. One was chasing a grasshopper. A little border collie yapped from the front porch.

Jimmy gathered his gear and said, "I hope they don't come out shooting."

I scoffed at him. But heading to the front porch, I changed my tune. Jimmy's gut was good. A man older than my father stepped onto the front porch, aiming a double-barreled shotgun at us. He hollered, "Git outa' here!"

I raised my hands. "Mr. Stubblefield? I'm Kat Coe with the newspaper. I just wanted to ask a few questions—"

Ka-Boom!

That old man fired that shotgun. It roared, and we jolted. He'd aimed it high and away from us, but it was enough to make you pay attention.

"Are you deaf?" he yelled. "I said leave!"

Jimmy tugged on my blouse. "That's a 20-gauge pump, Kat. Let's get out of here."

"We're leaving!" I yelled over the barking dogs as I walked backward. "I just want you to know that we know there are two sides to every story. We're here to tell your side if you'll let us. The cops will tell theirs."

Maybe seeing us retreat, I don't know, but the old man lowered the shotgun barrel toward the ground and came down the concrete porch steps. He was dressed in overalls and had a straggly beard.

I stopped and listened. "They came in here early this morning." He waved his free arm. "Tore up my house. Took my boy!"

"Jerry?" He was thirty-five, but I guess your son is always your boy. "Do you know why?"

"Because of that no-good son of a bitch Freddy Dickey, that's why. My boy ain't cookin' no dope." Again, the man waved his arm high. He was agitated and animated. "Dickey's running his head on everybody he ever knew, trying to get the heat off hisself. He'd throw his own mother under the bus if it'd buy him one less day."

Okay. They bust Freddy. He starts singing. Does that have anything to do with Callahan? I was still focused on the Bennett murder.

"Can I quote you on this?" I asked over the still-barking dogs.

He glanced over his shoulder. "Bozo! Shut up!" The pit bull was slobbering, yowling, and pulling on his chain. The old man walked toward it and kicked dirt in its face. The dog cowered, whimpered, tucked its tail, and quietened. My blood chilled.

The old man returned to us.

I asked, "Your name? I'll need it, to quote you."

"Harold. They call me Hal. Hal Stubblefield."

Hal was a little taller than Jimmy but sickly thin and pale with alligator-looking skin. His gray hair was thin. I think he was probably a heavy smoker and drinker. Sometimes, you can just tell. His mustache and the beard around his mouth were yellowed from cigarette smoke.

My gaze followed the sound of a creaking screen door. "Hal?" A woman stood on the covered porch. "Is everything alright out here?"

"These people are here from the news, Momma." Hal still had his shotgun aimed at the ground, but it could be pointed at us with the tilt of his wrist. "They're here about them arresting Jerry."

"Who arrested Jerry?" I asked.

The jail log listed Scott as the arresting agent, but Callahan could have been involved. I wanted to know. He'd be easy to ID.

"I don't know all of 'em. I know that weasel, Russo."

Dammit, was Callahan among them or not? It went directly to the Bennett case.

"Any others?" I tried again. "A great big guy maybe wearing a black hat?"

Hal slung his arm angrily. "Hell, I don't know! A swarm of 'em pulled up here, geared up like they was gonna storm Normandy Beach."

He'd remember Callahan if he'd been there in the black hat.

"Who else have they arrested?" A young woman emerged from inside the house. She was twentyish, tall and willow-thin, wearing a T-shirt and jeans. Light brown hair hung almost to her hips. "Did they arrest Danny?" Hers was a pouty, Cupid mouth. Heavy bangs fell into her eyebrows.

I glanced at my notes and then back at her. "Danny who?"

"Dickey. Freddy's brother."

The roughneck in Sambo's. I would have remembered his name had I seen it, but I double-checked anyway. "No ma'am. That name's not on this list."

She clasped her heart and peered at the older woman. "Thank the Lord."

I didn't remember seeing her in Sambo's that night when Danny approached me, but I'd been so focused on Callahan that I could've missed Farrah Fawcett throwing darts.

Hal scratched his cheek, then pointed at my notepad with a thick, longer-than-men-should-ever-wear, yellowish fingernail. "What other names have you got there?"

I glanced at Jimmy. "It's public record." I started reading names. "Kay Brown—"

"Oh, no, Auntie. They got Kay!" The young one clung to the old woman's arm.

"Keep going." Hal ordered, tipping the barrel of that shotgun back at us.

"Okay. You know they got Freddy a while back. And Kay and Jerry. Do you know Ben Sims? They arrested him a few days ago. Here's John Parker, Mike McCain, Bobby Dean, Angie Brown." I peered up at the girl. "Is she related to Kay?"

She nodded. Her hand was clasped over her mouth, her eyes wide.

I kept reading names aloud. None of them meant anything to me, but they did to the Stubblefields.

Hal backed up, sank onto the steps, and leaned against the brick banister wall. "Son of a bitch." He wagged his head.

"Enlighten us. What do you think is going on?" I asked.

Hal's wife snapped, "I'll tell you exactly what's going on. They've always had it out for our boy. They've tormented Jerry since he was eighteen years old. He's a good boy. Works hard. He's one of Gibco's best hands."

The bell in my head started dinging like the teletypes. The druggies and Gibson Oil.

I kept scribbling notes, avoiding eye contact. "Gibson Oil. Do the others work there, too?"

Hal answered, "Jerry, and Danny, and Ben. Kay and Angie, they're just girls they run with. They all went to school together. Mike and Johnny are welders. Bobby Dean's a pipefitter."

The old woman held open her screen door and waved to us. "Come inside. I want you to see what the police did to my house."

Jimmy and I followed her into the living room. It was in disarray; furniture moved around as if it had been ransacked. She pointed. "This is what the police do when they have a search warrant." Saliva spewed from her mouth as she spoke. "They tear up your house and leave you to put it back together."

"Did they take anything?" I asked.

"Something from Jerry's room," she answered.

Hal glared at her and knitted his brows.

"What?" I asked.

Hal snapped and waved his hand. "Nothing. Ma's mistaken."

"Can I take pictures?" Jimmy asked. "Of what they did to your house?"

"As long as you tell our side of this story. They're Gestapo." Hal wagged his finger at Jimmy. "You quote me on that. They're goddamned Nazis. Son of a bitching mother—"

"Hal!" His wife cut him off.

He growled and shut his mouth.

Jimmy snapped shots as Mrs. Stubblefield pointed to the disorder. Kitchen cabinets were rifled through; wall panels were removed.

This was as big a breakthrough as Bass letting us shoot inside that crime scene, only in reverse. I'd never heard of anyone getting photos of the aftermath of a police search warrant. They did, indeed, tear up the house and leave it for the homeowner to deal with.

"What's your name?" Jimmy asked her. "I'll need it for the caption."

She peered anxiously at her husband, who nodded. "Loretta," she said. "Loretta Stubblefield." Loretta was a hefty old gal who outweighed her husband, and she wore a mid-calf length cotton dress with big flowers that did her full figure no favors. She wore boxy shoes with white socks over ample calves.

"You're Jerry's mother?" Jimmy asked.

She nodded, lifting her eyeglasses to dab moisture in her eyes. "They hound our boy."

I asked Hal, "Did you serve, sir? In World War Two?"

"First Infantry. Omaha Beach."

"I appreciate your service." I offered my hand, and he shook it. Those fingernails made me cringe, and I could still see him kicking dirt in the dog's face, but I always offered my hand to thank the people who agreed to talk to me. "Can Jimmy take your picture?"

"No. I think we've gone about as far as we're going to go." Hal had become antsy. Maybe he regretted letting us in.

"I understand. Thank you, sir."

We left.

"Go to the courthouse," I told Jimmy.

He glanced at me. "Why? It's almost time to close. We won't make it."

"They had a search warrant. They've got to file it sooner or later. But you're right. Probably not today. What do you think they were looking for?"

"Drugs," he said. "What else?"

I said nothing, but my gut wondered if they weren't looking for stolen property. Something that connected the drug raids to Marilyn Bennett's murder. Why else would Callahan be working with Russo?

Lt. John Russo called a news conference at 6:30 p.m. at DPS headquarters, where he announced the seizure of another five pounds of crystal meth and the arrest of eight suspects believed to be involved in a multi-county methamphetamine ring.

Originally, such a briefing was called a press conference.

But broadcasters whined that using the term 'press conference' implied print journalism was more important than broadcast journalism. (As far as I was concerned, it was.) But everybody bowed to the broadcasters and called press briefings 'news conferences.'

It irritated the crap out of us, which was why we called them gang bangs.

Everyone was there. I didn't ask many questions. Having been to Stubblefield's house, I'd have more details than they would. All I needed from Russo were details on names, times, amounts, and street value.

I hung back. After the others left, I approached Russo, offering my hand. "It's nice to meet you in person," I said.

He smiled. It was a nice smile that seemed genuine. "You, too, Kat."

John Russo was not what I expected. A Department of Public Safety Lieutenant? I pictured him with short hair, either parted on the side or buzzed short, like most law enforcement officers. Russo's blond hair wasn't as long as Jimmy's, but it was way long for a cop and shaggy.

"I just wanted to talk one-on-one," I said.

He nodded.

"There's more to all of this than would appear on the surface." It wasn't a question.

"Now, why would you say that?" Russo's eyes were the color of my coffee at the end of shift—dark enough to get lost in. I'd guess Russo was five feet nine or ten inches tall, about the same height as Jake. Come to think of it, he was built about like Jake. I'd bet he was quick, like Jake.

"Why did y'all tear up the Stubblefield house?"

His obsidian eyes narrowed. "You talked to them?"

"We went to their house. We took pictures inside."

You'd have thought I held stink bait under that man's nose. He recoiled, and his upper lip curled. "I don't guess it would mean anything if I asked you not to run those pictures."

"If it's important to you, I'll do my best to make sure we don't. I doubt they'll want them anyway. But why ransack a house like that? What were you looking for?"

He pointed to the blocks of drugs laid out for the media to photograph. "They don't leave that shit sitting out on the kitchen cabinet." He paused, his eyes probing me. We'd never seen each other before. "Off the record. You steer clear of old man Stubblefield."

"Hal?" I asked.

His lip curled. "That old man's a rattlesnake. He's flat-ass evil. Probably behind Freddy. I can't prove it—yet. But someday I will."

I didn't expect that. "If they sell dope and make tons of money, why live in a house like that?"

Russo lifted his hands and shoulders. "Why do any of them live like they live?"

Dress him in sandals, an oversized, flowery shirt, and shorts, and John Russo could've passed for a beach bum.

With a threadbare Deadhead T-shirt on, he could fit in with the acid heads, but put that man, with his trimmed mustache and goatee, in a greasy, plaid cowboy shirt with white snaps, part his hair on the side, and he could've just come off an oil rig.

The one thing you would not guess Russo to be? A cop. So, this was an undercover officer. A chameleon.

Russo was no Callahan, but he was a nice-enough-looking man.

"Russo, were you looking for something else at Stubble-field's? Like, say, stolen property?"

He stared with an empty expression.

I tried again. "What was Callahan doing here this after-noon?"

He scoffed. He had a dimple of his own, but his laugh was haughty. "You know I can't tell you about another investiga-tor's business. Ask him."

"I did."

His gaze was intense. Russo was sizing me up as he fished in his shirt pocket and pulled out an unopened pack of cigarettes. "Yeah? What'd he say?"

"No comment."

Russo snickered as he tapped the pack of cigarettes against the palm of his hand, peeled off the wrapper, and pulled one out. "Even to you?" He tucked the pack back in his pocket. "I hear you're the new girlfriend."

"What does that mean?" I was beginning not to like him.

He lit the cigarette and inhaled, and our gazes locked to-gether. Russo exhaled and tucked the lighter into his pants pocket, never breaking his stare. "Now, Kat, you seem to be a smart girl. I didn't think that was a complicated statement." He aimed that cigarette at me and grinned out of the side of his mouth, smoke trailing out. "Not one that needs interpretation."

I stared at him, not knowing where he was going.

I guess he read my confusion because Russo shifted on his feet and craned his neck forward. "A word to the wise, Kat Coe. Callahan never keeps a woman long. After he gets what he wants, he moves on. Ask around. Callahan's left a trail of tears as long as the Brazos." He lifted both hands, still holding that cigarette in his right. "You're the new girl in town."

I think I vapor-locked.

I guess I kept staring, as I had at Prissy's desk earlier in the day, so confused. Was he married or a womanizer? Or both? Or neither?

Either way, that son of a bitch smacked my little red rubber ball heart into the dirt. I guess my mouth was open.

Russo lifted a shoulder. "Just don't say you weren't warned."

And there it came. Queasiness.

My head spun as I drove back to the newsroom, hearing their voices. *Maybe Mrs. Callahan will decide—Jack may make you choose—After he gets what he wants, he moves on.*

But then I remembered the look in Callahan's eyes—and that kiss. I wanted him to be who I'd believed him to be: the man in my dreams.

When I was a teenager, I dove into Lake Brownwood from a floating dock. The water was so deep and so dark that I lost my bearings. I thought I was swimming to the surface when I was actually swimming to the bottom. That same panic swept over me. I'd lost my bearings in Callahan's arms. What was up and what was down?

In the newsroom, that story trilled off my fingers. We had the press conference (I refused to call them news conferences), the mug shots, and the interview with the Stubblefields. Rhonda wasn't interested in the house photos, and I was glad. I prepared to dissuade her for Russo's sake, even if he had turned into an asshole.

Another front-page story and byline, below the fold, written on autopilot. My mind was elsewhere. Rhonda ran the President's address above the fold and kicked the council inside. They didn't vote on a bond election.

My desk phone rang. "Hey, beautiful. What are we doing tonight?" I heard his voice, and my stomach twisted. I hesitated. Too long. "Is something wrong?" he asked.

My head was swimming. I couldn't answer. I felt sick.

Alarm crept into Callahan's voice. "Katherine? What is it?"

I took a deep breath. "What do you want to do?" My voice was small, and I felt a lump in my throat.

"About what?" he asked.

"Tonight. What do you want to do?"

"Your place or mine. I'm tired of Sambo's. I want some alone time."

"Okay, you choose."

"You're safer at your place. I get you to mine, I'll be tempted not to bring you back."

My stomach. Wasn't right. Maybe I had Jack's bug. "Callahan? I think ... I'm not feeling good. Jack went home with a virus. Maybe we shouldn't."

He was silent for a long moment. When he spoke, his voice was smooth, low, coaxing. "No, Katherine. That's not what this is."

I wanted to curl up in a ball and cry. But I couldn't.

"What is it?" His tone was insistent.

"I guess maybe we need to talk."

"Okay. Let me pick you up. Or I can bring food to your house."

"Apartment," I said.

"Give me the address. I'll swing by and pick up—what? What do you feel like eating?"

I wasn't hungry at all now. "I don't know. You choose. I'm not picky."

"Do you care if I bring beer?" he asked.

"Not at all." I could use something to drink.

Maybe he read my mind. He asked, "Do you want something? To drink?"

"Wine."

"Red or white?"

"Red."

"Sweet or dry?"

I giggled. "Now you sound like the reporter. Dry."

His tone lightened. "I'm cuttin' out. I might beat you there."

I hung up the phone and rested my head in my hands, my elbows on my desk, my hair pushed back from my face.

"What's the matter, Kat?" It was Jimmy. He'd taken his shots of the confiscated dope and scurried to the council. "You were on top of the world earlier."

I sighed. "Everything." My eyes were filling with tears. But I wasn't going to talk to Mr. Snide about Callahan. I hid my eyes behind my hands, staring at the desk.

"What?" Jimmy seemed surprised. "Did they say you can't cover cops?"

I diverted. "I'm afraid they might."

He waved his hand. "I wouldn't worry about it as long as you keep kicking ass like you are." He walked off. "Goodnight."

I sat at my desk for a while, going over everything he'd said, and I said, and they said, buying time, trying to compose myself before I saw him.

Finally, I asked, "Rhonda, am I good to go?"

She gave me a thumbs-up and yelled across the room. "Great story!"

"Thanks."

Chapter 15

Could I have misread him that badly? Was he playing me just to get me into his bed? It's every woman's nightmare: finding out their words were spoken to deceive. Feeling used. He certainly tried hard enough to get me to go home with him last night.

Russo's words were still deafening.

I drove to my apartment as a moth flies to a flame, knowing the fire that was Callahan could incinerate my heart.

I caught my breath seeing him sitting with those long legs halfway up the stairwell to my second-floor apartment, leaning back casual-like with his elbows on the step behind him as if he were sitting in the rodeo arena.

He was something to see, even in silhouette.

I was so excited to see him at my apartment. But my insides trembled.

Seeing me, he stood, waiting as I approached. He kissed me softly as I met him on the steps.

I unlocked the apartment, turned on the lamp by the couch, and watched from the living room as he dropped his hat upside down on the coffee table, ran his fingers through his hair, set the sack of food on the dining room table, opened the refrigerator, and placed the beer and wine inside.

He turned around, his hands and back pressed against the refrigerator. "What's going on, Katherine?"

I blinked and averted my eyes, turning away.

"Katherine, look at me."

I did, seeing bewilderment on his face. "What happened since I saw you this afternoon?"

T.J. Callahan was an investigator. That soul-searching stare. He wasn't going to give up until he got the truth.

"Prissy said you told her we were dating."

His head tilted to the side. "And that's a bad thing because?"

"Because she said, 'What if I tell you he is married.'"

He closed his eyes and shook his head. "That won't happen again."

I'd had it bottled up. It came bursting out. "She said, 'You don't deserve him,' and I said, 'He'll decide that' and she said, 'Maybe Mrs. Callahan will decide that."

His eyes flashed. "Babe, I'll fix that."

I searched those eyes, wanting to see inside them. "Then tonight, someone else said, basically, you just use women. That you'd left a trail of tears."

He scoffed. "That fucker, Russo." It wasn't loud, but it was incendiary.

I fought tears. Always a love-struck schoolgirl in his presence, but I wanted the truth. And Callahan had the right to know what Russo said about him. Admit it or deny it.

"Russo said, 'I hear you're the new girlfriend,' and I asked what he meant by that, and he said, 'A word to the wise. Callahan never keeps a woman long. After he gets what he wants, he'll move on.'" I swallowed. "He said, 'Ask around. You're the new girl in town.'"

Somewhere during all that, his gaze left mine. It was roaming the room above my head. While I spewed it all out, Callahan had donned that protective mask no one could read.

He opened the refrigerator, pulled out a can of beer, popped the top, and stood tall, turning up that can. He drained it, crumpled it with one hand, and chunked it in the trash. He opened the refrigerator, drew out a second, pulled a chair from the table, and turned it to face me. He clomped the chair feet on the floor hard and sat in it.

That whole time, he never said a word. Nor had he looked at me again. I had no idea what was going through his mind. I was a statue, staring.

It felt forever before he leaned his head back and closed his eyes. "Fuck, it's a long fall."

"Yes, it is."

His gaze was back on me, narrowed accusingly. "And you believe him. You don't trust me." He stood and headed to the refrigerator. "I'll be on my way."

My heart stopped. "No, Callahan! I don't want you to go!"

He slammed shut the refrigerator door. "Then what do you want?"

"I want to trust you!"

His arms swung wide. "You don't think I want the same thing?"

I lost the internal struggle. Tears slid down my face. I closed my eyes, trying to fight them. I was back in that deep, dark lake, struggling to know which way was up and which was down. Drowning in emotion.

Big arms wrapped around me. Callahan's chin was on top of my head. He smelled so good. He felt so good. His voice was so gentle. "What does it take for you to believe in me?"

I peered up at him. "Truth. Is it true, what Russo said?"

He glanced away. I kept watching him as his eyes avoided mine. *Oh, God, he won't look me in the eye.* It's true.

When his gaze met mine, his expression and voice were neither angry nor apologetic—just flat. "I've dated my share of women. A couple of them wanted to get married. I didn't."

"A couple?"

He stepped back. "Hell, I don't know. It's not something you count." He paused, staring above me, maybe into the abyss of his past, until his eyes met mine, this time with fire in them. "I never promised any woman anything."

He walked back to the table and took a long swig of that second beer, still standing, those eyes roaming the empty air high in the room. "Russo's right about one thing." His gaze came back to me. "I can't think of a time it wasn't me who called it quits."

I moved to the couch, sank, leaned back, and closed my eyes. That first night, I knew that if I were after him, I'd have to stand in line. I was hollow. "I thought we were special."

That temper flared. "We are special!" He pointed to the door. "I told my sergeant about us today. Do you think I'd have done that if you weren't special? Hell, I told Clancy." He got even louder. "I told fuckin' Russo and Prissy. I threatened your pipsqueak photographer, remember?" He sneered. "Which wasn't hard, by the way."

He polished off that beer and chunked the empty beer can in the trash, hard this time. It clanged loudly. He pulled another from the refrigerator, popped the top, and aimed it at me. "What else do you want to know? Ask away."

"I don't know. It's just—when I'm with you, I feel wonderful. I was walking on clouds."

"So was I."

My elbows rested on my knees, and I pressed my hands against my temples, shaking my head. "Then Prissy keeps saying you're married. What Russo said. I'm afraid."

"Of what?"

"Isn't it clear?" I stood, yelling back. "Of falling for a man I don't know. Of getting my heart stomped all over again. Are you married but separated? An invalid wife? Divorce not final?"

He chortled snidely and spread the free arm wide, the one not holding the beer. "How many times have I got to say it? No."

"Why does Prissy keep saying it? Mrs. Callahan…"

He stepped toward me. "I don't know why she says it, but that's never going to happen again. I can promise you that."

"Have you ever been engaged?"

"Never."

I buried my face in my hands and quickly removed them, meeting his direct gaze. I had to know. "Is what Russo said true? Do you use women for sex and move on?"

His mouth fell open. He stepped back, looking at me as if I was Medusa. "How can you ask me that? What the fuck?"

It was like we were back in the parking lot. Callahan's face flushed, and the veins in his neck bulged. I thought he might explode. I was afraid he would leave. But he didn't. He ranted instead. "We're fucking adults. Adults go out. Sometimes, they have sex." He picked up the chair he'd sat in earlier and pounded its feet on the floor. Hard. The downstairs neighbors had to wonder what the hell. "No. It's not true. I don't feel like I used anyone. If that's the case, they used me, too."

I sat back on the couch. "But you ended it."

"Yeah. I did."

I peered up at him. "Why? Why haven't you fallen in love? Married?"

"Pretty fucking simple, Katherine. There's never been anyone I could see myself spending the rest of my life with." He sat in that chair and took another long swill of his beer.

Both of us were silent, me picking at my fingernails, him gripping that beer can, staring straight ahead. After a bit, he sighed deeply, his volume down, disappointment in his tone and body language. "I wanted to get to know you, Katherine. I thought you wanted to get to know me."

I turned my head, and our eyes met. "I do."

"Do you really want to know me?" I read his doubt.

With undeniable, unmistakable longing in my eyes, I answered with naked honesty. "More than anything in this world."

"Then come home with me." He stood and moved toward me. "I asked you before. It's clear now, you thought that was just about sex." He shifted his shoulders. "Did I want to make love to you last night? Well, hell, yeah." He stepped closer. "And if you'd be honest, you did too. Remember? I was there."

Our gazes were locked. "I can't make love to a man I barely know."

"You do know me!" He was loud again, his hands raised high. "How do you know anyone? Is it time alone? Or something inside? A deep connection? I thought that's what we had—you and me. I see all the way to your core, Katherine, and I like everything I see. You just can't seem to see me the same way."

His tone changed to resignation. "So, I confess. I wanted to make love to you last night. Hell, I'd make love to you right now, but that's not all I want. I want you to see my world—the one outside the police department—because I have one, you know. There's more to me than the badge."

Shame scalded my cheeks. Newspeople were so jaded—all of us. Trust didn't come easy for me. My gaze found its way back to him. "Do you still want me to know your world?"

"Yes."

"Don't break my heart, Callahan." My eyes probably begged.

He came to the couch and sat beside me, and those arms pulled me to him. Those arms. My head rested against his chest, and I heard his heartbeat. Slow, steady, strong. He spoke softly. "I have no intention of breaking your heart."

"You didn't intend to break anyone's heart. But apparently, you did."

He stroked my face, combing my hair back with his fingers brushing softly across my ear and down my neck, his eyes consuming me. "This is different, Katherine. We're different."

Our lips met, and we became lost in a kiss like the night before. Neither of us held ourselves back. Every time his lips touched mine, I wanted him so badly. All of him. Only this time, his hands didn't roam. He pulled away. "Grab a few things. I'll bring you back tomorrow."

Chapter 16

Callahan lived in southwest Taylor County, not far, he told me, from Abilene State Park.

It was after eleven o'clock on a moonless early spring night, and the sky was alive with a million twinkling stars when Callahan stopped his truck in front of a wide metal gate.

He got out.

With his truck door open, I inhaled the scent of cedar and listened to the symphony of the woods—frogs, cicadas, crickets. In the truck's headlights, I watched him unlock and open the gate. We drove through. He got out again, closed and locked it.

A porch light shone on a house, maybe a football field ahead up a dirt lane. There was a barn and pipe fence corral.

"I've got twenty acres," he said.

Parking by the house, he came around and opened my door. I stepped onto the running board as he offered his hand. I took it, stepping to the ground. It was a tall truck.

I tried to make out the surroundings, but it was impossible with no moon. The house was easy to see, with a yellow porch light shining by the front door.

It was a native rock house with a covered porch across the front. Rock columns were on either corner and on each side of the entry steps.

He led me through tall grass and up concrete steps to the wide cement porch. It was rocked halfway up on three sides and had a broad balustrade. If it were mine, I'd set potted plants on it. But it wasn't mine.

Callahan unlocked the front door, opened it, flipped a light switch, and stood aside, holding the screen door back to let me walk in. He hung his hat on deer antlers mounted on the front wall by the door. A straw hat was waiting there for summer.

It was a man's house with bare plank wood floors—I think they were pine or cedar, not narrow hardwood. It had high ceilings and scant furnishings. Old wallpaper covered every wall, even the ceiling.

A lone lamp sat on an end table beside a plaid-cloth couch on the facing wall.

He turned on the lamp, illuminating a big picture of horses on the wall centered behind the couch.

A native rock fireplace stood in the center of the left wall, with a trophy deer mounted above the wide cedar mantle. A portable TV with rabbit ears sat on a little table beside the fireplace. Callahan had a couch, a chair, one end table, and a coffee table. Big wood windows were curtainless.

No woman lived here.

Callahan handed me my bag and pointed. "My bedroom's down there. I bought Chinese in town. I'll be right back with it and the drinks."

My stomach caught. The bedroom.

He read me. "Don't worry. I'm not going to attack you. I'll sleep on the couch."

He flipped off the overhead light in the living room as he walked out, returning to the truck.

Setting my bag in the bathroom, curiosity drew me to the back bedroom. I turned on the light switch. It had more furniture than the big living room.

A king-sized bed with a tall headboard was centered against that outer wall. A side table and lamp stood on either side of the bed. There was a window on either side of the bed, too. But no curtains. On the wall adjoining the bathroom stood a cedar dresser with a mirror. On the opposite wall stood a tall chest of drawers with a small chair beside it.

My gaze locked onto the big bed. I closed my eyes, imagining. How many women has he had in that bed?

He was behind me. I turned to face him, my hands on his chest, peering up. He took my face in his hands and kissed me, lingering over his gentle kiss as he had the night before. He knew what he was doing. He knew that soft kiss was tantalizing enough to make us both want more. He pulled me to him tightly, and one more time, my desire for him bested my common sense as we lost ourselves in each other's arms.

But what if we made love, and he dumped me? Tomorrow? Or next week? I felt myself tensing.

He felt it, too.

Callahan drew back and took my hand. "Let's have a bite then we'll sit on the porch and enjoy a drink. Are you hungry?"

"Not really."

"Well, I am."

I followed him into the kitchen, where he opened a tall box of Chinese food and scraped fried rice and something into a bowl. "You sure I can't get you some?"

I shook my head.

He shrugged and began to eat, standing at the counter.

I watched him. "I'm here. What do you want, Callahan?"

He cut his eyes at me and scoffed, wiped his mouth with a cloth he yanked from a hook on the overhead kitchen cabinet, and said, "You know damned good and well what I want." He finished an egg roll in two chomps and wiped his mouth again, his eyes never leaving me. "The question is, what do you want? Damn, Katherine, your body screams one thing, but your mouth says something entirely different."

I bristled. "I don't want to be the new girlfriend. The new girl in town."

"I never said you were."

"Then what am I to you?"

His jaw tightened. "Honestly? I don't know."

I closed my eyes. Here it comes.

"For the life of me, I don't understand how you got so deep inside me." My eyes opened wide. He was pointing at the bedroom, and he was loud. "I fucking dream about you,

Katherine. I want you. All of you." He glared at me, and his voice turned snide. "Yeah, it surprises me too."

I couldn't speak. He didn't give me a chance. He tilted his head to the side, his gaze narrowly suspicious. "Prissy says you'll make your name here and move on." He nudged his head toward me. "Is that the plan? Get close to a detective, use him to get news, string him along, then, 'Adios, I'm off to the big city.'" He waved his hand at Adios.

The absurdity of it. Me toy with him? Waving his hand on. It was the comic relief I needed. I giggled.

He reached into the refrigerator, opened a fresh can of beer, took a long drink, and washed down his food. His gaze was intimidating. "No. I'm serious. Is that the plan?"

"I don't have a plan. I guess, when I first came here, that was the plan. It's what reporters do. We do good work to make a name for ourselves, move on to a newspaper with a larger circulation where we might make a living wage."

He wiped his mouth on his upper arm. "I should've known."

"No, Callahan! That was before you. I'm not going any-where. I'm not using you."

He didn't respond, and he didn't look at me again.

He reached back into the refrigerator, grabbed a backup beer, and strode out of the kitchen, across the dining room and living room, and out the front door. The screen door banged as I watched him disappear into the darkness.

What the hell? How did this get turned around on me?

I sat at the small kitchen table, taking in the old-fashioned room with hens and eggbasket wallpaper. The faded wallpaper was smoke-stained and grease-splattered behind the stove. The little breakfast table was against the dining room wall. It was old and square with spindle legs. Three spindle-leg, spindle-back chairs sat around it.

The back door and a propane stove were on the rear wall. The sink was in the center of the right side, with light green cabinets above and below on either side.

The refrigerator faced the sink, centered on the opposite wall.

I opened the fridge door. The wine bottle had a cork.

"Do you have a corkscrew?" I stood beside him on the porch.

He sat in a rocking chair, his head leaned back, his eyes closed. He'd turned off the porch light. The air was cool and aromatic.

Without acknowledging my presence, Callahan walked around me back to the kitchen, fished in a drawer, took out the corkscrew, opened the wine bottle, and popped the cork. He reached high in the cabinet, drew out a stemmed glass, and poured it halfway full of red wine.

"Bon Appetit." He offered the glass with no smile on his face or in his eyes.

Cautiously, I took it.

He headed outside again, leaving me standing alone in the middle of the kitchen with my glass of wine.

I'm not sure if it was his heavy tromping over the bare wood floors that vibrated the almost empty house or the screen door banging for the second time, but I exploded.

I slammed the wooden frame of the screened door open. It banged against the wall. "Really? You ask me out here to treat me like this?" My hands were on my hips, elbows out, my legs wobbly.

He looked over his shoulder and raked his eyes over me.

I sucked in a deep breath. *I knew that look.*

His voice was quiet. "Does it make any difference how I treat you, Katherine? You won't trust me." He turned away, peering back into the blackness. "You're just going to leave, anyway. I give up."

My heart almost burst.

I shrieked at him. "You give up? You give up? Because I won't hop into bed with you the first night?" Pointing at the house, I screamed at him, "How many women have you had in that bed?"

He shoved the rocking chair back with his legs as he stood, facing me. It swung wildly back and forth. "Goddammit! What kind of sex maniac do you think I am?"

He lowered the volume to a simmer. "You believe Russo—who's a drunk, by the way. You listen to Prissy, who's a lying bitch." He hit his chest with his fist. "But my word's no good!"

His gaze narrowed, fiery, and mean. "How about I go poking around in your past love life? Look at you. You're telling me you never broke a man's heart?"

Our eyes were locked as I trembled. My heart drummed so furiously I could barely breathe as I clutched the screen door. "Not that I know of."

He froze for a long second and raised his beer high and snide. "Well, Babe. There's a first time for everything." He tromped down the porch steps as I stood frozen, watching him disappear behind a curtain of fireflies.

Somewhere way off, coyotes yipped. An owl hooted. Nearby, a horse whinnied.

I returned to the kitchen, downing the glass of wine he had poured. I filled the glass again, guzzled it, and then poured another.

Light shone through the window over the kitchen sink. Peering out, I saw nothing.

I walked back to the porch. A tall outside light illuminated the horse pen. Another shone inside the barn. I watched silhouettes. He was out there with the horses, rubbing his hand over the muzzle of a tall one. A smaller one snorted and nudged his shoulder from behind.

Turning, he said something—I didn't know what—something comforting and low. He stroked the smaller horse's face and ran his hand along its back.

Speaking quietly, he rubbed them both, stroking their faces and ears. "Let's get some oats." He disappeared into the barn, a horse on either side of him.

Horses don't nuzzle heavy-handed men. They sense cruelty and shy away from the heartless.

That man invited me into his world, and my incessant accusations slashed him raw.

He did me a favor, and I didn't say thank you.

And he was right. Why in God's name would I listen to that bitch Prissy?

I never thought about hurting him, just about him hurting me.

I returned to the table, sat down, sipped from that third glass of wine, leaned my head back, and stared at the ceiling, remembering. Their words and his.

I don't think what he said pierced my heart as much as the look on his face before he said, "I give up." It was the same look I saw when he walked out of Raul Landeros's house—utter defeat. What Callahan hoped we had was as dead as Raul Landeros. I saw it in his eyes. I killed it.

With my elbows on the table, my forehead in my hands, my mind whirled, and I whispered, "Please, don't give up."

I didn't hear him come in.

When I got up from the table to refill my wine glass, he stood in the doorway to the dining room, leaning with his right shoulder against the door frame. Casual-like. His left arm was raised high, gripping the overhead trim. He was studying me.

I startled. "How long have you been there?"

"Long enough."

"I'm sorry."

He didn't acknowledge it. He asked, "You said your ex-husband's name was Jake?"

I nodded.

His hand still gripped that overhead door frame, his piercing gaze on me. "You said he's a rodeo man?"

"Yes, a bull rider." Where's he going with this?

He straightened, filling that doorway. "I never asked, and you never said. Were you married to Jake Satterwhite?"

I felt my mouth sag as I backed away from him.

He stepped toward me, and it was no longer a question. "You were Jake Satterwhite's wife."

I fumbled backward and bumped against the stove. "Yes."

A tense moment of us staring at each other. Callahan broke the gritty silence. "I'll be damned." He sank into the chair by the door, leaned his head back, and closed his eyes. "Son of a bitch. No wonder."

"No wonder what? You know Jake?"

He lowered his head, the corners of his mouth turning down as he met my gaze. "Yeah, I've been around him a few times."

"What do you mean, no wonder?"

He opened his mouth to answer, clamped it shut, and shook his head, averting his eyes.

"What do you mean?" I demanded loudly.

His gaze narrowed. "You know what I mean."

I've got nothing. "What's Jake got to do with you?"

Callahan stood; his face twisted. "He's why you can't trust!" His arm swung wide. "Everyone knew Jake screwed around on his wife, we just never knew his wife."

Hearing it was like diving into a high mountain lake. Ice water steals your breath. I froze.

He bristled. "Say something. For God's sake, tell me you knew."

It took a minute to break the chokehold on my throat. "I didn't know it was something everyone knew."

"It was."

I turned my back to Callahan. *Jake.* I left him and all the disappointment that went with him. Now, Callahan dragged him back.

I bit my lower lip, refusing tears, and faced him. Our gazes locked onto each other. "I want to trust you. But I wanted to trust him, too. He was my husband, Callahan. My husband looked me in the eyes—just like we are right now—and he lied, and lied, and lied."

We stared at each other as the clock over the stove tick ... tick ... ticked.

I reached into the refrigerator, drew out a beer, opened it, and set it on the table for him. I'd put him through hell. He deserved an explanation.

I refilled my glass of wine and took the chair facing him, losing the fight against tears.

He handed me the towel he used to wipe his mouth earlier and sat in the chair by the door, listening. Watching.

"We weren't getting along. I took off work to surprise him in San Antone, thinking it might make us better. I watched him ride. He was great, as always. When I went back to congratulate him—by the time I got through the crowd and found the trailer, he was with a redhead. She jumped up and asked, 'Who are you?' I pointed at Jake and said, 'I'm his wife.'"

I guess I fell silent, frozen in that painful moment.

Callahan brought me back, asking, "Then what?"

"I said, 'I had to see it with my own eyes.' I walked away and drove home."

He squinted. "You suspected?"

I avoided his unyielding gaze, answering into my wine glass. "I wondered. But anytime I questioned him, he'd get mad and say I was just being possessive. Insecure. We'd end up fighting and eventually making up."

My eyes met his as I confessed what I had just then realized. "I think I let him win those arguments because deep down inside, I didn't want to be right. The truth was—too awful to face." I closed my eyes. Tears dripped out, and I took a deep breath. "I was committed to my marriage." I paused, accepting the guttural truth as it occurred to me. "I guess I wasn't good enough."

Callahan scoffed, loud and snide. "You called me sexist because I told you to go cover a quilting bee, but it's your fault he cheated on you?"

I rested my forehead in my hands, talking to the table. I was exhausted. "When the one person who knows you better than anyone else on Earth prefers another woman, he's saying you're not good enough." I met his gaze and lifted a shoulder. "I wasn't good enough for him, anyway."

Callahan stood abruptly, shoving the chair back with his legs.

One step and he slapped an overhead cabinet door with his palm. It banged, and I flinched as he turned to face me. "No! He wasn't good enough for you. Dammit! If he didn't want to be married to you, he should have filed for divorce, not fuck around behind your back."

He fumed for a minute, standing, glaring at me. "I can't believe you, of all people, said that. You, little Miss Women's Lib. Can't you see? Women who blame themselves for their husband's infidelity are as sexist as it gets. You're treating yourself like a second-class citizen. The flaw's inside him. Not you."

Silence engulfed the room as I absorbed his words. Anger overtook his face. "A man doesn't have to hit his wife to abuse her."

"No, Jake never abused me."

"Oh, yes, Katherine, what he did was abuse. He was unfaithful, and then he made you think it was all in your head. That son of a bitch better hope he never runs into me again."

"I don't want pity."

"I don't pity you!" I jolted. That woke up the horses.

He kept staring. Glaring. Sometimes, I felt like Callahan consumed me with his eyes. He demanded, "Why'd you go to San Antone without telling him?"

"I told you. To surprise him."

"No. Maybe you didn't know you'd find him with another woman, but something inside said you might." He swung his arm wide. "There's nothing but jackrabbits and two hundred miles of lonesome between San Angelo and San Antone, but you drove it to face him on his turf. The rodeo arena."

He twisted his neck. "Damn, why can't you see? That took courage. That was brave."

My mind rewound.

It was an impulse decision. I had Jake's schedule. The San Antonio Stock Show and Rodeo was as close as he would be for weeks, and he hadn't asked me to join him there as we had in years past. Yes, I'd wondered if there was someone else. But with Jake, I always wondered.

Callahan returned to the table and picked up the beer I'd opened for him earlier, taking a long swill of it while still standing. "But I get it now." He aimed the beer at me. "That's why what Prissy said cut so deep. Tellin' you over and over again that I'm married."

"I don't want some woman to come up to me and say, I'm his wife."

He was quietly emphatic. "Katherine. I. Am. Not. Married. I never considered it."

His lone brow raised high as he pointed the beer at me again. "And then fuckin' Russo makes you think I'm just like Jake." He paused, taking a deep breath and clenching his jaw. His gaze was fierce. "There are men like Jake all over the fucking world, but I'm not one of them."

I blinked.

He didn't dip me into a vat of boiling oil. He dropped me back into ice water. I lost my air. Frozen.

I relived screaming at him, 'How many women have you had in that bed!'

I never once screamed that at Jake.

I saw again the hurt in his eyes when he said, 'No matter what I say, no matter what I do, you won't trust me.'

Callahan was right about all of it.

They accused and I quickly convicted him—driven by fear. My marriage to Jake rendered me incapable of trust. Why else would I have been so quick to believe anything terrible that anyone said about someone I adored?

I hid my face in my hands, unable to find words, laden with regret and dread. I ruined what might have been. I felt it in my heart. I'd seen it in his eyes.

At last, the words came. "I screamed at the wrong man." I'm sure my eyes begged forgiveness. "I'm sorry. I convicted the wrong man." I hung my head, too empty and too sick of myself to cry anymore.

Callahan gripped my forearm. "Look at me, Katherine." I did. He ran his fingers across my still-damp cheek and held my hair back. He spoke just above a whisper. "This is my home. You are the only woman I've brought here." He pointed to the bedroom. "There has never been a woman in that bed."

I burst into tears. The queasiness came back.

I should've eaten. I shouldn't have gulped the wine. I gagged and swallowed and covered my mouth with my hand. I didn't know someone could puke and sob at the same time, but I was about to.

He opened the refrigerator, dug around, pulled out a can of soda, popped the top, and set it in front of me, pouring the wine into the sink. "Sip on this," he said, leaving the room.

I did.

I drank the sweet soda and cried into that dishtowel.

He came back with a wet washcloth and offered it to me.

"Thank you." I spread the cold rag on my face.

"Hold it against your neck. It helps with nausea."

My stomach calmed. My tears subsided.

Callahan watched me in silence, sitting in that chair by the dining room door, and I managed to avoid his gaze, nursing the soda and pressing the cold rag to my throat.

At last, I asked, unable to look at him, "Do you want to take me home now?"

"It's too late."

I sighed with resignation, then lifted my head, chin high. Our eyes were locked. I'd face this truth head-on. "You're always the one to end it." I searched his eyes. "Tell me now. I need to know. Are you done with me, Callahan? Is it over?"

Silence.

Nothing.

He did not answer. He just stared back, his gaze narrow, probing.

I rested my forehead in my hands, eyes fixed on the table, waiting for his answer as I listened to the infernal ticking of that clock. I felt his eyes on me. It was unnerving.

Callahan lifted my chin. "Do you want it to be over, Katherine?"

Tears welled in my eyes again. "No. No, no, no."

"I can't be any more honest than I've been. The question is, can you, will you trust me?"

He became a blur. "Yes."

"I'm not Jake."

"I know."

He smiled softly and wiped my tears with his thumb. "No, it's not over. I don't know that I'll ever be done with you."

I moved around the table. He scooted his chair around and pulled me into his lap, and I buried my face in his neck, those arms wrapped around me, his hands in my hair, holding me tightly to him.

I loved his neck. I nuzzled it. I kissed it. And I almost said I love you. But I caught myself.

We kissed the way we did whenever our lips met, hungry for each other until he pulled away. "I'm going to prove to you that what's between us is more than sex." He glanced at the clock. "But we've got to get some sleep." His hand rested underneath my hair, across my neck and shoulders. "I'll take the couch and you can have the bed."

"I don't want to put you out of your bed."

"Then sleep beside me, Katherine. I won't—do anything."

In the bathroom, I dressed for bed, changing into a nightshirt. That was all I owned since the divorce.

When I entered the bedroom, Callahan had opened the windows on both sides of the bed. The room was illuminated only by the lamp on his bedside table. The alarm clock showed it was almost two a.m.

"I like the windows open. Is that alright with you?" he asked.

"It's wonderful. Do we have enough cover?"

"I've got more if it's not."

I crawled under the bed covers and pulled them around my neck, inhaling the night air. "What do I smell?"

In the dim light, he stood tall and pulled the shirttail out of his jeans. He unbuttoned his shirt. "Besides the cedar and horse barn?"

"I smell something sweet."

I watched him unbutton the cuffs. His chest muscles flexed as he slipped out of his shirt, one arm at a time, and my heart quickened seeing him that way. A powerful chest and shoulders. Think of the muscles a man uses in roping.

Dark hair grew on his chest, not too much, and a thin trail of dark hair grew down the middle of his hard abdomen, disappearing below the jeans. I don't know if he realized I shamelessly ogled him.

He seemed oblivious and pointed to the open window beside me. "There's an old lilac bush right out there. It's blooming."

"Lilac. It's wonderful."

He sat in the chair and pulled off his boots and socks.

I propped up on my elbow, watching. "Are you sleeping in your jeans?"

He grinned boyishly. "Babe, if you have any hope of me keeping my promise, I've got to sleep in these jeans." He turned off the lamp light and slipped under the covers beside me. "Are you warm enough?"

"Um-hum." His body radiated heat. I rolled, turning my back to him. It was safer. No matter how much I wanted it, I had too much to drink to make an important decision.

He lay on his side, one arm tucked under his pillow, and Callahan enveloped me with the other, pulling me against him. As he did, his palm brushed across my breasts. I don't think intentionally, but still, it was enough. A long minute later, that hand began to softly explore the curves of my body: my stomach, my waist, my hip, down my thigh. He met no resistance.

He stopped with a heavy sigh. Callahan brushed the hair from across my ear and whispered. "Katherine, you're not the new girlfriend. I want you to be the last."

His hand slipped under my nightshirt, and he cupped my breast in his hand, softly rubbing his thumb over it. I moaned, and just before I turned to him, he groaned. "Oh, damn, Katherine. I've got to roll over."

I let him.

I drifted to sleep against the warmth of his back, savoring his words, 'I want you to be the last.'

Chapter 17

He woke me sitting on the side of the bed, holding out a cup of coffee. Sunlight and a soft breeze streamed through the big, open, curtainless windows. I peered at him and rubbed my eyes. "What time is it?"

With the tips of his fingers, he brushed away a strand of hair clinging to my cheek, tucking it behind my ear. His voice was soft. "A little after seven. I wasn't sure what time you wanted to be back."

He set the cup on my bedside table, walked around, and slipped back under the covers. He already had a mug on his side. He'd propped pillows, there were plenty, leaned against them, and rested his hand on my shoulder. "Do you have any idea how beautiful you are, Katherine?"

Did he really say that?

I rolled to face him.

He peered down at me. "Have you ever been to Navarre Beach?"

"Near Destin? I've heard of it, but I've never been there."

"I went deep-sea fishing there," he said. "The sand is sugar white, and the water is almost green. But not quite. Your eyes are the color of the water at Navarre Beach. I've never seen eyes like yours. I get lost in them sometimes."

Pinch me. Is this real?

Men like him don't talk like that, but he didn't stop. "When the sun came through the window this morning, your hair glowed like copper. Your bone structure, your long neck, your perfect skin. I'm amazed at your natural beauty." He patted the mattress beside him. "Come here, Babe." He spread his left arm wide.

I propped my pillows against the headboard, grabbed that coffee from the bedside table, and leaned into him, kissing his chest. "Nobody ever said anything like that to me. Thank you."

"I don't know why not." He wrapped me in his left arm and snugged me tightly against him. "I've never been able to keep my eyes off of you."

"I always thought you were studying me."

He chuckled, tilting his head back. An impish grin spread across his face, forcing that deep dimple. His eyes glistened. "Studying," he chortled. "Yeah, I guess you could call it that."

I leaned my head back to peer up at him, and from this angle, I saw clearly a long scar along the left jawline. Callahan had a small dimple in his chin plus the one in his cheek when he smiled big like that. In my eyes, that face was perfection.

"How long have you been awake?" I asked.

His gaze was on me, tucked under his arm. "I don't know. A while."

I sipped my coffee, which was delicious, but it occurred to me, "We didn't go to bed until two, and you saw the sunrise. You didn't sleep at all, did you?"

"Yeah, I did. Some."

"Not enough. I should have slept on the couch. Or you should have taken me home, I guess."

With his left hand, he played with my hair. "If I wanted to take you home, I would've done it. I could've slept somewhere else. I didn't want to. I wanted you right where you were, beside me." He paused, adding, "I want you to believe in me, Katherine."

"I do." I hesitated, staring at my coffee cup as I confessed, "I wanted to make love last night."

He snickered and lifted that rebel brow. "You have no idea. But it hit me—we'd both been drinking, and you might wake up and regret it. I couldn't take that. No, I made up my mind if it happens, we'll both be sober, and you'll be the one to initiate it. It's the only way. It has to be you. You have to know this isn't just about sex."

I would have given myself to him right then—but he hadn't slept. It wasn't the time. I wanted him fresh when it happened.

He set his mug on the bedside table and rested his right forearm on his head, his gaze wandering the room. "The more I thought about everything, the madder I got." He tucked his chin to see me. "The way he treated you. The things Prissy and

Russo said to you. Hell, no wonder you were confused. I'll deal with them. Today."

My eyes misted. "I'm so sorry for the pain I caused you."

He shuffled around in the bed, repositioning, facing me. His brows were drawn together. "Katherine, do you trust me now? Believe in me?"

I stroked his cheek. "Yes. My fears and doubts are gone."

"Are you sure? What if someone else says something bad?"

"I already thought about that." I sat up on my knees. "Here's exactly what I'm going to do. I'm going to pull out my reporter's notepad and pen and say, 'I'll use your direct quote when I tell T.J. what you said.' And I'll come straight to you."

For the second time that morning, he tilted his head back and laughed—a good one like he'd done at Sambo's several times. He gripped my shoulders. "So, let's leave it all behind, Katherine. Your past, my past, last night. Let's don't drag it around with us. We start fresh today. Is that okay?"

"Absolutely perfect." I kissed him quickly and hopped out of bed. "Are you ready for more coffee?"

He held out his empty cup.

"Black?" I asked.

He answered with a foxlike grin. "Do you take me for a cream and sugar kind of guy?"

Chuckling, I took his cup, and he leaned back, resting his eyes while I went to the kitchen and freshened our coffee. He'd opened the window over the sink. The horses were in the corral. It looked like the Hill Country—rocky with cedar and mesquite.

In the bedroom, I offered him his cup and set mine on the table beside him. "Excuse me a second." I went to the bathroom, and when I returned, I stood by him.

Last night's five o'clock shadow was second-day stubble. He could grow a nice beard if he wanted. He peered at me cautiously over his cup of coffee.

"There's something I've meant to tell you, but we get sidetracked." His eyes grew suspicious. I showed him my palm. "It's about the Bennett case, and no, it's not for a news story."

Slowly, he nodded, his gaze wary. "I interviewed James Billingsly yesterday. It was off the record, but it's your case. I wanted you to know. It just got lost in everything else."

His stare went blank. That quickly.

"Mrs. Bennett went to his place for an oil change that day."

Callahan smirked. "Why do you think I picked him up that morning? Bass told me as soon as I got to his mother's place."

I should have known.

"And I never told you about the Gibsons. They approached me at Marilyn Bennett's funeral separately, but they both called me names and told me to leave the Bennetts alone."

His brows shifted high as he drank from the mug.

"Then yesterday, Jimmy and I went to this guy's house that the narcs picked up. Jerry Stubblefield."

Callahan's back stiffened, and his expression hardened.

"Russo's people picked him up for manufacturing and delivery, and I thought it might be a follow-up to the Freddy Dickey story."

"Katherine!" His loud voice woke up. "Old man Stubblefield's nuts." His brows scrunched. "You need to be more careful."

I sat beside him on the bed, excited to tell him my story. "He came out of his house with a shotgun and fired it into the air."

"Dammit!" *Maybe I shouldn't have told him. He wasn't taking this well.* He clomped his mug on the bedside table. "I told you. You could get hurt poking into the wrong places."

"He didn't fire at us. Just into the air."

Callahan used both hands to sit up straight in the bed.

I grabbed his forearm. It was hard as an oak limb. "I calmed Hal down and told him I understood there are two sides to every story, and I wanted to tell his side. So, they talked. They led us inside to show us how the cops tore it up looking for something. Anyway, that's not the point."

Fire sparked in those golden-brown eyes. He was testy now. "So, what is?"

"Jerry Stubblefield works for Gibson Oil. Several of those druggies do."

"No shit."

"Has it crossed your mind that maybe, just maybe, stealing rifles and jewelry and money to buy drugs was the motive behind Marilyn Bennett's murder? That maybe it wasn't Billingsly? Everyone knew how rich the Bennetts were."

He scratched under his chin, studying me. "Are we going to talk here as a couple or as a reporter and cop?"

A couple. I liked that. "This isn't for news."

"I've never thought James Billingsly killed Marilyn Bennett."

"Why?" I heard the surprise in my voice even if he didn't.

"Look at him. Billingsly could snap a woman's neck with a love tap. Her wounds don't fit him."

"Then why did you arrest him?"

Callahan held up his big hand and lifted his index finger. "Because he had motive." Another finger went up as he said, "An eyewitness put him at the scene of the murder." A third finger. "At the time of the murder." Three fingers up. "And we had nothing else. Nada. And one hell of a lot of pressure to act."

He squirmed in the bed, maybe getting comfortable. "And no, I don't think she was killed for drug money." He stretched like a cat, bowing that muscular chest, and he talked through a yawn. "I think Roxanne Gibson killed her out of rage over her relationship with Tex, whatever it was. She used the robbery as a diversion."

Callahan rolled his neck. "I'm trying to prove my theory that she enticed some drugged-out roughnecks to help her. She needed them to wrangle and tie up Mrs. Bennett. While they looted the house, she beat Marilyn Bennett to death herself."

He paused momentarily, seeing my jaw slacken and my eyes widen. His were, too. "I don't guess there's anything more I could do to prove how much I trust you than telling you all that. You being a reporter and all."

I adored him even more, if that was possible. "Why do you think it's her?"

"Mrs. Bennett's face told me everything I needed to know." He paused a long moment, staring into space, seeing what he didn't want to see. "Babe, her face was pulverized. Crushed. They didn't hit her in the back of the head and knock her out. They didn't shoot her or sexually assault her. No, her face was the target of that assault. Her cheeks, her jaw, her nose, her mouth, teeth, forehead, and eyes were all shattered. That tells me the assault was pure malice. Spite. Maniacal madness. Roxanne Gibson saw Mrs. Bennett's beauty as a threat, and she destroyed it. Yanking those earrings out said a lot."

My hand found my heart. "That's horrible."

"Yeah, it was. And some doors only open from the inside out."

Confusion was evident on my face.

"I need someone who was inside that house at the time to talk. Or I need to recover the stolen property. I don't have either. Yet."

"Do you know for sure that she and Tex were having an affair?"

He lifted a shoulder. "I don't know if it was sexual, but they spent a lot of time together. The gift of those earrings—that doesn't look too platonic to me."

"You know, I heard a rumor they'd been seeing each other even before Mr. Bennett died."

He nodded. "Yeah, something was up between them. But maybe it was lopsided. Maybe Tex felt that way about her, but she didn't feel that way about him."

"Then she shouldn't have accepted the earrings."

He lifted his empty cup. "Good point."

"Did you question Tex?"

He set his cup on the bedside table. "I didn't want to spook him until I had more than a hunch. Now he's disappeared."

I felt my eyes open wide. "Tex Gibson disappeared?"

"No one's seen Tex since the week after Marilyn Bennett was buried, and no one has filed a missing person report." He repositioned in the bed to face me. "Here's the deal. Years back, there were rumors about Tex and another woman. And one day, she disappeared. That woman's never been found." He rubbed his eyes with his fists and yawned, stretching his arms and tightening his muscles. "We'll find Tex someday at the bottom of Lake Fort Phantom Hill. Maybe with that other woman."

"And what about Billingsly?"

"He'll be released when I catch the real killer."

I sipped my coffee, pondering. "Do you think you'll find the Bennett stolen merchandise at one of these drug houses?"

That rogue brow shot up again, and I was pretty sure it was involuntary that time. "No comment. We've gone far enough."

I petted his cheek. "Are you hungry? Can I cook breakfast for you?"

His grin and his eyes told me he was exhausted. "I don't know, can you?"

"I can. But you need to sleep. Now." Holding his face in my hands, I kissed him gently. "I don't have to be at work until two. What about you?"

"I'll call later and tell them I'll be in this afternoon." With me out of the bed, Callahan dispersed pillows, stretched out, and rolled onto his side, hugging the pillow I'd slept on. "It smells like you."

I ran my fingers through his hair and kissed his forehead. "When do you want me to wake you?"

He glanced at the clock. "Give me until ten."

Quietly, I rummaged through Callahan's kitchen. There was not much to cook with or to put it on, nothing to serve a man for breakfast, but he had a couple of cast iron skillets, a propane stove, and a couple of plates.

Tiptoeing back to the bedroom, I whispered, "Are you asleep?"

He shook his head with his eyes closed.

"Can I drive your truck to the nearest grocery store? To get stuff to cook you for breakfast?"

He mumbled sleepily, "The keys are in my jeans. No, on the dresser, I forgot. Get money out of my billfold."

I glanced around the room. Callahan's jeans were folded on that chair by the chest of drawers. Now, he could sleep. He raised on one elbow, peering at me over his shoulder, the muscles in his shoulder and upper arm pronounced. Just look at him. "Can you find your way out and back?"

"I think so. But where am I going?" I took the keys from the dresser.

"The Gap. There's a little store. Go out my gate. The horses are in the pen, so leave the gate open. Turn left. Stay on my road until you reach the pavement. Take a right. That's Highway 89. It dead ends in Buffalo Gap. Take a left." He laid back down. "You'll see Stonewall's on the right, around a hard curve. When you come back, look at the odometer. It's exactly six miles from the railroad tracks to my road."

"What about the lock on the gate?"

"Code. 2255. Remember C-A-L-L."

"Go back to sleep. I'm sorry I woke you."

He raised his arm and aimed at the dresser. "Get money."

"Okay." Yes, I lied. I had to, or he'd argue, and I was determined to pay for something for once.

He drew up on that elbow again, looking at me over his shoulder with an afterthought. "Katherine? Can you see over the steering wheel? To drive? Reach the accelerator and brake?"

My head tilted back, and I laughed heartily. "I'm not short."

"You're not tall."

"I'll scoot the seat up. Relax. I've driven trucks." Just not one as big as his. "Go to sleep."

Chapter 18

I would dress for the day before I went to the Gap. In the bathroom, I slipped out of the nightshirt and into jeans and a fresh blouse I brought with me.

An old-fashioned porcelain pedestal sink stood in the middle of one long wall between the toilet and an ancient, open-faced, free-standing propane heater. A metal medicine cabinet hung so high above the sink that I had to stand on tiptoes to see myself in its small mirror. I needed a step stool.

A walk-in shower took up the outside wall of the bathroom. He must have had it put in after he bought the place. I had to grin at the clawfoot bathtub. Callahan couldn't fold himself into that.

Flowery wallpaper on the walls. No telling when this house was built.

I performed my morning routine there, even dolled up with mascara and lipstick, and as if I was going on a date, I dabbed on perfume. What a beautiful morning. I couldn't remember being this full of life. Waking in bed beside Callahan, listening to him—I shed my fear of him as a snake sheds its skin.

I peeked in on him before leaving. He was out.

I stood on the porch, assessing his world. A creek flowed fifty yards away on the right, parallel to the house. It filled a stock tank near the road. Both sides of the creek were lined with oak, mesquite, and cedar. A giant willow tree grew at the edge of the stock tank.

On the left were the tin barn and a pipe rail corral. A two-horse trailer was parked beside the barn, with a tractor behind it.

His horses were a tall, solid black gelding and a smaller mare. She was a line back dun. A water trough outside the barn. A haystack not far away.

Going down four wide cement porch steps to the native grass yard, I looked back at the house. It sat high off the ground. It was a pier-and-beam rock house with a high-pitched roof and shingles the color of cedar foliage.

Silent and serene, in stark contrast to his work world.

Callahan found a way to balance heaven and hell; one more time, I saw he was right. You couldn't know that man without seeing him here. He was so much more than the badge.

Driving into Buffalo Gap, I was reminded of college in San Marcos, the heart of the Texas Hill Country.

You crossed a creek and railroad tracks to enter the little town of Buffalo Gap. It was an oasis on the prairie with some of the most magnificent, ancient live oak trees I'd ever seen. Their canopy shaded the road through town.

I found Stonewall's Grocery easily. It was a native stone building on a cement slab with a low roof surrounded by spreading live oaks. Two old-fashioned gas pumps were in front, and there was a small asphalt parking lot. A rock bench with a cement seat lined the front wall. This was a gathering place.

Screen doors front and back welcomed the breeze. It was a pleasant, homey place with a butcher counter and chest-type drink box. And it had a smell of its own—a blend of country air, aged masonry, fresh produce, candy, and a water cooler.

After loading up with bacon, eggs, milk, bread, canned biscuits, and butter, I headed to the small checkout counter. I liked the earthy smell of the place.

An older woman glanced out the front screen door as she rang up my groceries. She eyed me cautiously. "Isn't that T.J.'s truck?"

"Yes ma'am."

She drew her mouth to one side. "What are you doing in it?" She was about my height with the thickness of age. Short, tightly permed, steel gray hair.

"Buying food for breakfast."

She adjusted the round wire-rimmed glasses on her little scooped nose and asked, "Where's T.J.?"

I smiled. "Asleep."

She stared for a moment, studying me. A young man with brown hair stepped beside her. "Mom, what is it?"

The woman nodded at me. "She's driving T.J.'s truck."

He looked at me the same way his mother had as if I were a serial killer. "How'd you get T.J.'s truck?"

I held up the keys. "He gave them to me." I couldn't keep from grinning. They were protective of him. "Is there a problem?"

The two exchanged glances. Both had blue eyes. "T.J. never lets anyone drive his truck," the man said.

"What's your name?" I asked.

"Dale. Dale Stonewall and this is my mom." He tilted his head. "My dad's out back."

I offered my hand across the counter. "My name is Katherine. Katherine Coe. Callahan gave me his keys and told me how to get here so I could buy groceries to make breakfast. I promise I didn't steal it from him."

It struck me then. He called me Katherine; somehow, that's who I'd become.

Dale nodded cautiously and took my hand but didn't shake it. I paid, and he handed me the sacked groceries. They watched as I took it, climbed into that big truck, and started the engine. He didn't let other people drive his truck. He didn't hesitate when I asked.

Turning onto Highway 89, I glanced at the odometer. Six miles.

I was happy down to my soul. I never felt like this before, not even with Jake. I didn't give a damn about what anyone said. I'd also made up my mind about something else.

Quietly, I slipped back into the house with the groceries and peeked into the bedroom. There was a soft snore. He was out. I closed the bedroom door silently.

I quietly prowled Callahan's house, getting to know it. I loved the big windows that opened so high, allowing fresh air to flow. I propped the wooden front door with the screen closed, allowing the outside to enter. The Chinese called it feng shui, a principle that free-flowing air promoted positive energy. I could buy into that here.

That back kitchen door didn't go outside. It opened onto a laundry room, an ancient stoop walled in to accommodate a washer, dryer, and storage shelves. With an exterior door and small windows across the back, I could see the backyard and the white rock hill beyond it.

I cleaned up our mess from the night before and straightened the house.

Scrounged and found an old, embroidered tablecloth in a kitchen drawer, spread it on the little table, and set it with dinnerware and folded paper towels for napkins.

Pre-heated the oven. Brewed a fresh pot of coffee.

I put the biscuits in the oven and fried bacon a little after nine-thirty. I waited until the last minute, knowing the aroma of frying bacon would wake any man. With the biscuits out of the oven and buttered, the bacon out of the pan, I fried eggs.

I was cooking the last egg when he slipped one arm around my middle and pulled me against him. He brushed my hair to the side and nibbled my neck.

Goosebumps.

"Nothing better than waking up to bacon and you."

A smile took over my face. Bacon got first mention. I chuckled. Men and bacon.

I was too busy flipping hot grease to turn around. I glanced up and over my shoulder. "Did you sleep well?"

"Yeah, thanks." He let go of me, taking in the room. "Look at all this." He stepped away, turning around. "You found the tablecloth. The table is set. Biscuits." He helped himself, taking a big bite of one. He talked with his mouth full. "Buttered. Damn. Delicious."

And he poured a cup of coffee. "Thank you, Katherine." His mouth was full. That man could eat more, faster than anyone I ever saw.

I took that last egg from the frying pan, set it on a paper towel to drain, and turned around to face him. He looked almost boyish just out of bed, his hair tousled, finishing a second buttered biscuit, holding his coffee mug in one hand. He had those jeans back on.

I couldn't stop smiling. He had biscuit crumbs on his chin.

Callahan watched me, I'd say warily, over his cup of coffee as I came to him. He set the mug on the kitchen counter and wiped biscuit crumbs from his face.

Our eyes were locked on each other.

"Breakfast is ready." I ran my hands softly across his chest, feeling his collarbone, shoulders, and biceps, never taking my eyes off him. "We can eat now. It's warm." Slowly, I trailed a fingernail down that delicious line of dark hair, stopping at his jeans.

My eyes were still on his as I unbuttoned that top button with one hand. "Or, if you prefer, we can eat after we make love."

I didn't have to say it twice.

We lay in bed, my head on a pillow in the crook of his left arm, which was wrapped around me. I was snug against him, my hand resting on that sexy abdomen. Neither of us spoke. Our desires had finally been satisfied. I was almost asleep when he pulled me on top of him. He did it gently, effortlessly.

He didn't speak.

Oh. One of us wasn't fully satisfied.

I smiled. "What?"

His eyes roamed my face. He didn't say a word.

I said three. "I love you." It just blurted out.

Something inside of me froze. My heart stopped mid-beat. Maybe my body tensed. How many women had said that to him afterward, only to have him run like a frightened buck?

My eyes and my face surely betrayed my fear.

Callahan stroked my face softly, his fingers resting in my hair, his thumb on my chin. "Katherine, if this isn't love, it doesn't exist." He grinned boyishly. "And no, I've never said that to anyone before."

I kissed him quickly and sat on my knees beside him, excited as a child at Christmas. "Say it again. I want to hear it."

His eyes glistened as his gaze unapologetically roamed my bare body. He studied it like a map. "What's your middle name?"

"Elise."

He repeated, "Elise." He ran his hands softly across my breasts, along my collarbone, around my shoulders, and down my back. "Katherine Elise Coe. I, Thomas Jefferson Callahan, love you."

I closed my eyes. Tears came to them.

His hands rested at the small of my back—he could reach around my waist—and he drew me to him. His grip was firm, his eyes intense. "Katherine, I've been in love with you." He pulled me into a kiss that was neither soft nor gentle. It was ravenous. And I trembled under the power of his passion as he took me, each of us drunk on desire, tasting and feeling each other, rolling in the covers, two bodies entwined as one.

At last, he rolled onto his back, pulling me on top of him, and with those big hands, he placed me exactly where he'd wanted me in the first place.

It took my breath. I closed my eyes.

He cupped my face in his hands, his voice like silk. "Katherine, let me see your eyes."

I opened them, expecting him to say something. But he didn't. He didn't have to. I saw the purist love I'd ever seen looking at me from those honey-brown eyes—and I melted into him. With a loud moan, I buried my face in his neck. My fingernails dug into his shoulders as every muscle in me clenched tightly, and my whole body quivered.

And when I did, he did, too.

It had never been like that.

Chapter 19

He flinched, clenching me tightly. I opened my eyes. The sun no longer streamed through the bedroom windows.

I peered at his face to see a tic in the corner of his eye, and I was startled. "What happened?"

No response. He still gripped me tightly, staring at the ceiling.

"Did you have a bad dream?"

He eased his grip on me. "I guess." Those umber eyes were wistful. Maybe even sad.

His expression, the sudden jerking, frightened me. Alarm rose in my throat. "What is it?"

"Nothing."

He still wasn't looking at me.

I reached and turned his face to mine. "Something."

Our gazes held. "I just had a bad dream, Babe. It's nothing to talk about."

Was that pain or fright in his eyes? "T.J.!"

"I don't want to talk about it," he said. A moment later. "I lost you."

I kissed his chest. "Honey, you're not going to lose me. I'm not going anywhere."

He shook his head with that sad smile. "Just leave it."

I turned onto my stomach, propped on my elbows, studying him. "T.J.? Aren't you happy?"

"Happier than I've ever been in my life." He shrugged a little, his brows lifting high. "I don't know, Babe. Maybe it scared me. I don't know what to say. It woke me up."

I stretched up and kissed his mouth. "You? Afraid? I don't believe that."

"I have fears, just like everyone," he said.

I sat up on my knees, facing him, comfortable in front of him in my nakedness. Not an onion skin layer of pretense was left between us. "What is your fear?"

He lifted a shoulder. "I don't know. Maybe, maybe losing the treasure just when I find it." I didn't have time to absorb that because he'd cut his eyes at the clock. "Oh, damn. We overslept."

He bolted from bed, went to the living room, and dialed a number, at ease in his own skin, too. "Clance, I'm running late." He listened. "No, just dragging ass." He glanced at me and winked. "Couldn't sleep. Tell Sarge for me, will ya?" He listened for a moment. "I'll be in as soon as I can." He started to hang up, then stopped. "Wait. Do something for me. Tell little Miss Prissy she and I are gonna have a talk when I get in, and she's not gonna like what I have to say." He listened. "Yeah, tell her just that. I want her to stew on it."

He disappeared into the bathroom. When he returned, he slipped on jeans, saying, "I guess we're going to have to start this day."

I lay on my back, arms folded behind my head, savoring the sight of him. I'd seen the love inside those eyes. He satisfied me beyond my dreams and made me feel safe.

"You haven't had enough sleep," I said.

"It'll have to do." He came to the bed and stood over me. "I need to tell you something."

Peering up, my brows lifted. That didn't sound good.

"I told you I never said 'I love you' to anyone, and it hit me a minute ago. That's not true. And one thing we're going to be is honest with each other."

I held my breath. I'm sure my eyes were big.

"I did say it. I was young. Not long after I got back from the war. I thought that was what I was feeling." It was a melancholic smile. "That wasn't love. When I broke up with her, the way she looked at me—after I told her I loved her, and I took it back—I swore I'd never say that again until there was absolutely no question. And I haven't. Not once, until just now."

He sat beside me on the bed. "I'm thirty-three years old. I know exactly what I feel. Exactly what I want. And what I want is you." He glanced around the room. "This." He leaned over me, resting his weight on one hand. "I told you I love you. No doubts. You said you love me, and I believe you. I know it's one hell of a plunge but, I want to go to sleep beside you and wake up beside you forever. If you'd be willing."

Did that mean what I thought it did?

It took a moment to sink in. I sat up straight. My eyes must have been saucers because they felt big. "You want to get married?"

His face flushed, and he straightened, glancing away.

I kissed his shoulder and grasped that powerful arm. He could reach around my waist with both hands. I couldn't reach around his bicep with both of mine. I spoke softly, "Look at me, please."

He did, but he didn't let me speak. "I'll be a good husband to you, Katherine. You'll never have to worry about me being unfaithful. Or wonder where I am. I won't abandon you."

Unexpected tears. What a crybaby I'd become in his arms. "I just gave myself to you. Completely."

He wiped tears from my cheeks. "Does that mean you'll marry me?"

"T.J., I'm yours."

Mischief spread across his face and into his eyes as his rebellious brow arched high. "Yes, or no? Will you marry me?"

I tilted my head back and laughed with glee. "Yes, I'll marry you. Nothing in this world would make me happier than to be your wife."

He hooted, scooped me out of bed, messed up covers and all, and he twirled me in a circle. "When?"

My arms were around his neck, head back, my smile as wide as the Texas sky. "Whenever you want."

He held me in the air like a child, my feet off the ground. "Do you want a big wedding?"

"No."

He lowered my feet to the floor. "Then what are we waiting on? Tomorrow. We'll buy the license tomorrow and we can get your ring."

"Rings," I said. You'll wear one, too?" Jake never did. He said it was dangerous, that men lost fingers wearing rings.

"Of course. You can pick it out. A gold band?"

"I'll take one, too," I said. "You chose mine."

He kissed my hand. "You need diamonds."

"I had diamonds. I'd rather wear the gold band that you chose for me. Pure, unending love."

He cupped my face in his hand. "If that's what you want."

"Thomas Jefferson Callahan, all I want is you. Us. This. Forever."

We clung to each other, standing in the bedroom for a glorious moment, fresh air streaming through the windows, carrying the fragrance of lilacs. I felt T.J.'s heartbeat against mine.

Joy. That was the word.

I never imagined this kind of joy.

He glanced at the bedside clock. "What the hell? Work can wait a little longer." He smiled wide, the dimple deep. "What do you say? Let's consummate our deal."

I laughed genuinely. "I thought we just did.

That rogue brow. "Babe, I'm good to go."

And we were back at it again.

After he showered and dressed, we headed to town through Buffalo Gap. Both of us were in blissful daydreams. I was already moving my furniture into his house, figuring out what would fit where.

"Can you take a week off when we get married?" he asked.

"I have vacation time. I think Jack would let me off."

He gripped my hand. "You want to see what color your eyes are? Let's go back to Navarre Beach. I'll take you deep-sea fishing."

"Sounds wonderful. Then we can take our time moving all my stuff into your house. That's going to be a lot of work, you know."

He cut his eyes at me. "Our house. And I've got a trailer. We can probably get it all in one load."

"Our house. I like that. But you may not realize how much furniture I have. Do you care if I plant a flowerbed? Put potted plants along the porch? Curtains?"

"Babe, it's your house now. Do anything you want." He cut his eyes at me with his mischievous grin. "Just don't paint anything pink."

I giggled like a schoolgirl.

A minute later, he asked, "Are you going to ride Ginger?"

"The little dun? Sure."

"She's perfect for you."

I knew a little about horses. "She's beautiful. What's the big one's name?"

"Blackie."

"Do you rope on him?"

He took his eyes off the road for a moment. "Me and Blackie won San Angelo three years ago." He tapped his belt.

"Really?" That was a big deal. I hadn't realized.

He cut his eyes at me. "That's when I met…"

I covered his lips with my fingers. "No. We finished that book last night. Threw it away."

What a wide smile. "You're right." He spread his right arm across the back of the bench seat and tilted his head to summon me. "Come here."

I scooted beside him, my left hand resting on his thigh. Then it hit me. "You realize people will think we're crazy."

"Do you think I give a shit what anyone thinks?" His brow furrowed. "Are you having second thoughts?"

I kissed his cheek. "Not a crumb." We were entering Buffalo Gap. "Stop at Stonewall's."

"Why?"

"Because I'm pretty sure, they thought I killed you and stole your truck. I thought you might let them see you're alive."

T.J. got a big laugh out of that. We walked into the store with him holding my hand.

Seeing him, Mrs. Stonewall exclaimed. "T.J.! It's been a while." Her eyes gravitated to our hands.

"I know, Margaret." He took off his hat. "I've been working a lot. I want y'all to meet Katherine." He glanced down at me. "Coe." He smiled. "She's going to be Katherine Callahan just as soon as I can make it happen."

Dale's face lit up. "Your wife! Wow!" He came around the counter and patted T.J. on the back, smiling. "I never thought I'd see this day." Dale's gaze zipped my way, and he nodded. "Congratulations."

"Thank you." I couldn't quit smiling.

Mrs. Stonewall came and hugged T.J., turning to me. "I'm sorry, dear. I never dreamed."

I assured her, "It's fine. I loved you being protective of him."

T.J. pulled me close, his arm around my shoulder. We stood there for a few minutes while they chatted about the goings on in Buffalo Gap. He bought each of us a soft drink and headed to Abilene. We were both going to be late.

The land flattened out, with fewer trees than on Highway 89. I watched flat farmland fly by my window.

T.J. brought me back inside when he said, "I'm hoping to break the Bennett case today." He'd thrown that cop mask out the window. "If I can wrap this up, we can be in Florida next week."

"Today?"

He took his eyes off the road for a fleeting second and smiled. "It's my lucky day."

That it was.

A few miles later, I asked, "Is Russo really a drunk? Are you two going to have it out?"

He checked his side mirror. "The truth is, Russo's one hell of an investigator, and I've never seen his drinking affect his work. I was just pissed, and he's been pissed at me. We work together so, yeah, it's time we get that straightened out. Especially after that shit he told you."

"Why, T.J.? Why's Russo mad at you?" I asked.

He cut his eyes at me. "Because I dated a secretary at DPS. He introduced us. She wanted to get married. I didn't. She's cried on his shoulder ever since."

I nodded. "Okay. I get it now." I nibbled his ear, whispering, "Too bad for her. You're mine now."

He turned his face for a quick kiss and grinned. "You're damned right. I'm yours. Pretty soon we'll have rings to prove it."

Oh, God, this is a dream.

I stretched out, riding with my back against the passenger door, my bare toes tucked under his thigh, watching him. I liked looking at him. Last night, even when I woke up this morning, I never imagined this.

I am going to be his wife. I'm living a fairy tale.

To the world, T.J. Callahan was a hard ass. Jimmy called him a Nazi. He had seemed almost invincible to me. Bigger than life. I had come to know the real him. Angry, frustrated, yearning, dejected; tired, hungry, and finally satisfied.

Happiness radiated off him when he scooped me out of the bed and twirled me around the bedroom.

"While you got dressed, I made you a sandwich." I held up a brown paper sack. "Bacon and egg." He looked at it with surprise. He hadn't noticed it before. "We never ate, remember? You didn't have any plastic bags, so it's wrapped in paper towels, and I found one sack in the kitchen. We've got to get some groceries and staples."

He snickered. "Babe, my staples come from the drive-through window on the way home."

"Yes. The kitchen trash is full of your staples. Do you realize how much money you'll save eating breakfast and dinner at home instead of in the drive-through?"

"So, you're thrifty too?" He glanced at the brown sack lunch again. "I haven't had one of those since elementary school. Only married guys bring sack lunches from home."

"Well honey, I guess you're going to have a whole new lunch crowd pretty soon."

That fast.

Everything changed. Everything was different. An unexpected anxiety pulsed through me, and I shivered. Out of nowhere, his job frightened me. I didn't have to close my eyes to see him walk into Raul Landeros' house with his arms spread wide. No weapon.

I turned my head to peer out the window at freshly planted fields, row after row, zipping past. Little green shoots peaked above the brown earth as far as I could see.

I turned back, watching him drive with his elbow in the open window. My heart thumped rapidly in my chest. This is crazy. What's come over you? There was no reason for me to feel anxious. He's going to the jail to question some people. That's not dangerous. He does it all the time.

This makes no sense. This was the happiest day of my life, but my skin began to tingle. It was a panic attack. Yes. But why?

I lifted my eyes to heaven and closed them. *Please, God, keep him safe.*

His beeper vibrated as we pulled up to my apartment. Checking it, he asked, "Can I use your phone?"

"You don't have to ask."

He picked up the telephone in the apartment and dialed a number as I took my bag to the bedroom. It was time for me to shower for work.

"Callahan," I heard him say. He listened and replied, "I've got to run by the office first, but I'll be there." As he started to hang up, he stopped himself. "Russo, you and me, man. It's time we had a meet-and-greet." He listened. "I'll see you before long."

I laughed softly. I knew what that meant. Did Russo?

T.J. glanced around the apartment, seeing me watching from the bedroom door. His brows drew together. "Is all this stuff yours?"

"Yes, I got the furniture in the divorce. I told you, there's more at my parents' house."

"Damn." He whistled. "Satterwhite bought it?"

Of course, he would assume the man bought it. "No. I did."

He smiled. "Then let's pack it up. I don't care how many loads it takes. We're not living apart another night. Not any-more." Callahan crossed the room and picked me up, holding me tightly against him, my arms around his neck as we spun in a circle.

Oh, my, yes. He could dance.

He kissed me quickly. "We're going to have a wonderful life together, Mrs. Callahan."

"I'm going to be Mrs. Thomas Jefferson Callahan. I can't wait."

He hefted me higher. "You're the only Mrs. Callahan there ever has been or ever will be." He kissed me again, this time deeply. "I'm gonna spoil you rotten." He lowered me to the floor and turned to leave.

"Wait." I ran to the pantry and grabbed a bag of potato chips. "Have these with your sandwich."

"See there, you're already spoiling me." He winked, holding up his chips. "I'll see you after work. Wish me luck, Babe."

Chapter 20

I sat in a stupor in the lobby of the hospital emergency room. Alone. My mind was dead. I closed my wet eyes to see him walk out my door, holding the sack of potato chips with that beautiful smile. *'Wish me luck, Babe.'*

I was too in shock to cry, reliving the morning, hearing him say, 'I could do this forever if you're willing ... You're the only Mrs. Callahan there ever has been or will be.'

I was so excited to go to work and tell them I was marrying Abilene Police Detective T.J. Callahan, the most wonderful man in the world. But I never shed that worry.

Jack was still out sick. Rhonda assigned me to follow up on yesterday's big drug roundup and localize a national story on inflation. It wasn't all cops all the time. Several people were out with whatever bug Jack had. The rest of us pulled double duty.

Jimmy stopped by my desk. "You want to go check the search warrant from yesterday?"

I stared at him. Blank-faced. I wasn't sharp for some reason.

He squinted. "The search warrant for Stubblefield's. Remember? They were supposed to file it."

"Oh, yeah." I waved my hand, poo-pooing him. "I doubt it's been filed yet." That was true. I peered at Jimmy. "We're getting married."

"What?" He shouted over the teletypes.

I laughed out loud as Rhonda peered at us from across the room.

The teletypes quietened. "T.J. and I are getting married," I said again.

Jimmy stepped back. Was that shock or disdain on his face? "Well, that's just one hell of a whirlwind romance." His arms swung wide, the expression accusing. "You haven't known each other for a month."

I blinked, still grinning. "I don't guess things like this have a timetable." I returned to my story.

Jimmy stood at my desk as if he somehow thought my marriage was up for debate—and then we both froze as a frantic cry came across a scanner. "Ten-thirty-three!" A breathless man yelled, "Shots fired! Officer down!"

The paralyzing call pierced the newsroom. Everyone stopped what they were doing to stare at the scanners.

Another man shouted, "Officer down! Repeat! Officer down! Roll ambo! 545 Stubblefield Road, Tye!"

My jaw dropped, and my heart stopped.

My ears began ringing loudly, yet I heard a man yell, "Two deceased!"

They might as well have shot me in the head.

I knew it was him.

Police dispatch, the fire department, EMTs, and officers in the field shouted on top of each other.

I can't say who covered the story. I didn't.

I remember Jimmy yelling, his mouth moving, his arms waving. I couldn't hear what he said because of the deafening, high-pitched roar in my ears. My whole body was numb. Only my eyes worked.

Rhonda stood at my desk. She was saying something. That was it. The last thing I remembered—their mouths moving. Me not hearing. The numbness.

I barely remembered driving to the hospital.

For some time, I'd sat alone, my hands squeezed between my knees, wide-eyed and waiting. They wouldn't let me go back. I wasn't next of kin.

"Kat?" My gaze traveled to the voice. It was Russo. He ushered me. "Come with me. Hurry."

My heart rebounded. "He's alive?"

"He's asking for you." Russo gripped my upper arm tightly, guiding me. His face was gray as he walked fast.

"But he's alive?" He was dragging me. "Russo?"

"You've got to hurry."

"Russo!"

He would not stop walking. "Stubblefield shot him."

I stopped. "But he's going to be okay? Right?"

He lifted his brows and shook his head. "I'm sorry, Kat. Hollow point."

I was blank.

"Hollow point bullet, Kat. It mushrooms on impact. Hit him center chest."

I gasped. "Tell me he was wearing a vest."

Russo's lips drew tight as he ushered me into the room where T.J. was surrounded by doctors and nurses.

He was watching for me. Our gazes caught, and T.J. tried to smile. He stretched out his arm, and I ran to him. Those beautiful eyes fastened on me. "Katherine ... Callahan."

I kissed his hand, holding it, our gazes latched. "You're going to be alright."

I wanted to pet his face but I couldn't get that close. "I love you, T.J. Fight, baby, fight. You can beat this—"

His hand fell limp. The heart monitor screamed.

So did I. *"Nooooo!"*

Somebody shoved me. "Get her out!"

The horrifying, ear-splitting machine kept shrieking. People were yelling.

I screamed as I reached for him. "Nooooo! T.J. Nooooo!"

For more than five years, I watched people as they lost loved ones.

Some people stand silently in shock, stupefied by their loss. Others weep softly, standing alone. Some people sob loudly, clinging to the nearest shoulder.

A few fall to their knees.

And some people scream. They wail at the sky and claw at the earth. I always swore I'd never be one of them. I'd have more dignity.

I didn't.

As John Russo dragged me back out of the emergency room, I kept reaching for T.J., crying, "Nooooo! T.J.! Nooooo!"

I sank into a lobby chair, shaking my head and screaming at the top of my lungs so that heaven had no choice but to hear. "Nooooooo!"

I couldn't breathe.

This isn't happening. This is another dream. Wake up from the dream!

But it wasn't a dream.

And I heard him. I saw him saying, 'Death is part of life.' I saw his face, the face I loved, as he said, 'Look it in the eye and accept it.'

I turned my eyes toward heaven, shook my head, and hollered again. "No!—No!—No!" I would not accept his death. *"Noooo!"*

People stood back, gawking. I saw them. They weren't important. I didn't care about them.

My eyes closed. He held me in the air, smiling so widely his dimple showed. 'You're the only Mrs. Callahan there ever has been or ever will be.'

And I sobbed. Uncontrollably. Until I could not breathe.

I have no idea how long it was before someone touched my shoulder. "Kat."

I glanced up at Russo. "Go away, Russo!" I slapped him, flailing my hands. I didn't want to be comforted. I shrieked at him, "Get away from me! Get away!"

He did.

Russo backed off, watching me as if I were a wild animal caught in a trap. You can't help an animal like that. They're too consumed with fright and pain. They'll hurt you if you try to release them. So, he didn't try.

Shaking the arms of my chair, I wailed as loud as I could, "Why, God? Why?" And something inside of me quietened. I stilled, frozen, wide-eyed.

Clancy came, standing by Russo. I felt their eyes on me. Louisa was there. People I didn't know. Maybe they thought I'd become catatonic because they spoke as if I were not present. But I heard Russo tell them, "I can't get near her. Callahan asked me to find her and bring her to him, so I did."

"How'd you know where he was?" someone asked.

"I'm a fucking cop. I know how to find things out." Russo peered at Clancy and Louisa. "They were holding hands when he flatlined."

"Oh, no!" Louisa cried out and covered her face with her hands.

My tears came back.

Russo stretched his arm toward me. "How is that even possible? How can two people get that crazy about each other that fast?"

"Because they are soulmates." It was Louisa's voice.

Russo scoffed loudly. "Fuck, Louisa. Don't try to feed me that bullshit."

Louisa bit back. "You don't believe in soulmates?"

"Santa Claus and the Tooth Fairy."

I peered up as she jabbed her finger at Russo. Her cheeks were red. "Well, that shows what little you know, John Russo. Great minds have recognized the existence of soulmates all the way back to Plato. Some people try to explain it, but no one can. No more than we can explain the human soul. Can you see a soul, Russo? Or explain it? No. But just as people have souls, some people have soulmates. Their love is so strong it outlives their bodies with their souls. The bond of love unites them one lifetime after another."

Russo had become slack-jawed as Louisa gnawed on him. She pointed at me. "I've watched them together. I felt the force between them. Trust me. She and T.J. are soulmates."

Clancy said, "I think I know what you're talking about. They were arguing in the parking lot one day, and I told them they looked like a married couple bickering and, shit, man. Callahan took my head off. He didn't want me interrupting their fight."

"Exactly." Louisa glared at Russo. "If you saw them together, you would know."

Russo had bounced back from his tongue-lashing. "Bullshit. Both of you."

Louisa covered her mouth with her fingertips, shaking her head softly. "I cannot believe Callahan is gone."

Russo faced her and said something I couldn't understand because I was sobbing again.

Louisa's voice was loud and emphatic. "We must pray now together, for Thomas Jefferson Callahan."

It brought me out of my stupor.

"Louisa, will you pray with me?" I stretched my hand toward the blur of her, and she came to me with outstretched arms, wrapping them around me tightly as I stood to meet her. I buried my head in her shoulder, crying. "I don't want to live without him."

"Russo! Tell her, now!"

"Kat, he's in surgery. I tried to tell you."

I froze, covering my open mouth with my hand.

He came to me. Gripping my shoulders, Russo crouched low so that our eyes were level, and he searched my face; I guess he wanted to be sure I was sane and wouldn't slap him again.

He said, "Kat, when an officer dies in the line of duty, the doctor comes out and tells us. I've lost brothers before. I know the routine. If we knew he was gone, we wouldn't have just left you there crying. One of us would have taken you home, but we had nothing definitive. So, I finally went back and demanded some answers. They took him into surgery right after we left."

I blinked. "So he's alive? T.J.'s alive?" My knees were weak. "Please, don't give me false hope. Are you sure?"

Russo glanced at his watch. "It's more than two hours. No one has come out to say he didn't make it. I take that as good news."

I collapsed into my chair, weeping again.

"Now, we must all pray." Louisa summoned the men, extending her arms. "Come. The more prayers the better. He is still in danger."

Russo looked at the others and then at her. "You go ahead."

"I've been praying," Clancy said. "We've been partners since the academy. He's my brother." They walked away.

I held Louisa's hand as she prayed aloud in Spanish. I didn't understand her words, but I knew her meaning, and I said my own prayer silently, begging for his life.

Louisa made me understand. You can't see gravity, but you have no control over it any more than we had control over the force that drew us together. I understood the familiarity of that first kiss, why I'd felt as if I was back in the arms of a long-lost love—because that's exactly what it was for both of us.

I understood why he wouldn't give up, even when my doubts slashed him raw. 'How do you know anybody?' he'd asked me. 'Is it time or a deeper connection? I thought that's what we had.' T.J. was so much more intuitive than me.

Finally, our dreams made sense. We'd been together always, and no matter what, if we lost each other in body—someday, somewhere, we would be together again. Bodies are lost. Souls are not. Our love lived with our souls.

The men came back a while later. I'd collected myself enough to speak. "We're getting married," I told them.

"Wonderful!" Louisa hugged me, apparently the only one surprised.

Russo flashed a cagey grin. "Yeah, I heard. We had a meet and greet."

That brought a smile to my face. I wasn't sure Russo knew that I knew what that meant—or if he knew I knew what it had been about.

"He told me, too," Clancy said, and his face was kind. "I never saw him any happier, Kat. Congratulations."

Russo hum-hawed for a moment before he squinted at me. "Do you have any idea how many women have wanted that big lug to put a ring on their finger?"

"He's not a lug!" Nobody was ever going to insult him again to me.

Russo laughed loudly, and others joined in. "You've got to lighten up now, Kat. He's going to make it."

"You know, Russo, I don't care how many women want him." I tapped my chest with my fingers. "He's mine. T.J. Callahan is mine."

A smile spread across his face, lighting up those black eyes. "Yes, ma'am. That he is."

We went back to waiting in silence as one officer after another began filing into the lobby, gathering around us and offering their sympathy. His sergeant, the man I'd seen pat his back at Landeros' house, stood before me and offered his hand. Detective Sgt. Tom Berry introduced himself. "T.J. told me you're getting married. You have a good man."

I thanked him.

"He's strong. He'll come through this." The sergeant hugged my shoulder before joining Clancy and some others. Someone brought me coffee. Nobody tried to carry on small talk. We waited as one big family. Because Callahan loved me, they embraced me as one of theirs. Me, the cop reporter.

I don't know how many hours we waited before a nurse approached. "Mrs. Callahan?" she asked.

I clenched my eyes tight, terrified of what she might say. I held my breath.

"They said you can wait in his room. They'll take him to Intensive Care when he comes out of recovery."

I stood. "T.J.'s alive? He's out of surgery?"

"Yes."

The room erupted.

Louisa and I hugged, crying on each other's shoulders.

Russo and Clancy bear-hugged and patted each other on the back as men do. All across the lobby, men and women cheered and hugged and applauded. People I didn't know embraced me.

The nurse addressed the crowd of cops. "Detective Callahan is out of surgery but he's not out of danger. Doctors can only do so much, so if you're a believer, keep praying." Then her gaze settled on me, her hand extended. "Come with me."

I glanced at Russo and Louisa. "Do you want to come with me?"

"Only two can go back," the nurse said.

"I have to get back to work anyway." Louisa squeezed my hand. "Please, let me know how he is. Tell him I was here."

I kissed her cheek. "I will. Thank you, Louisa. I heard what you said. It explained so much."

"What? That you are soulmates?" She smiled and tapped her own heart. "In here, you knew. That kind of love will not be denied. I watched you. I knew."

Russo offered, "I'll wait with you if you want me to."

I had liked him, then loathed him, and now he felt like family. I think that's what law enforcement people do. They fight among themselves like brothers and sisters, but when the earth opens up and swallows one of them, they remember they are family.

Chapter 21

Russo and I waited in a small, brightly lit room on the third floor of Hendrick Medical Center. The medical complex on Abilene's north side served the same geographical area as the newspaper.

They gave Callahan a private room, maybe because he was a policeman.

And because he'd called out for me, called me Katherine Callahan in front of the doctors, they assumed we were married. The nurse called me Mrs. Callahan.

We waited silently in hard plastic chairs for a long while until I finally had the presence of mind to ask, "What happened?"

I guess Russo was ready to talk because he opened up like floodgates in May.

"Freddy Dickey happened. Freddy knew how much time he was facing with us catching him with that much dope. It's his third strike. He wanted to make a deal, hoping for leniency at sentencing. He said he knew what happened inside the Bennett house. I called Callahan.

"Freddy told T.J. that Jerry Stubblefield and Ben Sims paid him for a load of meth using cash they took from the Bennett safe. We seized that cash in our raid on his place. Sure enough, their fingerprints were on it, but there was no way to tie it directly to the Bennett safe."

"What about the stolen rifles and jewelry?" I asked.

"Freddy said they were sitting on the merchandise until things cooled down since they were flush with cash. So, Callahan didn't have anything but Freddy's word, which isn't worth much to a judge. Callahan didn't want to tip his hand by bringing Stubblefield or Sims in for questioning. They'd spook and run. But we all figured if they whispered it to Freddy, they whispered it to someone else, so we started building cases on their known associates. Just get 'em in jail legitimately and hold them 'til they hurt enough to talk."

Russo's brows climbed high on his forehead with a teasing grin. "Kat, you only check the Taylor County Jail logs. We've got associates of Freddy Dickey, Jerry Stubblefield, and Ben Sims in four different county jails.

"Anyway, a chick in Cisco said Sims told her they robbed Bennett's house, but he never mentioned anything about a murder. So, Callahan had two people fingering Stubblefield and Sims, which gave the theory more credibility, but he still had no evidence.

"It doesn't take long for hardcore users to start crashing when they miss a few fixes. And they hurt. I mean, they physically and mentally hurt." He patted his shirt pocket. "Speaking of fixes, I need a smoke."

I gripped his arm. "Don't you dare. You've got to finish this."

He shot me a dammit look and went on. "The jail called this morning. Sims said he'd talk for leniency, so I paged Callahan. Sims told him Jerry offered him a 50/50 split if he'd help rob the Bennett house for cash, rifles, and jewelry. Sims swore he didn't know anyone would get hurt. Said Roxanne picked them up at an oil rig near Clyde. They snorted meth together." He paused. "Do you have any idea what a stiff snort of meth will do to a woman the size of Roxanne Gibson?

"Apparently, she called Marilyn Bennett saying they needed to talk. Marilyn said she would wait up. When Mrs. Bennett opened the door for Roxanne, the two men stormed in behind her and tied Mrs. Bennett to a dining room chair. Sims said they left her with Roxanne while they helped themselves to the master bedroom and study."

T.J. figured it out perfectly.

Russo stood and began to pace as he talked. He'd been sitting for too long and needed a fix of his own, a smoke. Maybe a drink. "Sims told Callahan he saw Roxanne backhand Mrs. Bennett a couple of times but said he and Stubblefield went off looking for valuables. Said he didn't see her kill Mrs. Bennett."

"How do you know all this, Russo?"

He drew back, maybe surprised at my naivety. "I watched the interrogations. We do that to protect ourselves. The more witnesses to an interrogation the better, in case they say we coerced them."

I didn't know that.

"Callahan needed something Bass Bennett could identify as belonging to his mother. This afternoon, Sims told him they stashed everything in an old truck inside the garage behind the Stubblefield house. T.J. got a search warrant, and we went back. As soon as we stepped out of our cars, before Callahan could even show him the search warrant, Stubblefield stepped out of that dark garage and fired."

I closed my eyes. "Where is he now? Stubblefield?"

"On a slab In the morgue." Russo leaned his elbows on his knees, resting his forehead in his hands, and shook his head. He exploded. "Fuck, fuck, fuck!" Each fuck got louder. "Dammit, I should've shot sooner."

I pressed my fingertips to my eyelids, fighting the vision of T.J. lying shot on the ground. "Did you get the stolen property T.J. wanted?"

"Everything but the earrings." He took a deep breath and peered at me. "She probably kept them for herself. Callahan's guess was Tex gave them to Mrs. Bennett and somehow, Roxanne found out. Hell hath no fury."

"I can't imagine what either one of them sees in that man. He is so ugly."

Russo tilted his head back and snickered. "He may be, but they say old Tex is hung like one of his racehorses."

"Oh, gross, Russo!" I backhanded his shoulder, cringing at the thought, laughing with embarrassment. My cheeks were red. "I can't believe you said that."

He kept laughing, a belly laugh that brought tears to our eyes. We both needed that relief.

"Where is she?" I asked. "Roxanne Gibson?"

He wiped his eyes. "Who the fuck knows? Sicily would be my guess."

I lowered my head, resting it in my hands. "I'm sorry I went crazy and slapped you."

He lifted a shoulder. "You thought he was dead." He patted his shirt pocket. "Truth is, I still can't believe he's alive." He pulled out a pack of cigarettes, tapping the box on his open palm.

He stopped and stared into the room's emptiness, and his face grew long.

He held the unopened pack of cigarettes mid-air. "Out of the corner of my eye, I saw Stubblefield step out of that garage with his rifle aimed at Callahan. I just didn't ... couldn't move fast enough. Callahan dropped as I fired."

He peered at me with such remorse in his eyes. "Stubblefield hit him center chest, Kat. Took him down. Then we find out Stubblefield used fucking hollow points?" He shook his head. "Men don't live through that."

My tears were back, but Russo kept talking. "What do you do for a man shot in the chest? He's covered in blood, but you know, he's bleeding more on the inside than outside, and you can't stop it. It's not like a shot in the arm or leg you can put a tourniquet on. It's not like a heart attack; you could do CPR. And the pain? My God, the pain of a gunshot to your chest?"

Russo tucked the pack of cigarettes back in his pocket, rested his face in his hands, got up, and walked away from me.

I watched. He stomped his foot. "Fuck! We were all so fucking helpless." He turned, and his gaze met mine. "The first thing he said when I got to him was, get Katherine."

He sat back down and patted my shoulder. "But he made it this far. If anybody can pull through it, Callahan can." He slapped his thighs and stood. "Now, dammit, Kat, you got all the goodie out of me. I'm done." He fished out his pack of cigarettes. "I want a smoke and a drink. Maybe two or three. I'll check on you later."

I reached over and squeezed his hand. "Thank you, John."

"For what?"

"For killing Hal Stubblefield. For staying with T.J. and getting me. Staying with me." I held onto his hand, not letting him leave. "One last thing. I heard over the scanner two deceased. I thought he was one. Who?"

"Oh." It was like he forgot. "When I shot Stubblefield, some girl fired at me. Clancy took her out."

I closed my eyes, taking it all in. "It's surreal."

"Yeah, dammit. Now I owe Clancy my life."

Chapter 22

Russo had gone home when they brought T.J. to his ICU room.

I got out of the way and focused on him as attendants came through with I.V.s, tubes, and machines. I couldn't see his wound. A sheet and dressings covered him.

He lost so much blood; his normally bronzed skin was pale. I couldn't imagine the pain he suffered.

"It'll take a while for him to wake up," the nurse said. "He's been under anesthesia a lot longer than we like to keep them under. But a wound like that takes time to repair. You've got time to go home and rest." She was an older, heavyset woman.

"Thank you but I can't. When he opens his eyes, I want him to see me."

She smiled, put her arm around my shoulder, and squeezed. "Have faith, dear." She tilted her head toward the door. "There's coffee around the corner."

I sat with T.J. all night, my chair by his head, speaking softly near his ear, stroking his forehead and bicep as if I were soothing a sick child. I think I fell asleep, my hand on his arm, my head on his bed.

A rim of gold peaked above the eastern horizon when I felt him stir.

I opened my eyes to see his gaze roaming the room. His eyes were wide, maybe frightened. He couldn't speak, and with that breathing tube down his throat, he couldn't even smile.

I stood. His gaze gravitated to me, and he lifted his hand.

I kissed it. "I'm here. I'll be right back." I rushed around the corner to summon the nurse. She came to his bed, turning on the light above him. I'd been sitting with just the dim nightlight.

T.J. tried to speak, but he couldn't. He became agitated, trying to pull at the tube. That temper.

"Stop it!" The nurse scolded him, showing him her palm and ushering him to be still. "You'll rupture something." She loomed over him. "The doctor is coming. He'll take that out when he sees you're awake."

Callahan seemed to settle down, his eyes finding mine again. I kissed his forehead. He rested his eyes, and I whispered to him. "The doctors said you'll be fine now."

Actually, they hadn't said anything. But I had prayed, as had everyone else, and I was working on faith.

He nodded, just barely. The slightest movement with that thing in his throat could scrape his windpipe. "I haven't left you, T.J. I won't leave you." I kissed his face again, my eyes damp. "I'll never leave you."

He blinked, nodded slightly, and closed his eyes. He was still feeling the effects of the anesthesia. When the breathing tube came out, they gave him an injection to put him back to sleep. They would keep him sedated until his pain level became bearable.

I met his family later that morning. His father, Tom, was as big as T.J. with a bronzed face and buzzed white hair. Tom had big hands that felt like leather and eyes the color of the sky in spring.

T.J.'s eyes came from his mother, Mary Alice.

His younger brother, George, was the tallest of the bunch. Rawboned with light eyes like his father, his hair a sandy brown. "Clancy told us you're getting married," George said.

I smiled with pride. "Yes." What a terrible first impression he must have of me. How awful I must have looked with swollen eyes, awake most of the night. My face felt puffy.

George eyed me cautiously. "I'd like to say congratulations. I know my brother wouldn't have asked if he wasn't sure, but I want to make sure, you're sure."

"I am."

He set his jaw, and when he did, he looked like T.J. "Don't hurt my brother. You'll have to deal with me and Mother." He raised a lone brow. "And you don't want to mess with her."

I assured him, "You don't have to worry about us."

As the morning progressed, more people came. Clancy, Judge Riley, and Pat. Then I spotted Jack, the first person I'd seen from the newspaper.

"I'm so sorry," Jack offered his hand. I took it, and he drew me in for a hug. "I came last night when I heard, but they said you were with him upstairs in Intensive Care."

I was glad to know he cared. I introduced my city editor to the group. Jack and Bill Riley, the newspaper's city editor and county judge, already knew each other.

Jack said, "I had no idea about you and Detective Callahan."

"I was going to tell you, but you were sick."

Mary Alice butted in. "They surprised us all."

"Not me." Pat Riley entered the conversation. "I saw the way they looked at each other, the way T.J. held her hand the whole time we talked at Sambo's. I told Bill, I'd never seen him hold anyone's hand like that and the very idea, he wanted us to convince her to go out with him." She chuckled. "I felt it."

That made me smile.

I told Jack, "If you want me off cops, I understand."

"Why would I want you off cops? Nobody has ever worked that beat the way you have."

I glanced at the crowd and whispered. "Can we speak in private?"

Jack eyed the circle. "Sure."

We walked several yards away, taking two chairs, and I confessed. "I don't know if I can cover cops anymore. I'm sure they told you how I lost it when I heard the scanner."

Jack's smile was fatherly. "What do you think I'd do if I heard on the scanner that my wife or kids got shot? Do you think I'd finish reading copy? Any of us would have reacted the same way." He waved his hand. "Screw the story. It's family first." He nodded at Callahan's mother and brother. "They're your family now."

"I know he is, but Jack, I really lost it. If some reporter had come up to me last night, when I thought he was dead—I'm not sure what I would have done. I might have choked him. It's made me question everything I do."

Jack's face fell. He stared at the floor for a long stretch. "Well, kid, I don't know what to tell you." He glanced at Clancy and several police officers gathered around with George, Mary Alice, and the Rileys. Jack nodded at the group. "What they do, you can't put a value on. Society can't function without law and order." He turned his head and faced me squarely. "But democracy can't exist without us. Think about it. Any self-governing society is dependent on an informed electorate. That's what we do."

His brows drew together. "Power is an aphrodisiac. It's human nature for people with power to take advantage of it. Men who carry guns, politicians who levy and collect taxes—they can easily abuse their power if someone's not watching and telling voters what's going on. Don't underestimate the importance of a free press to democracy."

He nodded back at the group of cops who were laughing and visiting. "They put their lives on the line, literally." His gaze came back to meet mine. "No, we don't do that. But imagine there is a scale that balances the importance of public safety against the importance of an informed electorate. They balance out pretty damned even." He aimed his finger at me. "Don't underestimate the importance of what you do."

He made me want to cry again. I hugged his neck. "Thank you, Jack. I never thought about it that way."

"Well, you're not as old as I am." He smiled as he stood. "Now, you stay with your detective this week. Take next week, if you have to, but I'll need an answer soon about whether or not you're coming back."

I hugged him tighter than I ever dreamed I would. "I promise, I'll keep you updated."

He agreed.

And that became our ultimate question: Would I return to being a cop reporter? And would Callahan go back to being a detective?

For days, doctors kept him sedated, partially because of the pain level but also because the massive blood loss strained his kidneys. Recovery would take time.

I remained at his side as one week rolled into two. The newspaper paid me, but I knew they couldn't keep it up much longer, so at the end of the second week, and Callahan still hadn't been sent home, I asked for a temporary leave without pay.

Jack agreed to keep the position open for a few more weeks. I had enough savings to make do.

People took turns sitting with T.J., but I only left his side for a little longer than it took to shower and return.

They let him stay awake longer and longer each day.

One day, Louisa visited him when Mary Alice was spelling me. I heard them talking as I returned.

Mary Alice said, "You know, he wouldn't have been the first Callahan to die in the line of duty. Tom's uncle Charles, T.J.'s great-uncle, was the sheriff of Nolan County at the turn of the century. He was shot and killed by a drunk cowboy. And T.J.'s great-great-grandfather was killed at the Battle of Agua Dulce. They say a Mexican ran him through with a sword."

"Say that again."

Judging by their faces, neither realized I'd come into the room. They each turned, startled.

Mary Alice responded with surprise in her own eyes. "I said, T.J.'s great-great-grandfather Alexander Callahan was killed at the Battle of Agua Dulce. Near Matamoros. My boys are sons of the Republic of Texas."

"A sword?" I asked.

Mary Alice frowned. "That's what they say. Why?"

I shuddered, and they saw it.

Mary Alice demanded. "What is it?"

I spoke to Louisa. "I dreamed one night he was fighting with other men in tall grass. A bunch of men, not in uniform, with rifles and swords. Lots of haze and smoke. Gunsmoke, I don't know, but out of nowhere, I saw someone run a sword through T.J., through his side, and he looked me right in the eyes as he fell to his knees." I closed my eyes against the vision.

"It was so horrible … I never could go back to sleep." I peered at Mary Alice. "I never told him about the dream. I couldn't."

Louisa's eyes glistened with moisture.

"What are y'all talking about?" Mary Alice demanded. T.J. looked like his dad but he had his mother's eyes and her short fuse.

Louisa replied matter-of-factly. "They are soulmates."

Mary Alice guffawed. "Soulmates." She waved her hands. "Pssh!"

Louisa shook her head and peered at me. No convincing some people. I wasn't going to try. I couldn't. I just felt it.

Was it possible? Could T.J. have inherited the soul of his ancestor?

Louisa read my mind. "Me personally, I don't believe souls travel far. I think it's possible."

Mary Alice's gaze moved from Louisa back to me, her expression telling us we were stark raving mad. "Alright, smarty-britches. Educate me on soulmates." Her voice dripped with sarcasm.

I was studying T.J., his face peaceful in a drug-induced sleep. "I just know it's real."

Louisa was the professor in the room. "Mary Alice, I'll tell you like I told John Russo. Some things are beyond our understanding, but we know they exist, right? You can't see gravity, but you know it exists, right? You cannot see an atom, but you know it exists. You can't see the human soul, but you know we have one, right?"

"Yes, I believe we each have a soul," Mary Alice replied.

"And our souls are immortal, right?"

"That's my understanding." .

"Well, some people have soul mates. It's that simple." She nodded at T.J. sleeping, me standing beside him, my hand on his shoulder. "Their bond of love is so strong it outlives the body inside the soul. I believe T.J. and Katherine have shared many lives. They have loved each other and lost each other time and again, and with each lifetime spent together, their bond becomes stronger. That's what I believe." Her eyes lingered on T.J. "The first time he saw her he knew." Louisa's focus moved to his mother. "I saw your son's eyes. And if you'd seen the way he looked at her, you'd have recognized it, too. No force of man was going to keep those two apart once they found each other."

Mary Alice stood. "You truly believe that?" Pretty clear that his mother found the idea ludicrous. She dismissed Louisa with a wave of her hands.

Louisa lifted her shoulder. "Like I said, some things are beyond human understanding."

"How do you know so much about this?" Mary Alice's tone was accusatory.

Beautiful Louisa smiled sadly. "Because I lost my soulmate ten years ago." My hand clasped my heart seeing her charcoal eyes well with tears. "But I'll find him again. Someday." Her gaze shifted to me. "I knew exactly what you felt when you thought he was gone."

Chapter 23

When T.J. was released from the hospital, bluebonnets and Indian paintbrushes blanketed the pastures.

As his health improved, I felt comfortable staying away longer. His family and mine spent a weekend moving me out of the apartment and into the house just before he came home. I wanted everything perfect for his homecoming.

My parents brought my furniture, which was stored in Brownwood.

Mary Alice and my mother helped me arrange and decorate while Tom, George, and Dad lugged furniture.

Coming through the front door for the first time, Callahan froze and turned his circle, soaking it in. He smiled. "Is this the same house?"

The living room and dining room floors were covered in room-sized braided wool rugs. My furniture merged with his to transform the house into what it was meant to be: welcoming and alive. No more bare, vibrating plank floors or curtainless windows.

Callahan and I sat on the front porch late one afternoon in the ladderback rocking chairs with a little table between us that held two glasses of iced tea. He watched Blackie and Ginger in the pasture, and I watched him.

"Do you believe in soulmates?" I asked.

I never told him what Louisa said.

"I never did until you."

"When I thought I'd lost you, Louisa said we were soulmates. Russo laughed at her, but she insisted."

"I would've laughed, too if I hadn't lived it." Callahan repositioned, his eyes meeting mine. It was his specialty, I'd decided. He'd perfected the piercing gaze and the soft kiss.

He said, "I don't think anyone can believe in soulmates unless they find theirs. Babe, there's not another woman on this earth I'd have married. Just you."

I stroked his cheek, felt his beard, and smiled. "You need a shave."

That grin. "I'm rebelling. I might quit shaving altogether."

"Really?"

"Naw. I'll shave here in a few days. Just being lazy."

I knelt beside his chair. "We are forever, aren't we? I mean, not just until death do us part. I mean forever."

He kissed me sweetly, his thumb rubbing my chin. "Yes, ma'am."

I returned to my chair, and we rocked silently a while longer. There was something I wanted to tell him, but I hadn't decided how.

"Clancy got a full confession." It was another one of his pronouncements, out of nowhere.

Surprised, I asked, "When?"

"He called his morning."

"And you're just now telling me?" I couldn't believe he sat on it this long.

He winked. "Stubblefield and Sims both came clean. Finally."

I knew he hated not being in on wrapping up that case. "Clancy got a warrant to arrest Roxanne, but we'll never be able to serve it. She'll never step back in America."

"Tell me." I wanted the rest of the story, as Paul Harvey would say.

"First of all, they were all three wired to hell that night on Freddy Dicky's meth. Roxanne snorted plenty when she picked them up; the men had been doing it all day.

"When they got inside the Bennett house and got Mrs. Bennett in that chair, Roxanne demanded she confess to her affair with Tex. She wanted Marilyn to admit she slept with her husband. But Marilyn kept saying they were just friends.

"They said Roxanne went ballistic, jerked the earrings out of Marilyn's ears, and said, 'I have a pair exactly like these. Mine are yellow diamonds. Custom made.'

"She took the earrings and held them underneath a lamp, peering at the inside of the earrings and said, 'Same jeweler.

Custom made." She screamed, 'Tex gave these to you. My husband gave these to you. Don't you lie to me.' And that's when she started hitting Marilyn, wearing gloves.

"When Marilyn started bleeding, Roxanne called for the men to find a pillowcase. She put it over Marilyn's head, so she wouldn't get bloody, and just kept pounding her face."

"*Geez.* Talk about cold-blooded. What with?"

"Neither man was sure. At first it was just her hand, but I guess her hand got sore. She found something and wrapped it inside a towel from the kitchen."

"A while later the men came back telling Roxanne they needed the combination to the safe. When Marilyn refused to give it, Stubblefield started in on her, Roxanne cheering him on. He could hit a hell of a lot harder than Roxanne Gibson.

"Marilyn finally gave them the combination and told them where her jewelry was. She told them how valuable that painting was and said, 'Take everything and leave me alone. We have insurance.'

"They got the safe open, put everything inside pillowcases and got the hell out of there."

"How valuable was that painting?"

"Bass told me it was worth half a million dollars."

I shook my head softly in disbelief. "Those druggies wouldn't know what to do with a painting like that."

"Roxanne kept it," he said.

"Did Marilyn ever admit having an affair with Tex?"

T.J. lifted a shoulder. "Not that they ever heard."

"And Tex? Is he dead?"

"I'm sure he is."

"Wow." I sat there, trying to absorb it all.

But T.J. didn't dwell on anything. His mind moved on. A few minutes later, he peered up and pointed. "I want to put a ceiling fan on the porch here. It's nice now but it'll get too hot to sit out here this summer. I need to fix that." He winked. "I like sitting out here with you."

"I'm working on flowerbeds." I tapped my temple. "In here."

"You work away," he quipped. "I'll help when I can."

"I think I'll line them with field rocks. Purple sage would look nice in front of the porch."

He snickered. "Help yourself. We've got plenty of rocks and sage." His attention was high over the corral.

"What are you watching?" I asked.

He pointed. "Peregrine falcon. Look. On top of that light pole."

I'd never have noticed. We kept rocking in the peaceful country quiet. I'd never known silence, so accustomed to the roar of the newsroom. The faint squeak of our rockers was the only sound.

No. I heard bees buzzing, too. Somewhere.

I remembered something I'd intended to ask for some time.

"You know that night, when you were shot, everyone in the department came to the hospital but Prissy. I wondered why she didn't show."

T.J. snickered. "You won't be bothered by her again."

My eyes grew wide, filled with curiosity. He'd never mentioned her.

His dimple was showing. "I sent her packing."

I guffawed, slapping the arms of my chair. "T.J.! You did not!"

"I did. She tried to poison me against you. She tried to make you believe I was married, which she knew was a fucking lie. When I got to work after I left you, the first thing I did was tell Clancy we were getting married. Then I called her into my office with him there. I wanted Clancy to be my witness so she couldn't accuse me of doing something different.

"When I told her we were getting married, you should've seen the look on her face. I said, 'Prissy, just so you know: Katherine is the only Mrs. Callahan there ever has been or ever will be.' She just stared at me with those bug eyes, and I said, 'There are openings in other departments.'"

I squealed with delight and clapped my hands. "I had no idea!"

He took the last drink of his iced tea, clomped his empty glass down loud, almost as one of his pronouncements, and said, "I told you I'd fix that. Clancy said she gave notice a few days later."

I leaned over and kissed his lips gently. "You know you're my hero, right?"

He pulled me into a deeper kiss and wouldn't let me go. "I want you," he whispered. "It's been too long."

I kissed him quickly, pulling away. "When it's time." He wasn't in physical shape for us to go there. I shook my glass. "I'm empty and so are you. Do you want more tea?"

He glanced at the western sky. "I'd take a beer."

"I need to check on dinner, anyway." Taking both glasses, I went inside.

As I said, furniture brought the house to life. All the money he'd spent through the years on horses and trailers and feed and saddles, buying the property and tractor, I spent on furniture and artwork and rugs and dishes and cookware and whatnots. Things that help make a house homey.

I refreshed my tea, checked the casserole in the oven, returned to the porch, and handed him an opened beer. He peered at me with surprise. "You don't want one?"

"I better not," I said.

He eyed me keenly. "Why? You need to keep a clear head?" He flashed that mischievous grin. "What if the time is now?" His eyes glistened like I hadn't seen in weeks. He was feeling his oats again.

"What time?" My mind was elsewhere.

He raised that lone brow and shamelessly ogled me. "That time."

His chest was still bandaged, but he looked strong as a plow horse to me. I couldn't help but laugh as his intentions became clear. "I don't think you are physically able yet."

His eyes glowed like warm honey. "That part of me didn't get shot, Babe."

We laughed together, and he flashed his impish grin, the one with the dimple. "You know, I'd let you do most of the work."

I laughed so hard that tears came to my eyes.

He laughed with me. "Don't make me laugh. It hurts," he said.

"I didn't make you laugh. You made yourself laugh." We kept giggling. "I'm all yours when you're ready."

He stood, holding out his hand. "Babe, I've been ready."

"First, we need to talk about something. It's important."

"Okay." He still stood, his gaze questioning.

Still sitting in my rocker, I peered up at him. "Christmas."

He sat back down with confusion all over his face. "Christmas? What about Christmas?"

"Remember when we were talking that night at Sambo's, and I said, 'If we can't talk about work, what will we talk about? And you said, 'How about Christmas? Will we spend it at your folks or mine?'"

He lifted his hands, bumfuzzled. "Okay."

"I think we'll be spending this Christmas at home."

He cocked his head and shifted his shoulders. "Katherine, where are you going with this?"

I couldn't suppress my wide smile. I was toying with him, and it was pure fun. "Count back."

He lifted his hands again, looking around, bewildered, as I expected him to be. Men can be so clueless about some things. I took his hand with a soothing tone. "Honey, when we made love, that's been what? More than a month ago?"

His eyes roamed the sky as he pondered. "Damn, we are past due."

"In more ways than one."

"What?"

"Well, honey, we weren't exactly thinking straight. Neither one of us used protection. There'd never been a reason for me to take birth control pills and…"

He leaned toward me with his eyes as wide as I'd ever seen them. "Are you telling me we made a baby?"

My heart caught. Was he upset? "I haven't been to the doctor but nothing's happened. And something should have happened."

He was loud. "Are you serious?"

I smiled with relief. That was a beautiful smile. "I think we're going to have a Christmas baby."

He tilted his head back and hooted like the day I said I'd marry him. "Oh, damn! Katherine!" He slammed his hands on the arms of the chair and stood, turning in a circle—the way he did sometimes. He stopped, facing me, and spread his arms wide. "Come here! A baby? I'd pick you up but I might spring a leak."

He grabbed me and winced. We embraced—gently. My ear rested against his chest, and I heard that steady heartbeat. "I can't believe it. A baby." He kissed me quickly. "One time. You and me. We made a baby."

"Honey, it was more than one time."

"Still. We're going to have a baby. I've never thought about a baby—ever."

Another second of apprehension, a tightening in my chest. "I can't be sure until I go to a doctor. Do you still want to get married, either way? Are you happy?"

"Don't be ridiculous. Of course." He gathered my hair, holding it back at the nape of my neck, peering down at me. "If I hadn't gotten shot, we'd be married now. What are we waiting on? Let's go get the license."

Striated clouds glowed pink and orange as the sun sank in the west. "It's too late today," I said.

"Okay, tomorrow."

I touched his chest. "Are you up for it?"

The dimple came back. "Babe, if we can make love, I can drive to town and get a marriage license." He took my hand. "Come on. I'm ready for my test."

We married in a simple ceremony at the house, standing before the fireplace. Judge Bill Riley officiated. Louisa stood beside me. She felt like a sister. And George was Callahan's best man. Our parents were with us. We exchanged gold bands. That day, in the eyes of the State of Texas, I became Katherine Elise Callahan, although, as far as he and I were concerned, we married when we made love.

That next week, the doctor confirmed what my body told me: T.J. and I would have a baby in late December. I was so excited—our baby. I couldn't wait.

As we lay in bed one night, he said, "There's one question left."

"Um-hum." I was almost asleep. I wasn't sure if he was talking to himself or me.

"Am I going back to the force?"

That woke me. I didn't know he'd seriously considered not going back. I rolled over and asked, "What do you want to do?"

His arms were folded behind his head. He cut his eyes at me. "Dad wants us to move to Ballinger." His gaze began to move around the ceiling. "He wants me to ranch with him, lease more land, and give up law enforcement. So does Mom." He cut his eyes back to me. "Do you want me to give up law enforcement?"

I'd thought about how dangerous his job was and how hard that had been to live through. "I think it would be selfish of me to ask that of you. I love you T.J., and I want you to do what makes you happy. What do you want?"

He rolled onto his side, facing me, propped on his elbow. "I don't want to hide from life." He stroked my hair, rubbing strands between his fingers. "Katherine, you know, what happened with Stubblefield was a fluke." His gaze left my hair, finding my eyes. "Chances of something like that happening again are one in a trillion. Besides, ranchers get killed, too. Tractors roll over and bulls kick."

I touched his cheek. "Do what you love. But will you make me a promise?"

"Depends."

"Promise me you'll wear a vest when you serve search warrants. And when you go into hostage situations."

He ran his finger along my lips, tracing the shape. "Normally, I do. I'm not sure why I didn't that day." He nodded. "Yes, I will make you that promise. But, Babe, a man can't wear a vest all the time and like you said, even with a vest, Raul could've shot me in the head. The way I see it, God's going to take us all when He decides to take us. He had every opportunity to take me, and He passed. I think now I understand why."

"Why?"

"Because He knew then, I was a father. He kept me around to take care of you and our kids."

"You'll be careful?" It still scared me, remembering him walking into Raul Landeros's house with those arms wide. "Keep us in mind?"

"Every minute every day." He sat up straight in the bed. "And what about you, Katherine? You faced old man Stubblefield with a shotgun aimed at you. I don't see you hiding out here from life. Babe, whether you're in the newsroom or not, when God calls Thomas Jefferson Callahan, I've got to go. You could be sitting out here, and someone would drive up and tell you. Would that make it any easier?"

I glanced away, refusing to think about it.

His voice softened. "Look at me." I did. "Stubblefield could've just as easily shot you the day before. I don't think you realize you take risks, too. Without a gun or a vest." He stretched out flat on his back, his arms folded behind his head again. "I never told you about a dream I had."

I sat up. "You said your dreams would embarrass me."

"Most would've. But one night I had a nightmare from hell. I was holding you in my lap, like a baby, and you died, right there in my arms. I shook you, trying to wake you up, but you were gone." His eyes closed. "I woke myself up, hollering. I didn't even try to go back to sleep." Those brown eyes settled on mine. "I can't even imagine what you went through when my heart stopped."

"I don't want to remember. But I'm going back to work when you do. I just wanted to stay with you until you were strong again."

I'd had so much time to think about everything. I'd looked at reporting from both sides now. What Jack said that day was spot on.

"News is an integral part of democracy, but I've come to realize you were right, T.J. People don't need to know everything."

He surprised me when he replied, "But we do need to know what's going on around us. You're in the best position of anyone to decide what to put in a story and what to leave out." He sat up again. "But Babe, work or don't work, that's up to you. When the baby comes, you'll stay home, I hope. At least until they start school."

"With a baby, do we have the money for me not to work?" I had wondered about that.

He cut those eyes at me. "Lots of guys have wives and kids at home. Don't you worry about money. You leave that to me."

I chortled inside. Oh, how I loved my old-fashioned husband. A part of him wasn't from this century.

But I'd be happy to let him care for me and our children if that's what he wanted to do. And I'd take care of him and them. How I changed in his arms. "I can write. Try to sell stories," I said.

Then it dawned on me he said, until they start school. They. "Just how many kids are you planning on us having?"

There came that beautiful, wide smile with that dimple, the glimmer in those eyes I adored. "I don't know." He twisted his neck a long, slow twist. "Our kids? I'll take as many as you and God'll give me." He kissed me goodnight and turned off the lamp light.

We spooned, his big hand tucked beneath my breasts, his favorite way to fall asleep. I remembered the night after our first kiss when he said, 'When you're in that bed all alone, you just remember I would've held you all night.' He would have. Thomas Jefferson Callahan, my husband. Yes, we were meant to be.

Silver light streamed through the open window beside me, ruffling the curtain. "T.J.?"

"Um-hum."

Fireflies twinkled outside my window screen. "If you die before me, I'll find you again."

He stroked my hair away from my ear. "Babe don't die before me. I can't take it."

"But what if I do?"

He pulled me tight against him, his big hand back in its favorite place. "I'll find you, Katherine." He kissed my neck. "I promise. I always will."

I exhaled a deep sigh of contentment as I closed my eyes, savoring the warmth and strength of him engulfing me, and I wondered—*how many times have we said that to each other?*

About the Author

P.J. Jones is a native Texan who received the Readers' Favorite True-Crime Gold Medal Award of 2022 for co-writing *The Evil I Have Seen: Memoirs from the Case Files of Detective Lt. Robert (Robbo) Davidson, ret.* During her journalism career, she received the Sunshine Award from the Society of Professional Journalists, served on the Board of Directors of the Freedom of Information Foundation of Texas, and was a founding member of the Alabama Center for Open Government.